Charlie Owen enjoyed a thirty-year career in the police service, serving with two forces in the Home Counties and London, reaching the rank of Inspector. *Horse's Arse* is his first novel. He is married with six children.

# HORSE'S ARSE

# CHARLIE OWEN

**headline**

Copyright © 2007 Charlie Owen

The right of Charlie Owen to be identified as Author of
this work has been asserted by him in accordance with the
Copyright, Designs and Patents Act 1988.

First published in 2007 by
HEADLINE PUBLISHING GROUP

First published in paperback in 2007
by HEADLINE PUBLISHING GROUP

1

Apart from any use permitted under UK copyright law,
this publication may only be reproduced, stored, or transmitted,
in any form, or by any means, with prior permission in writing of
the publishers or, in the case of reprographic production, in accordance
with the terms of licenses issued by the Copyright Licensing Agency.

All characters in this publication are fictitious and any resemblance
to real persons, living or dead, is purely coincidental.

Cataloguing in Publication Data is available from the British Library

ISBN 978 0 7553 3684 5

Typeset in AGaramond by Avon DataSet Ltd,
Bidford on Avon, Warwickshire

Printed and bound in Great Britain by
Mackays of Chatham plc, Chatham, Kent

Headline's policy is to use papers that are natural, renewable and recyclable
products and made from wood grown in sustainable forests. The logging
and manufacturing processes are expected to conform to the
environmental regulations of the country of origin.

HEADLINE PUBLISHING GROUP
A division of Hachette Livre UK Ltd
338 Euston Road
London NW1 3BH

www.headline.co.uk
www.hodderheadline.com

# Acknowledgements

I first sat down to write this book a few years ago to fill my days off work whilst I recovered from an operation on my back that had gone wrong. The idea of writing a book came initially from my wife who was probably increasingly fed up with my 'cabin fever'. Had she not pushed me, I doubt *Horse's Arse* would have seen the light of day — some might say she has a lot to answer for.

I also owe my sincerest thanks to two old friends, Martin and Tracey Kosmalski, who looked after me during an awful period and helped get me back on the path to recovery. They helped me get admitted to the Lister Hospital in Stevenage, and it was there that I began to recover from my illness. Some of the book was written whilst I was there and I thank Martin, Tracey and their daughters Jo and Gemma for their support and friendship at a difficult time.

Vast amounts of the book were written at the Police Convalescent Home at Goring where I spent some considerable time recovering. My thanks to the staff there and to my fellow 'raspberries' and 'window lickers' who offered encouragement when they became aware I was attempting to write a book. Here it is: I hope you enjoy it!

I also owe a huge debt to my friend Richard Tucker, who pestered many of his contacts in the publishing business and eventually got in to see Kerr McRae and Martin Fletcher at Headline. They had a punt on an outsider and I hope this Horse comes in for them!

Finally, I offer thanks to my wife Karen. She has been my sounding board, constructive critic and proofreader throughout the writing of this book. She knows it inside out, probably as well as I do, and still laughs at the same passages. She has encouraged and supported me throughout and I dedicate this book to her.

This novel is from start to finish entirely a work of my imagination and the characters, companies and their actions in the story are entirely fictional.

# Foreword

This is a story about a fictional sub-divisional police station, set in a fictional county in the mid 1970s. The sub-division is phonetically known as Hotel Alpha, but such is the disdain the officers feel for the town they police, it is generally referred to as Horse's Arse.

If the world had an arse, then Hotel Alpha would be its piles.

It is not a popular posting, generally reserved for the more aggressive and belligerent officers of the Force.

This is an account of how the Job used to be done. This is the way it was, but never will be again.

# Prologue

Handstead lay about fifteen miles north of Manchester from which the town had been aggressively populated and expanded during the 1950s, when a far-sighted Manchester City council had indulged itself in early ethnic cleansing and moved thousands of its most troublesome tenants out into the sticks.

Promises of a new life in new homes, and even jobs in the burgeoning petro-chemical industry, had drawn them like flies round a dog turd to the brave new world that was Handstead. The ancient old town that had merited a mention in the Domesday Book all but vanished under the concrete sprawl of the New Town.

The dream proved short-lived, and by the early 1970s and the departure of its major employer the town was a waste of ghetto-like estates, desolate windswept shuttered shopping parades and looming tower blocks. Many of its inhabitants, long since released from the burden of gainful employment, lived out their lives in alcoholic and drug-induced hazes between trips to pick up what the state gave them without question. Their benefits were supplemented by petty and occasionally serious crime, robbing and raping each other and creating a reputation for themselves that spread to all corners of the county and beyond. Handstead villains, men and women, had spread the word and their exploits were related with pride from generation to generation.

Without question the very worst of the estates was the Park Royal. With its solitary pub, depressing regulation shopping parade, featureless council houses, unkempt gardens and abandoned cars, the estate was home to some six thousand inhabitants. The few decent souls amongst them lived out their lives in silent fear, dreaming of the day Handstead Council rehoused them. The place was a dump and the local police had done little to address the problems. Efforts to house a home beat officer and his family on the estate were quickly abandoned, after the house was stoned and the officer's children were attacked in their front garden. Why the locals were so anti-police wasn't immediately obvious, but over the years the mutual hatred between the residents of Handstead in general and the Park Royal in particular and the local police had gone unresolved.

The Force's answer had been to use Handstead as its penal colony, and the town was therefore policed by a motley collection of alcoholic, sexually promiscuous and generally undisciplined misfits. None of them laboured under any misapprehension as to their place in the food chain either. They knew they had been condemned to spend their careers at Horse's Arse; some because they were serving 'sentences' for offences committed elsewhere, others because that was how the dice had rolled when their initial postings were being decided. Blissfully unaware, they were almost true Stoics. Powerless to do anything about their fate, they calmly accepted the inevitable shitty end of the stick and tried to make the most of their situation. The attempt regularly manifested itself in outrageous abuses, but they took a perverse pride in policing Horse's Arse notwithstanding. They recognised better than most what a hopeless task they faced, but revelled in their Canute-like resolve to hold the tide of shit at bay as best they could. They made a difference, albeit a small one, and enjoyed the 'rather you than me mate' looks they got from colleagues who worked elsewhere. It never occurred to any of them to apply to transfer out of the sub-division. What would be the point? It would never be allowed: they were destined to stay there so best get on with it. How often had they been told, 'If you can't take a joke you shouldn't have joined the Job'? Some joke. They recognised their own frailties, but that was where they parted from the ancient doctrine of the Stoics. The faults of others, particularly the local villains, were never forgiven and they were policed with extreme prejudice.

Making a difference: that's what it was all about for the Handstead force.

The new Handstead police station perfectly reflected its surroundings. As was the habit, it had been built alongside the old classic Victorian police station which had become offices for the local council. Typical drab 1960s architecture, warped metal window frames and a peeling noticeboard displaying faded 'Wanted' posters of villains probably long since dead told an onlooker everything they needed to know about the place. The station had an unloved air about it and bore the scars of many a past siege when the locals had gathered to vent their spleen at the perceived excesses of its inhabitants.

The local magistrates' court had been built alongside the police station and was connected to the cell area by a subterranean tunnel. The tunnel ensured that prisoners could be taken straight to the dock without passing through any public areas, and also provided the officers on night duty with the opportunity to hold mock courts. Many a puzzled magistrate wondered about the sanity of the overnight drunk he had just fined who thanked him profusely for overturning the death sentence imposed on him the night before.

It was the busiest sub-division in the county in terms of the numbers of prisoners locked up, coming close each year to nicks in larger towns. Officers at Horse's Arse had arrest records that were the envy of most of their colleagues around the county, but then if you spent your working day immersed in a sewer it was almost inevitable that you ended up with a few turds in your pocket.

Of the three shifts worked at the station, Early Turn was generally the quietest, since most of the low-lifes rarely ventured out of bed until after lunch, and officers cleared up after the night before. The day would inevitably get busier as Late Turn (2 p.m. to 10 p.m.) progressed into Night Turn (10 p.m. to 6 a.m.). Friday and Saturday nights were usually the busiest, with the Late Turn officers working through until 2 a.m. to assist their hard-pressed colleagues dealing with pub fights, assaults, violent domestic disputes and every conceivable type of drunken behaviour. During long hot summers (fortunately rare) every night resembled Friday and Saturday, and Late Turn officers would end up working a week of twelve-hour shifts.

# Chapter One

'Another six, darling,' shouted the drunk leaning heavily on the bar. The room was packed, the jump itself awash with beer from the overflowing pint glasses that were arranged in two long, straggling lines along its length. The bar towels lay submerged in liquid, and cigarette butts floated in their dozens in the two ashtrays at either end of the bar.

The drinkers stood shoulder to shoulder facing the two bartenders, shouting at the top of their voices, looking like a drunken terracotta army. The bartenders, both women, were beginning to wilt under the pressure, which had increased tenfold since 10 p.m. Other drinkers at the bar had vacated their spaces to accommodate the influx and now stood or sat at tables at the back of the bar area watching in silence as the newcomers got it down their necks as quickly as possible.

As they stood alongside each other pouring another pint each, the younger of the two women whispered to her companion, 'They're like animals.' Briefly looking up from the drink she was pulling to glance at the baying mob in front of her, she added under her breath, 'Look at them.'

'Don't,' replied her more experienced partner. 'Just smile, get their money and look grateful.' She slammed a pint down on to the bar top. 'Anything else?' she asked the bleary-eyed specimen in front of her.

'Just keep them coming, darling, we've got a long night ahead of us,' he shouted, before belching loudly and continuing: 'We'd better have some pork scratchings to be going on with.'

She shuddered as she turned back to the packets of crisps and peanuts on the wall by the optics. Someone farted, long and loud above the raucous din, and the bar erupted in whoops and cheers. As she tossed half a dozen packets of scratchings on to the bar, she glanced over at the younger girl who was making her debut behind the jump that evening. She was no longer watching the drink she was pulling but looking open-mouthed at the fat, balding, middle-aged man in front of her. The beer was overflowing into the slop tray and on to the floor.

'I'll need some peanuts for the youngster please, sweetie,' the fat man said. His flies were open and he'd pulled his penis out of his trousers and was stretching his foreskin from side to side imitating a feeding chick in its nest. He was sweating like a rapist, eyes fixed on the girl. The older woman shook her head, rolled her eyes to the ceiling,

2

reached over to take the overflowing pint glass and emptied it over the fat man's crotch.

'You slag,' he shouted, as his companions cheered loudly and cleared a small space around him as he put his tackle away.

'Put Jenny Wren away, Trevor, and behave yourself,' she said. 'Pay no attention, darling. He's always getting it out but God only knows why. It's like a cock, only much smaller.'

'Bitch,' snarled the fat man as he pushed his way through the throng to dry himself off in the gents.

'Off for a Spanish hand gallop, Trevor?' shouted one of the crowd, prompting prolonged and almost hysterical laughter. The group had only been drinking for fifteen minutes, but each of them had bolted four pints of either bitter or lager in that time, and still had plenty more to get through up on the bar.

'They're like animals,' repeated the younger girl, tears welling in her eyes.

'Don't worry, love, they've only got half an hour. They'll be on their way soon enough; just try to ignore them,' her friend answered as she pulled another pint. 'Wash some of these empties for me and catch your breath. You'll get used to it.'

Not a chance, thought the young girl, resolving to never again set foot in this bear pit.

The tempo increased as the group became aware that

time was short, and more and more of the beer spilt on to the drinkers as it was thrown down their necks. Each of them was gasping for breath, gagging and belching as he moved on to the next pint. The wooden floor at the front of the bar grew slippery, and pork scratchings, crisps and peanuts crunched underfoot. Every one of the group was smoking, and a thick pall of smoke hung just above their heads and meandered around the cheap, yellowing ceiling bulkhead lights. The room was spartan and strictly functional. Its role was not to provide solace or relaxation, but to sell alcohol cheaper than anywhere else in town. And sell it they did, in volumes that raised eyebrows at their supplying brewery, which responded with bigger and better discounts.

'I'm absolutely fucked,' burped one of the group, holding the rail on the front of the bar with both hands, head bowed to the floor. His companion tipped his head back and drained the last half of his pint. He glanced at his watch.

'Fuck me, we should be downstairs and you're driving,' he said to his mate. 'It's half past, lads,' he shouted at the top of his voice. The noise subsided as the group grumbled and drank what remained in their glasses, and, in some cases, what remained in other unattended glasses. Then, wiping their mouths on the backs of their hands, talking too loudly and doing up their jackets, the Late Turn police officers lurched out of the bar and downstairs for four hours' public order duty in Horse's Arse. Calm returned to the bar and the other drinkers resumed their conversations as the loud, echoing voices faded down the stairwell like the Zulus departing from Rorke's Drift.

'They're straight out of the zoo,' said the young girl again, coming round into the main bar area to start clearing the debris. Her older companion remained behind the jump, mopping the bar top. She smiled, but said nothing. She'd worked there for three years and had felt exactly the same at first. But very quickly she'd become fond of these rude, drunken, obnoxious, sexist, racist, bigoted hooligans who seemed to live only for their next drink and shag, and told the most extraordinary stories she had ever heard. It was their stories that had softened her. She'd caught snippets of their hollow-eyed conversations about what they'd seen and experienced and she gradually understood that they needed somewhere to rage and shout at their fears, frustrations and demons. This bar was their pressure valve. They didn't drink anywhere else because their behaviour wouldn't be tolerated, but here they could drink to forget and comfort themselves, throw off the restraints of normal acceptable behaviour, and scream at the moon.

She understood why they let their hair down the way they did. She didn't approve, but she understood. As they'd grown used to her being around, they'd stopped showing her their knobs, mooning at her, sneezing cockles, whelks and bacon rinds on to the bar, and constantly trying to shock and appal her. Some of them grew comfortable enough with her to talk candidly about what they had seen and done. She felt like a priest in the confessional as infidelities, misdemeanours and other acts verging on the criminal were unloaded on to her. They told her everything and what they told her would have been dynamite in the wrong hands. But then, as she often reasoned with herself, who the hell would believe half of the stories she could recount?

If the Hoop and Grapes public house had had a piano player, he'd have stopped playing as the doors to the bar opened and the group walked in. As it was, the two men standing at the bar looked round, and a couple at a table glanced over at them. The relief manager looked up from the sink where he was washing ashtrays in preparation for closing up for the night to see who had come in. He had no idea if they were regulars – he'd only been there two weeks – but something about the newcomers made him uncomfortable. The size of the group for a start, all male apart from a sole female who seemed to be joined at the hip with one of the men who it immediately became apparent was the leader of the group. He was speaking quietly to four members of his gang, two of whom left and went out into the car park, the others going to either end of the single bar and then into the gents before returning to the leader and whispering into his ear. This strange behaviour attracted the full attention of the four other customers and the relief manager. Almost as one, the four drinkers got up and made for the door, nervously passing through the group still clustered around the entrance. Nothing was said. As the door shut behind them, with a leaden feeling in his stomach the relief manager saw a chair being wedged under the handle. He knew he was in trouble, but with past experience of griefy pubs he was able to recognise the fact and do something about it. Quickly, he went to the storeroom at the back of the bar where the only phone was and dialled 999. Speaking as quietly as he could into a cupped hand, he asked for police attendance as he believed trouble was imminent. Then he went back into the bar. How right he was. All fifteen of the strangers now stood there, smirking.

'What can I get you?' he asked genially.

'Lagers all round, you wanker,' said the apparent leader to raucous laughter, 'and get a fucking move on. We're thirsty.'

'Lagers it is then,' he replied as jauntily as he could through gritted teeth, his heart thumping, praying the Old Bill wouldn't hang about. He reached up to get a glass from the shelf above and began to pull the first pint, avoiding eye contact with the group who were staring quietly at him.

'You're too fucking slow. Couple of my lads'll give you a hand,' said the grinning leader. He nodded at two of his gang, who vaulted the bar and grabbed pint glasses from the draining board.

'Hey, hey, hold on,' shouted the manager, stopping his

pouring. 'Get the fuck out of here, all of you.' He moved towards the nearer of the two intruders and grabbed the grinning thug by the arm. 'Come on, get out, get out, now.' The response was an elbow driven into his face and he went down, blood gushing from a split lip. That was the signal for the rest of the group to swarm over the bar like marauding pirates and begin to loot everything they could lay their hands on. The contents of the till quickly vanished into various pockets, as did the cigarettes from the cabinet on the back wall. Bottles of drink were taken from the cool shelves and drunk straight down before being thrown out into the bar area and smashed against walls. The stunned manager struggled to his knees as the maelstrom ebbed and crashed around him and shouted again, 'Fuck off, you bastards. I've called the police.' This prompted one of the rampaging gang to pull a vodka bottle out of its optic and smash it over the manager's head. He slumped back down and was battered completely senseless as the gang put the boot in, hoofing him around the floor of the bar like a football. His head was flicked from side to side as the kicks rained in, blood spraying around in a mist like an ever-open aerosol can. Suddenly the leader called for quiet, as he became aware of a loud banging on the front window. Looking over he saw the pale faces of the two young gang members he had sent out into the car park as lookouts. They looked worried and were gesticulating wildly for him to come to the door. He walked over, kicked away the restraining chair, opened the door and stepped out into the porch where the two lookouts waited.

'Old Bill,' he said grimly as he heard the approaching sirens. 'Time to go. You two fuck off quickly. I'll be in touch.' He hurried back into the pub and headed for the cabinet to finish stuffing packets of cigarettes into his jacket pockets, followed closely by the female gang member. As he passed the unconscious manager he kicked his head contemptuously and smiled. The thug who had felled the manager with the vodka bottle was standing alongside his prostrate body still holding the broken neck of the bottle. He grinned at his leader's gesture of contempt and then quickly crouched down and stabbed the jagged edge into the back of the manager's head. He looked up at his leader for a sign of approval, only to be disappointed to see complete indifference at his act of deference. Shrugging, and throwing the bloodied bottle neck to one side, he too began to beat a hasty retreat.

The gang had waited too long. As the leader returned to the front door and peered out into the darkened car park, a police car and van careered to a halt outside.

'Fuck it, out of the toilet windows,' he shouted and led the charge away from the door. At the toilet door a panicked bottleneck ensued, while the front doors to the pub crashed open and two extremely large policemen carrying truncheons burst in and quickly appraised the scene of devastation before them. Others rushed in behind them, and then the whole group noticed the trapped gang and charged at them in their bottleneck. Some of the gang, including the leader and the girl, made it through the small window in the toilet, but for the remaining eight only a fearful beating at the hands of the police remained an option. They knew it, and once escape was no longer viable they turned to fight like cornered rats. They were no match for the superior numbers ranged against them, all of whom had had a good drink too, and were soon hammered into submission and arrested. Some rudimentary first aid saved the relief manager's life and he was eventually removed to the intensive care unit at the local hospital with severe head injuries. One of the more sober police officers was despatched with him on a deathwatch.

The eight prisoners were dragged to police vehicles where further summary justice was administered before they were taken to the police station for processing. The dice had been rolled and the game was on.

# Chapter Two

Six a.m. the following morning. A freezing cold January morning. It was still dark and pissing down. The Night Turn had been busy: the cells were full and the atmosphere in the nick matched the weather.

'D' Relief had arrived in silent dribs and drabs with the air of condemned men. Wordlessly they had changed into uniform and now sat in the muster room waiting to hear what the coming day held for them. No one spoke.

It was the first day at Handstead for one of 'D' Relief's sergeants, Mick Jones, recently arrived after a spot of bother with the wife of a fellow officer at an outlying rural nick. He was terrified and it showed. He had stood nervously, shifting from foot to foot behind a lectern as the Early Turn officers had silently filed in and taken their seats. He was sure that one large, unshaven, dark-haired officer with bloodshot eyes had passed him, turned slowly to look at him and revealed a set of vampire's teeth – he may even have hissed at him –

11

but it could have been a trick of the light. He hadn't slept for days before coming to Handstead. Colleagues at his previous nick had tried to console him when news of his enforced move had come through, but, as one by one they'd crossed themselves and promised to light a candle for him, he knew he was doomed. Not only was he now at Horse's Arse, but he was on 'D' Relief. Rumour had it that the Four Horsemen of the Apocalypse had declined moves to 'D' Relief.

Pop-eyed, he looked at his audience and they glared back at him.

'Morning, everyone,' he said. He actually squeaked, his throat was so dry, so he coughed loudly and tried again.

'Morning. I'm Sergeant Mick Jones. Spot of bother at Alpha Sierra, so here I am.' He laughed nervously, and on his own. In reply the vampire sitting in the front row leant to one side, removed his teeth and farted loudly.

'Jesus Christ,' Jones said quietly to himself and looked desperately to the door where Inspector Greaves, 'D' Relief's 'leader', stood looking out of the window. He was off with the fairies and Jones was on his own. Greaves was wearing a pair of carpet slippers, which he had walked to work in, and he now stood in an ever-increasing puddle. He was unshaven and saw nothing as he stared out of the window. Eighteen months at Handstead on 'D' Relief had broken him.

The vampire, 28-year-old Sean 'Psycho' Pearce, turned to

the officer next to him and said in a stage whisper, 'Who's this knob?' Jones heard him and shrank further into himself. He forced himself to look at the officers ranged in front of him and quickly wished he hadn't. They continued to glare at him.

Sitting at the back were the Grim Brothers, who would not have looked out of place in the front seat of a hearse. Indeed, neither would have looked odd in the coffin in the back. They crewed the area car, call sign Bravo Two Yankee One, and were a cold, brooding pair with a reputation for violence that kept them apart from the rest of the group. They worked and drank together, kept watch for each other, and according to Psycho Sean had probably been separated at their birth to a Rampton inmate. Jim Docherty was a dour, pale-faced Geordie in his early thirties with breath that could strip wallpaper. He loved his job, which he saw as a very simple one. Arrest villains, fit them up if necessary, kick the shit out of them – job well done. His partner in crime, Henry Walsh, took a similar line and between them they had established a reputation in the town as a pair of unscrupulous hard bastards. The locals hated them, and whilst their colleagues regarded them warily, their arrival at a pub fight was always as welcome as the appearance of the Seventh Cavalry. Unfortunately, their arrival at non-violent situations had a habit of shortly preceding a fistfight. Henry, known simply as H, had joined the Force straight from school and could never be described as the stereotypical copper. School had been a prep school in Kent followed by a minor public school in Devon, which he had left with a rudimentary education, a raging thirst and a desire to experience life outside a secluded valley. The son of a naval officer who had served around the world, Henry had been at boarding school from the age of eight, rarely seeing his parents or younger brothers. He was fiercely independent and emotionally retarded, but soon found the job he had been born to do. He revelled in the macho world of the police and discovered that being born with fists like granite gave him a distinct advantage. He was also marked out from the rest by his less hirsute approach to personal grooming. Whilst his colleagues, including Jim, favoured a collar-length, over-the-ears style with full sideburns, H preferred his blond hair cut in a tight flat top – a style achieved in a local knife and fork establishment to the accompaniment of 'Something for the weekend, sir?'. He enjoyed the comparisons, often made, to a German Panzer tank commander.

The Grim Brothers had made Bravo Two Yankee One theirs and no supervisor had ever been inclined to separate them. Many took the view that with them working together at least trouble was confined to one job at a time. Now the pair looked at Jones and then at each other.

'Complete twat,' said Jim and H nodded in agreement. They always agreed.

\*

The officer to whom Psycho Sean had offered his opinion of Jones was Dave 'Bovril' Baines. Bovril had gained his unusual nickname after a drunken coupling with a nurse at the local hospital. After several hours of frenzied activity the unfortunate woman's nether regions had become dry, and in an attempt to avoid serious injury she had asked Baines to use some lubricating jelly from a jar on a shelf above her bed. He had grabbed a jar, smeared a huge handful of its contents into her crutch and got stuck in again. Her screams had chilled his blood, as had the horrendous brown stains on both their bodies and the bedding. The discarded Bovril jar on the floor calmed him somewhat before he beat a hasty retreat leaving her dousing herself at the sink. He had related the tale to the rest of the group later and was quickly saddled with a nickname that would stay with him for the rest of his life. Even his mother now referred to him as Bovril, but innocently assumed that it was as a result of his childhood addiction to the stuff.

Bovril didn't respond to Psycho's observation, but privately agreed with him. A formidable shagger, he drew the line at going after colleagues' partners, but had a rendezvous planned for that morning with the girlfriend of a greengrocer who left for work shortly after 6.30 a.m. As soon as this pointless muster was over he would be on his way. He worked as hard as he had to, but he really had only one interest in life: sex, and lots of it. A previous supervisor had once memorably remarked that it was a shame he was such a lazy bastard. If he'd been able to get up in time he'd have shagged the crack of dawn. Even at this ungodly hour Bovril was thinking about sex. He cast a glance behind him at Amanda Wheeler, known as the Blood Blister, 'D' Relief's only WPC, briefly considered having a crack at her later, thought better of it and went back to sleep.

Amanda Wheeler had seen Bovril leering at her and wondered if her hour had come. Every fibre of her fifteen-stone body yearned for him. The red, bloated face that had earned her the nickname – often shortened to just the Blister – glowed more than usual as she lusted after him. She'd previously made him an offer at a party he all too easily refused.

'I'll need a couple more gallons and a lobotomy,' Bovril had gallantly told her. Despite the rebuff, the Blister was still very much in love with him. A veteran of the old Women's Police Department that had dealt with female prisoners and juveniles between office hours, the Blister found her new role an onerous one. She was vehemently opposed to the Equal Opportunities gurus who had got her into this mess and longed to turn the clock back to when she was the secret other half of a detective inspector who kept her on her back and in the dry. Now the Blister sighed deeply and took another long drag on her cigarette, drawing the smoke deep into her ruined lungs.

She blew the smoke vacantly at the neck of the officer

sitting in front of her. He had a large spot forming in his hairline and was rubbing it with his fingers. Alan 'Pizza Face' Petty was covered in spots and one more would make no difference to the stick he got on a regular basis. Each new arrival on his body was a fresh worry for him to pick and scratch at. With only three months in the job he was the butt of every practical joke and was little more than an errand and tea boy. He'd not been allowed out in the cars yet and spent his days wandering aimlessly around the depressing pedestrianised town centre taking regular calls to deal with shoplifters at the only supermarket. The other officers in the group generally ignored him. Recently turned nineteen he was no match for them and could feel himself unravelling.

He lived in horrendous lodgings in the town with an old puff adder of a landlady. She was unprepared for a lodger who worked shifts and the only meals she served were breakfast, lunch and dinner. Too bad if he was working nights. He'd considered moving into the local YMCA hostel, but H had convinced him he'd be raped by the legions of homosexuals that inhabited the place. He'd lost a stone in weight since joining and his physical and mental deterioration was becoming a real worry to his doting parents. When he'd gone home for a weekend, haggard and hungover following a 'D' Relief invasion of Calais, his reaction of 'What the fuck is that?' to the lovingly prepared Sunday lunch had his mother in an apoplectic fit. Only his heart-rending apologies had persuaded his father not to phone the station to complain about his son's rapid descent into moral hell. He sat there totally alone amongst the group.

Next to him was Ray 'Piggy' Malone, so called because of his uncanny resemblance to a Vietnamese pot-bellied pig. He crewed one of the beat vehicles with whoever happened to be spare. Piggy had the gait of primitive man and with his ever-open mouth and a forehead that protruded far enough to keep his feet dry had convinced his colleagues that he was the missing link. He spent large periods of the year off sick with a bewildering array of illnesses and injuries, all of which he managed to obtain doctors' certificates for. Never one to miss an opportunity, he had plunged down flights of stairs in sudden power cuts, slipped on wet floors and been deeply affected by the carnage at road accidents. He had let it be known that he had instructed his wife to arrange for him to be deposited in the back yard of the nick in the event of his passing away at home. This would ensure that his demise would be recorded as happening on duty, thus ensuring a huge payout. The fact that he personally wouldn't benefit had apparently not occurred to him – but then he was extremely thick.

Piggy was sitting next to the officer he was due to crew a vehicle with that morning, Alistair (generally known as Ally) Stewart. Ally was one of the smallest officers in the Force at

5'7¾'' – he had convinced his recruiting officer that he would grow to the required 5'8'' but never had. Southern police forces regularly made up their recruiting shortfalls with expeditions to the frozen, rickets-riddled wastes of the north where the unemployed masses jumped at the prospect of any employment, regardless of its locality. Consequently every force south of the Watford Gap had its fair share of unintelligible (to the southern ear) Geordies, Scousers, Jocks and northerners of every description. Yet even they drew the line at Ally, the runt of the litter with his shock of ginger hair, broad Glasgow accent, permanent angry pink complexion and physique to match the 'before' model in the Bullworker adverts. What he lacked in physique and size, however, he made up for with his dreadful 'small man syndrome'. He was also the most vehement religious and racist bigot and kept a large poster of the Pope in his locker, which he would headbutt before starting work. 'There ye go, ye Papist bastard,' he would bellow before making his way to Muster. However, his worst excesses were reserved for anyone unfortunate enough not to be a white Anglo-Saxon with milk-white skin. Some years ago he and H had travelled into the centre of Manchester on a train and after a few stops Ally had noticed that he and H were the only white occupants in the carriage. He had put his nose in the air, sniffed theatrically and said very loudly, 'Can ye no smell that, H, the smell of unwashed baboon?' H always maintained that they were not attacked only because none of the other travellers could understand Ally's accent. Ally was constantly in trouble and could wallpaper his flat with the discipline notices he had been served with over the years. He was however one of those coppers who knew instinctively when something was not right. Having stopped a black cleaner early one morning, searched him and found a £90,000 cheque the cleaner had just stolen from an office, he was asked by the custody sergeant why he had stopped him.

'The bastard had no socks on,' Ally had solemnly replied.

He was not in a good mood that morning after the Grim Brothers had noticed as he got changed that his pubic hair had vanished overnight. A one-night stand with an Australian barmaid had left him crab-infested, and his golden plumage had subsequently succumbed to a razor wielded by an Indian doctor who seemed to bring unusual glee to his task.

'Try not to move too much,' he had told the appalled Ally as he moved his rapidly shrinking penis from side to side with his thumb and forefinger as he shaved him. 'One slip and I could lop the poor little chap off.'

Ally promised himself he'd set fire to the rag-headed little bastard if he ever came across him on a dark night.

'Fuck me, Ally, it looks like a strangled chicken,' Jim had shouted in the locker room. Ally didn't get much in the way of female company and he felt hugely aggrieved that he had been infected by a chance shag with a woman of the right hue. He resolved to persecute all Antipodeans in the future as they were little more than white wogs.

'Are we going out today or not?' bellowed Psycho Sean, shocking Jones from his living nightmare. Of all the misfits before him, Jones knew that Psycho presented the biggest threat to him. He breathed insubordination and a sixth sense told him that Psycho would be the source of most of his troubles. He was right, too. Psycho was a real beast of a man, of average height, but as wide as the proverbial shithouse door. His breadth of shoulder and depth of hairy chest matched his enormous physical strength, but whilst he had been at the front of the queue when they handed out physique, he had obviously been elsewhere when looks were doled out. He was as ugly as a monkey's arse, memorably described by Bovril as looking 'like a bulldog licking piss off a stinging nettle'. All efforts to tame his unruly mop of dark, wiry hair met with failure and his swarthy, pirate-like, but bloodhound-jowly complexion was highlighted by a huge port wine birthmark on his left cheek. 'The ugly fucker's mother used to feed him with a catapult,' declared Bovril, but quietly so the monster didn't hear him, snap his back and drink the marrow from his spine.

Psycho had only been at Handstead for eighteen months after a period of suspension from duty following a complaint of unreasonable force made against him at his last nick. Off duty, he had wandered into a gents' lavatory in a department store where he had been propositioned by a clearly blind or mentally defective menswear department fairy at the urinal alongside him. Having punched the confirmed bachelor into the middle of next week (not unreasonably, most objective observers had reckoned) the enraged Psycho had overstepped the mark and rammed the unconscious man's head down a toilet which he repeatedly flushed. The man stood a good chance of drowning before other members of the public had intervened. Psycho had been arrested whilst throttling two of the fairy's saviours on the floor of the gents. Incredibly, the Deputy Chief Constable had reluctantly reinstated him without any discipline charges after it came to light that the geldings in the Complaints and Discipline Department had bent one too many rules in their efforts to get him sacked. The only punishment as such was his enforced move to the penal colony at Handstead. He had resumed normal service virtually fireproof and been sent to Horse's Arse, where he quickly gained a reputation for being totally mad. He wasn't mad – he just didn't care any more. He knew he'd have to seriously fuck up before the Job tried to get rid of him again and his conduct became more and more bizarre.

Stories about his manic behaviour were legion, and all true. The Grim Brothers had once, very reluctantly, taken a call on his ground when he couldn't be contacted and were astonished to pass him driving the other way in a lorry taking his HGV test in half-blues. He even had the balls to flash his lights and blow the horn as he passed them. He'd been spotted serving behind the bar of a rural pub on nights, and on more than one occasion found in his beat vehicle having his one-eyed piccolo played for free by a local tom. But nothing ever happened to him, and in truth the group quite liked him because life was never dull when he was around.

Divorced, he lived alone in a squalid flat outside Handstead, which was regularly used by the Relief for huge alcoholic binges. It was rare for an outsider to attend these orgies, but those who had spoke of them later in hushed, awed tones. The dust was still settling after the last party, during which a very pissed Pizza had spent several minutes trying to get the toilet door open but found that it opened only about six inches before stopping with a loud clunk, no matter how hard he pushed it.

Flat on her back on the toilet floor, the girl Psycho was drunkenly ravishing had taken several firm blows to the top of her head, and it was some time before Psycho noticed that she had passed out. She had been doused with beer to rouse her, dressed and put in a taxi still groggy and not quite sure what had happened. Psycho had sought out Pizza and flattened him with a punch to the back of the head. Pizza came round some time later in Psycho's bed to find him gazing lovingly at him, licking his lips suggestively and indicating an open jar of Vaseline on the bedside table. Pizza had fled in horror and spent the next couple of hours with a hand mirror between his legs before confirming that his cherry was still intact.

Jones shook his head to clear his racing mind and made a start. His pre-prepared muster sheet contained the names of everyone who should have been on duty, and to his undisguised delight they were all there. He assigned them to their beats for the day, read them some briefing notes concerning outstanding stolen vehicles and crime trends, briefly mentioned the assault on the pub landlord the night before, and ran for the door. Greaves was still staring out of the window and didn't see him go. Jones vanished into the sergeant's office along the corridor and sat shaking at a desk. At least, he consoled himself, things couldn't get any worse.

The muster over, the group began to drift up to the control room to pick up their personal radios and vehicle keys. Bovril didn't hang about and the Grim Brothers were still in the muster room as he raced his vehicle out of the back yard and off to his rendezvous with the greengrocer's girlfriend. The Night Turn Bravo Two Yankee One crew were still not in and the Brothers had some time on their hands. They had been after a disqualified driver for the past month, and, having finally found his vehicle parked two streets from his home on the Pound Court estate and positively identified him in the flesh, were hopeful of securing his capture during Early Turn. They discussed their prospects for the day.

'He's due to draw his dole this morning,' said H, 'and

there's no way he'll walk into town. Five quid says we have him away this morning.'

'Not a chance,' responded Jim. 'I think it's a dead cert we'll have him today. How about we let him run first?'

'What, a little chase?' said H, a broad grin spreading across his face.

'Why not? Five quid says he does a runner when we stop him.'

'Done,' said H. 'He'll shit his pants the moment he sees us and won't be able to walk, let alone run.'

They wandered up to the control room and arrived there as the Night Turn crew walked in. Terry Hughes and Barry Field looked shattered. They saw the Brothers and Hughes tossed the car keys at H.

'All yours, H. Got a full tank and all your kit. It's running like a dream.'

'Busy one, I take it,' said H.

'Fucking murder,' replied Hughes. 'Haven't stopped all night. We've had Alan Stanley banged up since eleven o'clock and still haven't interviewed him.'

'Give him to the CID,' suggested Jim.

'Not a chance,' said Field. 'Besides, have you been down the cells this morning? It's heaving. Huge punch-up at the Hoop and Grapes last night where the landlord was GBH'd. They've got eight in for that all too pissed to interview until later this morning.'

'What you got Stanley for?' asked H.

'Going equipped. Gave him a pull on the Roscoe industrial estate and found two huge screwdrivers tucked down the back of his trousers. I think we got him too early. Still, there've been a few breaks up there lately we can put to him.'

'Good luck, boys,' chorused the Brothers as they made their way out of the back door into the yard. They had nicked Alan Stanley two years ago in a stolen motor and knew he wouldn't give Hughes and Field the time of day. He would admit nothing and had a reputation with the local police for being impossible to interview. His forte was to sit, arms folded, smiling, and refusing to even admit who he was. It could be very frustrating. Which had made it all the more surprising when the Brothers gave evidence in court of full and frank admissions to numerous offences made to them by Stanley. He had gone berserk in the dock and had eventually been forcibly removed to the cells. He was duly convicted and got three months, all on the strength of evidence given by the Brothers. Stanley had committed some of the crimes the Brothers had allocated to him, but the majority were nothing to do with him. Jim and H had gone to the cells after sentencing, and as Stanley had raged at them with tears of frustration running down his face, H had quietly said to him, 'Fuck you, Stanley. You were due.'

Bravo Two Yankee One was a liveried Ford Escort RS 2000 with a pair of earshattering air horns and the crews loved her. As sure-footed as a mountain goat and with awesome acceleration, she convinced them that there were few drivers out there with either the skill or the horsepower to get away from them. H and Jim carefully checked the vehicle and its equipment before settling themselves.

'Ready?' H enquired.

'As ever, H. Let's go and lay our hands on that little shit.'

H manoeuvred Yankee One through the tight back yard and up to the huge razor-wire-topped back gates that enclosed it. An intercom box on the wall controlled entry and exit and H pulled up smoothly alongside it. He pushed the speak button and was answered by the switchboard operator in the control room.

'Yankee One out and about please, Sarah,' said H.

'Good luck, boys,' said Sarah, pushing the exit button. 'And good hunting,' she added as an afterthought.

Jim picked up the handset from the dashboard and booked on with the main Force Control Centre. 'Hello Delta Hotel, Bravo Two Yankee One, show us On Watch please.'

An operator acknowledged him and Jim sat back in his seat. Yankee One moved slowly, and with an unmistakable air of menace, out into Horse's Arse.

Back in the cell area, Sergeant Andy Collins surveyed the evidence of the Night Turn's endeavours. Fifteen prisoners lodged, most of them extremely drunk, for offences ranging from grievous bodily harm to being drunk in charge of a pedal cycle.

Collins had been round the block a couple of times and

was totally unflustered by the miscellaneous assembly before him. He was a huge man with a head of iron-grey hair, hands like hams and a cigarette permanently clamped between his lips. He dealt firmly with all his prisoners and was politeness personified until they stepped out of line. Many a lippy young pup had discovered that man could after all fly. His power of punch had earned him the accolade of 'the Anaesthetist' and he really came into his element dealing with those who considered police officers to be their social inferiors. The last to try it on had been a corpulent 60-year-old accountant, nicked by Pizza for drink driving during the last set of Nights he'd worked. Standing before Collins as the circumstances of his arrest were explained, he had begun by sneeringly telling the officer how much he earned every year.

'How much do you earn, *Cunt*stable?' he slurred.

'I'm a sergeant,' Collins had replied pleasantly, 'and you probably earn more in a month than I do in a year. Now where do you live?'

'You can poke it up your arse, you grey-haired twat,' continued the accountant. 'I'm very good friends with some of your superiors, you retard.'

Collins's face had begun to redden, and Pizza, recognising the danger signs, took a step back. But Collins didn't hit the man. Instead he simply took the cigarette out of his mouth and said, 'OK, let's log your property. Put everything on the table.'

The accountant smugly emptied his pockets on to the table and stood with his arms defiantly folded.

'All of it,' commanded Collins quietly.

'What?'

'All of it. Strip, you fat bastard.'

'What . . . what do you mean?' the accountant stammered, unfolding his arms as the colour drained from his face.

'Get your clothes off, fat boy. I'm going to have a look up your hairy starfish to see what you've got hidden up there.'

'You can't do this. I know you can't,' the man whimpered.

'STRIP, YOU FAT CUNT,' roared Collins, getting to his feet and showing his full size. 'Do it now or I'll do it for you.'

Slowly the accountant stripped in front of the scornful Collins and the hugely amused Pizza. As he removed his shapeless baggy underpants and stood holding his manhood like an errant schoolboy, he thought his degradation was over. But he was wrong.

'Bend over and pull those lardy cheeks apart, fat boy. Pizza, have a gander.'

Meekly the accountant bent over and pulled his backside apart.

'Blister, get in here,' Collins had shouted and obediently the Blister had walked in from the front office.

'Ever see tackle that small before?' Collins asked her, indicating the accountant who was looking in abject horror over his shoulder at the Blister, his backside still held wide open in both hands.

'Only on a humming bird,' she replied crushingly before leaving.

Collins really went to town on him shortly before he put him on the breathalyser machine. 'Listen,' he said in a conspiratorial whisper, looking round in case they were overheard, 'I might be able to help you beat this. My experience is that the more physical exercise you have, the lower the level of alcohol in your breath.'

'Really?' said the fat accountant, all ears.

'Yes. My advice would be to get some strenuous exercise in quickly.'

'OK, OK,' replied the accountant eagerly.

'On the floor then, fat boy, and give me fifty push-ups,' said Collins.

'Fifty?' queried the accountant who couldn't remember when he'd ever done one.

'At least,' replied Collins matter-of-factly.

Wearily the accountant got to the filthy floor of his cell and fifteen minutes later looked up at Collins who was sitting on the bench picking his fingernails.

'There,' he gasped, red-faced and perspiring heavily, 'fifty push-ups.'

'Took your time, didn't you?' snapped Collins dismissively. 'Right, up you get and give me fifty star jumps – got to get that alcohol out of your body, lard arse.'

Twenty minutes later the accountant collapsed in a heap, panting like a greyhound, drenched in sweat.

'Fuck me, you'll get nowhere like this. On your back and let's have fifty sit-ups,' said Collins, pulling him over on to his back where he lay like an overturned tortoise.

'I can't,' sobbed the accountant, 'I can't. I'm exhausted.'

'I thought you wanted to hang on to your licence,' said Collins. 'Obviously I was wrong. Never mind. Come on then, let's get you on the machine and get it over and done with.'

'No, no, I'll try,' moaned the accountant, desperately heaving his flabby body from the floor. He managed an extremely painful three sit-ups before he vomited. 'I can't do any more,' he cried.

Collins allowed him to clean himself up and then hauled him to the breathalyser machine, where the exhausted accountant blew twice over the legal limit and looked in horror at Collins. 'But you said . . .' he started.

'There you go, some you win, some you lose,' said Collins, shrugging his shoulders and then taking the accountant's arm and frog-marching him back to his cell.

The accountant was a changed man when he left two hours later with a charge sheet and bail notice in his breast pocket. He shook hands with Collins who playfully ruffled his hair for him. Thanking the sergeant for his kindness, he fled the station close to tears.

Collins was a superb judge of human nature and

character and had become an expert in exploiting them. It was his greatest gift.

He glanced again at the fifteen names in his charge that morning and thought he recognised most of them, particularly the eight nicked for the GBH on the pub landlord. They were all members of the so-called Park Royal Mafia, arrogant young thugs who were a constant source of trouble in and around the town. Collins picked up his phone and dialled the CID office. He'd seen the Early Turn CID officer slink in just after 6 a.m. hoping that nobody would clock him and spoil his day just yet. Early Turn CID at Handstead was the shitty end of the stick because you got to deal with most of the crap locked up overnight. And generally there was plenty of it. Collins waited patiently for several minutes until the phone was answered abruptly.

'CID,' barked a male voice.

'Andy Collins in Custody. Who's that, please?'

'Oh, hi, Andy. Sorry. It's Bob Clarke. How's it going?'

'Very much business as usual, Bob. Got a shedload down here for you. Want to pop down so we can run through it all? We've got eight Mafia in.'

'Great,' replied Clarke wearily. 'Yeah, I'll be right down, Andy.'

Clarke replaced his phone and sat rubbing his throbbing temples for a while. He'd had a skinful the night before; his eyes looked like a racing dog's bollocks and he was suffering.

He'd contemplated going sick but his DCI had been at the same do with him and questions would be asked if he failed to show. The next CID officer was due in at 8 a.m. and he knew that the rest of the day would now be spent trawling through the cells with him. They would inherit all the paperwork and the associated inquiries to get on with. He looked at his in tray which contained the pile of paperwork and inquiries from the past two mornings spent in Custody, and wondered when he would ever find the time to complete it.

Clarke had served at Handstead in uniform before escaping to CID and latterly to a Regional Crime Squad. He'd completed his five-year secondment to the squad before returning to Force and had been horrified to learn he would be going back to Horse's Arse.

'Why, what the fuck have I done?' he'd pleaded with his Detective Chief Superintendent on the squad.

'Sorry, Bob,' the DCS had said, 'out of my hands now. I hear the place is like a fucking war zone and they need some old heads. You're in the frame, old mate,' and poured him another very large Scotch from the bottle he kept in his bottom drawer.

'Horse's Arse, Horse's Arse,' Bob had kept repeating to himself. 'Jesus Christ. Horse's Arse again.'

Now Clarke pulled himself gingerly from his chair and walked down the one flight of stairs to the ground floor, through the front office and the station sergeant's office, and into Custody. Collins looked up and smiled at him.

'Hello, Bob. Cheer up, I think we'll be able to deal with most of this lot without involving you, but the Mafia are yours.' He passed across their eight custody records. Clarke recognised all but one of the names.

'Never heard of Morgan, Andy. Is he definitely Mafia?'

'Oh, yes. Been with them about two months and made the most noise when he got lifted. He's sobering up quicker than the others and I think his arsehole's dropped out. First time he's been nicked as an adult and it's dawning on him that he's all on his lonesome and in deep shit.'

'I think we'll concentrate on him first up, then,' said Clarke.

'Most definitely,' said Collins, who'd spotted the opportunity earlier and had intended guiding them in that direction anyway. 'Who's on at eight to help you?'

'Benson,' grinned Clarke.

Andy Collins and John Benson were very old mates and Collins gave a low, knowing chuckle when he heard his former partner's name.

'This stupid little shit doesn't know what's coming, does he?' he said, taking the custody records back from Clarke.

# Chapter Three

The Brothers had made their way to the Pound Court estate and driven quickly past their target vehicle. It was in roughly the same place but facing in the opposite direction to when they had last seen it.

'Been used, then. Today's the day,' said Jim quietly as he gazed out of his window. 'He won't be on the move until later. Spin past his house, H, and let's see if there's any sign of life.'

H nodded and turned Yankee One towards Bolton Road where Frankie Turner lived. Light drizzle had begun to fall and the still dark streets shone like black marble. The intermittent wipers made an oddly comforting sound and the Brothers listened with little more than passing interest to the early morning radio traffic and static. Yankee One swished quietly the short distance to Bolton Road through streets lined either side by parked cars and ruined, rutted, iron-hard grass verges.

Frankie Turner was a 35-year-old unemployed carpet fitter who was serving a two-year driving disqualification for his second drink driving offence. He had driven from court the day he was disqualified and had continued to drive his unregistered, untaxed and uninsured Ford Cortina ever since. He kept the vehicle a short distance from his home but had made the mistake of initially dumping it outside the bungalow of a sprightly 80-year-old widow. She knew Frankie and had remonstrated with him one morning about leaving the rusting hulk outside her house. He'd responded with a torrent of abuse and she'd reciprocated with an anonymous phone call to Handstead police. The Brothers had taken the job, and after some routine inquiries, Frankie was now in their sights.

They drove past his house without slowing looking for signs of movement. All the threadbare curtains were drawn but a weak light glowed in an upstairs bedroom and two full milk bottles stood on the doorstep. The overgrown front garden had a variety of broken children's toys deep in the long grass and the front door was in such poor repair that the Brothers had initially not been able to see the number on it. Most of the pebble-dash around the door had fallen away, exposing the brickwork, and the single pane of glass had long ago been replaced by a sheet of plywood.

Upstairs in the lit bedroom, Frankie Turner lay fast asleep in bed whilst his common law wife sat on the edge of the mattress breastfeeding their fifth child. The infant shared the room with his parents whilst the other four children, all under six years, were still asleep in rooms across the landing. Frankie had not been in long after a hard night with his card school. He'd gambled and drunk away what little money the family had, but consoled himself with the thought that he'd collect his benefit that morning. Perhaps the ugly cow wouldn't notice. Not that he was bothered if she did. She'd remonstrated with him once and he'd punched her front teeth down her throat. Now she had nothing to say about anything. The gurgling child disturbed Frankie who rolled over and yelled, 'Keep the fucking brat quiet, woman,' before pulling a pillow over his head. She briefly considered lying across it and smothering the bastard, but knew she was physically no match for him and didn't need another hammering. Silently she wished him the very worst.

Outside, in the dark and increasingly heavy drizzle, listening quietly to the radio and passing occasional comment on what they heard, were the answers to her prayers. The Brothers were now killing time until Frankie made his move. They reckoned he'd leave for the benefit office about 9.30 a.m. to give himself plenty of time for the 10 a.m. opening. Even if they missed him going, they knew they could get him on his way home.

They cruised the north area of the town doing nothing more than showing the flag to the few residents out and about. Without looking at him, H silently contemplated his partner of the last two years. Jim was a man of few words who chose his friends carefully and remained fiercely loyal to them once chosen. He was slightly over six foot tall and very slim, with not an ounce of excess fat on him. His three years' service with the Parachute Regiment had included a tour of Ulster and he had been in Londonderry on Bloody Sunday. That was shortly before he left the army to become a police officer, and there was little doubt in H's mind that events in Ulster had fashioned the man he now worked with. He never showed any fear or hesitation, and to those who knew him only slightly he appeared withdrawn and almost shy. With H, he had immediately felt comfortable, and despite their hugely different backgrounds they had gelled immediately.

Married with two young children, Jim was a devoted family man. Whilst he enjoyed a drink with the Relief, he never strayed and always went home. For a man who worked the way he did, H always felt that was something of a paradox. They were inseparable at work but strangely saw little of each other off duty. The fact that they lived some distance apart had something to do with that, but subconsciously both the Brothers kept their work and home lives as separate as possible. Neither ever took the job home with him, preferring not to inflict what he had seen and done on his unknowing family. Both men, from decent families and with inherently honest intentions, had adopted personae and characters to fit the environment in which they worked and their families would never have recognised the pair at work.

H had a daughter a little over nine months old, who in his eyes was the best thing ever to happen to him. She was the surprising product of a lengthy, loveless and soulless marriage from which he frequently sought relief. But he was discreet and went to great lengths again to keep that compartment of his life separate from the others. Some of the Brothers' colleagues considered their lack of banter and conversation to be a sign that they merely tolerated each other. The reverse was true. Each knew the other inside out and could predict how he would respond in any situation. They knew instinctively who would throw the first punch and when. Conversation was often superfluous.

H took Yankee One back into the near vicinity of Frankie's car and parked up on a used car forecourt, in amongst the cars for sale. Frankie would have to pass them on his way into town.

The first watery glimpses of daylight began to filter through the high reinforced windows of the cell in which Danny Morgan sat nervously on the hard wooden bed. Other than a badly stained toilet, the cell was empty. The toilet was full to the brim, but could only be flushed from outside the cell and his requests to have it flushed had all been firmly rejected. The cell stank of its many past occupants and the yellowing gloss walls were covered in graffiti, much of it dated by its various authors. A lot of it concerned the officers responsible for their arrests, but a surprising amount related to real or imaginary grasses held responsible for the writer's predicament. There really was little honour amongst thieves.

Morgan had read it all a dozen times since he had woken and as the minutes passed he began to ponder on his plight. He had turned seventeen just two months ago and within weeks of his birthday had begun to run with the Mafia. He had been born and bred on the Park Royal, and it was the natural progression for a youth of little intelligence and even less imagination. His first few weeks had involved not much more than some window-smashing, a spot of shoplifting and the stoning of a passing police car. He had got away with that, as he had with numerous minor crimes as a juvenile, but now he was in deep, deep shit and he knew it.

The Mafia decision to 'run' the pub on the neighbouring Lower Park estate – which simply involved jumping the bar, threatening the staff and then serving themselves for free all night – had gone horribly wrong from his point of view. Generally nobody resisted, but this time the relief manager of the Hoop and Grapes had fought back. Before he fought back, he'd phoned the nick, and of the fifteen Mafia kicking the shit out of him, eight had been captured in the pub. Morgan, on his first major outing with the Mafia, had smashed the vodka bottle on the manager's head and then stabbed him in the back of the head with the broken neck of the bottle. He'd been nicked trying to get out of a toilet window, covered in the manager's blood with shards of glass in his clothing and hair. He was fucked, and as he sat on the bed, shoeless and wearing a white paper suit to replace his own clothes which had been seized as evidence, he began to weigh up his options.

The uniformed officers who'd nicked him had taken a little payback on him with their sticks and his body ached from the beating. He could cope with that – what he couldn't handle was the prospect of prison.

'They'll love you in Strangeways, pretty boy,' one of the officers had sneered. 'You'll end up with an arschole big enough to turn a bus round in.'

'Yeah? Well fuck you,' Morgan had shouted as he tried to brave it out in the cell corridor, largely for the benefit of the other Mafia he knew were also there. He'd been lifted off his feet by a ferocious kick in the bollocks and had vomited from the pain. He felt dreadful and genuinely feared for his safety now. A huge, grey-haired sergeant had come into his cell earlier and lifted him from the bed by his windpipe.

'Your mum's not coming for you, boy, and you can poke a solicitor up your arse,' he'd growled at him. Collins had seen the fear in Morgan's eyes and knew he was nearly broken. 'You tell the nice detectives what they need to know and you'll be on your way. Otherwise – well, you don't want to think about otherwise.'

He'd thrown Morgan back on to the bed, smiled at him

and left, slamming the door behind him. The echo lasted some seconds. Morgan had called out the names of some of the other Mafia he knew had been nicked but had got no response. Some of them had heard him calling and were worried. He was young and soft, and they knew the police would go to town on him first. Morgan had quickly become a liability and a very real threat to their future liberty.

As he sat wringing his hands together, Collins came to the feeding hatch at the cell door. 'Breakfast, Morgan,' he called, and placed a paper plate with bacon, eggs, beans and toast on the open hatch next to a steaming cup of tea. Morgan's heart and spirits soared.

'Thanks,' he said, getting to his feet and moving towards the hatch. As he reached out to take the plate and cup, Collins hit them both with the flats of his hands, sending the scalding tea into Morgan's chest and the food on to the filthy cell floor.

'Got to be quicker than that, boy,' the sergeant said quietly.

'You cunt,' screamed Morgan, staggering back holding his scalding chest and slipping on what remained of his breakfast. 'You fucking old cunt, you've fucking scalded me. Look what you've fucking done.'

Collins unlocked the cell door and walked slowly up to Morgan. He took the cigarette out of his mouth as he spoke. 'That's a very naughty word to use,' he said. 'Don't you ever call me old again,' and he punched Morgan between the eyes with a jab that would have felled a bison and Morgan never saw coming. Morgan slumped back on to his bed semi-conscious, only vaguely aware that the sergeant was leaving the cell.

The phone on his desk was ringing as Collins settled back into his chair and replaced his fag. He picked up the receiver.

'Custody.'

'Dr Collins?'

He recognised the voice immediately as John Benson's and smiled. 'Hello, John. How's things? Has Bob Clarke spoken to you yet?'

'Yeah, he's just getting the interview ready now. Can we come down in about five minutes?'

'Should be fine, John. Patient's prepped and ready for his operation.'

'Fucking hell, Andy,' said Benson. 'How bad is he? Is he going to be able to talk to us?'

'He'll be fine, don't worry. Just a local anaesthetic, nothing serious.'

Benson knew exactly what had happened. The CID had come to rely on Collins 'prepping' their subjects prior to interview, but on a number of occasions they'd had to deal with prisoners barely capable of speech.

'I fucking hope so. We're going to need the names of the little shits that didn't get caught last night.'

'Relax, big man, you'll get what you need. See you in five minutes,' said Collins, putting the phone down.

In the CID office Benson turned to Clarke who was busy putting the finishing touches to a contemporaneous interview that Morgan would later sign. It was a work of art, complete with requisite crossings out, spelling mistakes, and gaps for inserting names, and amounted to a full and frank admission that implicated all the Mafia team that had been in the pub.

'Andy's prepared the patient,' Benson said.

Clarke looked up from his desk, which was strewn with statements concerning the attack on the landlord. He looked slightly worried. 'How bad is he?'

'Says he's OK. I said we'll be down in five minutes.'

'I fucking hope so. I'm nearly done, John. Have a look for me, will you?' He handed the completed pages of the interview to Benson, who quickly scanned the questions and answers. He nodded admiringly.

'Very nice. Still, I think we'll have some sport with the little bastard as well.'

Even though they had more than enough forensic evidence to nail Morgan, Clarke and Benson wanted much more. They knew that the other, older and harder members of the Mafia would refuse to speak to them, or even acknowledge their presence in the same room. They also knew that the manager and his staff would be intimidated in the weeks to come and their few independent witnesses would slowly but surely stop talking to them. They were confident the manager would pick out most of the culprits on the identification parades they planned to hold, but getting him to court would be much more difficult. It was always nice to have an early confession naming names along the way. They'd worry about court appearances later.

'You about done, Bob?' Benson opened his desk drawer and removed the items he needed for the coming interview.

'Finished,' Clarke replied, boxing the papers neatly between his hands. 'Got one for me?' he asked, indicating the interview items Benson was holding. Benson tossed one towards him, and he caught it in mid-air and tucked it into his trouser pocket.

The pair strode purposefully out of the CID office and down to the custody block where Collins looked up and grinned as they entered.

'He can't wait to see you two.'

'I'll bet,' said Clarke. 'How is he?'

'Cooking nicely. Should be about done now,' said Collins, collecting his cell keys and leading the CID officers down into the dingy cell corridor. He peered through Morgan's cell door peephole and saw that Morgan was now sitting on the edge of his bed holding his head in both hands. He sprang to his feet at the sound of the key in the lock and backed against the wall as Collins walked quickly towards him like the executioner come for his man shortly before the 9 a.m. drop. Theatrically, Clarke stepped in front of Collins and put an arm across his chest.

'No more, Andy, he's had enough. Come with us, son. We've got lots to chat about, haven't we?'

Morgan almost ran into Clarke's welcoming arms, passing Collins like a recently beaten dog. Father-like, Clarke put an arm round his shaking shoulders as he led him out of the cell into the corridor and towards the nearby interview room.

'Bloke's a fucking basket case,' Clarke said pleasantly.

'You're not kidding. Fuck me, I thought he was going to kill me. What's up with him?'

'Always been like that, but he's slowing up a bit now. Still got quite a punch on him, though.'

Morgan ruefully rubbed his forehead, which felt as if he'd been kicked by a horse. 'He fucking decked me back there. I'm going to have his job, the old cunt. I want to complain about him.'

Clarke guided Morgan into the interview room, followed closely by Benson, who was grinning from ear to ear.

'Who do I complain to . . .?' Morgan had started before Benson punched him as hard as he could in the back of the head. Morgan crashed face first into the far wall and slumped to the floor. His nose had burst on impact and the front of his tea-stained paper suit began to turn crimson. He shook his swimming head and turned, wide-eyed and open-mouthed, to face the CID officers. As his vision cleared he saw the man who had floored him. Benson was as large as his mate Collins, with jet-black, shoulder-length hair parted on one side, huge sideburns and a Frank Zappa moustache. His deep-set, piggy brown eyes sparkled with malicious glee and he smiled as he spoke to Morgan.

'I deal with all complaints at this station. Who exactly do you want to complain about? Tell me what happened and I'll see to it that the culprit is dealt with immediately.' He towered over the prostrate Morgan and stood with his hands on his hips.

'No one, no one. I've made a mistake,' said Morgan slowly.

'I like you. You remind me of when I was young and stupid.' Benson reached down, took hold of the hair at the nape of Morgan's neck and lifted him from the floor. Morgan screamed in agony and clutched desperately at Benson's huge hand as the detective led him to a wooden chair behind a desk. The chair faced away from the door towards a blank wall, thus ensuring that interviewees would only be able to concentrate on their interrogators. Benson pushed him into the chair and he and Clarke pulled up chairs opposite him. Morgan sat trembling looking at them, rubbing his neck and occasionally wiping his still bleeding nose. His eyes were the size of saucers and he was panting with fright.

'Do you smoke?' asked Benson.

'Yeah.'

Benson took a packet of cigarettes from his jacket pocket, handed one to Clarke, took one himself and lit both with a lighter. He took a deep drag and blew the smoke towards Morgan who looked questioningly at him.

'I wasn't offering you one, you prick.'

Morgan looked desperately at Clarke, who was blowing smoke rings to the ceiling. Clarke smiled. He and Benson were only warming up.

'Got something for you to sign, young man,' he said, indicating the papers on the desk in front of him.

'You're having a fucking laugh. I ain't signing fuck all.'

The CID officers looked at each other and raised their eyebrows.

'That suit looks uncomfortable,' said Benson.

'It's fine. You bastards took my clothes.'

'It's all messed up. Looks like you've dribbled down the front.'

'That old cunt chucked tea all over me.'

'And there's claret all over it.'

'You should fucking know.'

'Take it off and we'll get you a clean one once we've sorted things out.'

'Bollocks. My brief will want to see the mess I'm in.'

'Brief? Which fucking brief would that be? No one knows you're here, you twat.'

Morgan swallowed hard. 'I ain't taking it off. It's fine.'

'It's upsetting me, all that mess. Best you get it off,' said

Benson, getting to his feet and walking round the desk to stand behind Morgan. 'Let me give you a hand.' He tore the flimsy suit off Morgan's back, throwing handfuls of paper over his shoulder until Morgan sat hunched and completely naked in his chair. Benson returned to his seat. He and Clarke smoked another cigarette each and stared at Morgan who remained still, his head down, looking at the floor.

'Don't know about you, John, but I can hardly see the short-arsed little bastard. I can't talk to the top of his head,' said Clarke.

'Stand up, boy.'

'Bollocks.' Morgan had a spark of spirit left.

'On your feet,' hissed Benson menacingly through clenched teeth.

Morgan raised his head when he heard Benson's chair scrape as he pushed it back and walked around the table.

'UP,' Benson screamed, taking hold of Morgan's hair with both hands and yanking him to his feet. Morgan yelped with pain and grabbed at Benson's hands in a vain attempt to free himself.

'See him properly yet, Bob?'

'He's too small. Still can't see enough.'

With one hand, Benson reached down and grabbed Morgan's testicles, and in one agonising movement lifted him on to the table. Bent double with pain, Morgan crouched there with tears running down his face as the two detectives watched him dispassionately. As the pain eased he gradually stood upright, clasping his aching genitals in both hands. Benson and Clarke began to circle him like vultures. Morgan turned with them, desperately trying to keep both in view. Benson then produced the essential interview item he had brought with him from the CID office: a two-foot length of industrial packing band which he began to stretch. Morgan stopped turning and stared at him.

'We're going to need your signature on this interview and some names, son.'

'I can't do that, you know I can't,' stammered Morgan. 'Fuck off, you bastards, you know I can't.'

Behind him, Clarke stretched his own two-foot elastic band wide and released it with a resounding thwack into Morgan's buttocks. Morgan collapsed screaming on to the table before crashing to the floor. A deep purple welt was already in evidence as the detectives hauled the sobbing boy to his feet and threw him back on to the table. Then the interview began in earnest.

# Chapter Four

Piggy and Ally had left the station shortly after the Brothers and made their way directly to the rear of a 24-hour transport café just off the nearby motorway. The proprietor, standing at the front window, saw their panda car pull up and raised his eyebrows to the heavens. Another two free breakfasts pissed up the wall, but when he recognised Piggy struggling out of the driver's seat he knew only two breakfasts would be a right result.

'Doreen, that greedy fat fucker's back. How are we for everything?' he shouted over his shoulder towards the kitchen.

Doreen knew whom he meant and walked to the window wiping her hands on her filthy apron.

'Oh, Christ,' she sighed, 'he doesn't stop. Do you think he ever bothers to eat at home? Look at the size of the bastard.'

Piggy was waddling, at speed for him, towards the back

door, rubbing his hands together at the thought of a lovely big, free 'fat boy' breakfast. He saw the owner and his wife looking mournfully out of the window and waved cheerfully.

'Morning, Derek. We were just in the area,' he shouted. 'Any chance . . .?' He knew full well there was every chance of a freebie.

'Can't even get my fucking name right,' hissed the owner, smiling through gritted teeth and waving back. He walked to the back door, opened it and greeted the two officers like a maître d', albeit an unshaven, twenty-stone one clad only in a pair of filthy tracksuit bottoms and a string vest.

'Hello, boys, how's things? Fancy a spot of breakfast?' he said, standing aside as Piggy bustled in.

'You're a diamond, Derek. Only if you can spare it. Something smells good,' Piggy said cheerfully, pulling up a chair to the table in the middle of the kitchen. He glanced towards the main serving hatch to the café. 'Business good, then?'

'Can't complain. Good days and bad days, you know how it is,' replied the owner, looking anxiously at his customers who had also seen Piggy and Ally arrive and were clearing their plates as quickly as possible.

'What can I get you, boys? The full works? Cup of tea and bread and butter with it?' He was keen to get his unwelcome visitors on their way as quickly as possible.

'Hope it's real butter, not that shit you normally slap on', said Ally sourly, standing by the door with his hands in his pockets. The owner laughed nervously.

'Nothing but the best for you, lads. Doreen, full breakfasts for the boys with all the trimmings,' he shouted towards the back of the kitchen. With her back to them, Doreen didn't reply, but cleared her throat and spat quietly into the frying pan as she cracked some eggs on the rim. Piggy smiled contentedly as he listened to the contents of the pan start to sizzle.

'Can't beat a good fry-up on a shite morning like this,' he said to no one in particular.

'Since when did the weather become an excuse for you to fill your face?' said Ally, pulling up a chair opposite him. Piggy ignored the barb and again glanced at the rapidly emptying café.

'Where the fuck are they off to in such a hurry? This place is normally heaving. Hope it's nothing to do with us, Derek,' he said in all innocence.

'Christ no, of course not. Probably all got things to do. They'll be back later, don't worry.'

Piggy couldn't give a toss if they came back or not, but felt he should show some sort of gratitude for his free breakfast. 'Well, I hope not. I know it must be difficult to make a business like this profitable.'

Especially when a fat bastard like you eats me out of house and home for fuck all every time you turn up, thought the owner venomously as he placed mugs of tea in front of the officers with a big cheesy grin. Ally said nothing but took his mug in both hands and gingerly sipped the weak brown liquid. He immediately spat it on to the floor in a huge spray.

'Fuck me,' he yelled. 'Is it me, Piggy, or is this tea absolute piss or what? Have you had your knob in the tea pot?' he bellowed at the startled owner. Piggy looked at his partner in horror. He could see his free breakfast disappearing into the distance.

'You've put that fucking evil long life milk in it, haven't you?' continued Ally, who was eyeing the remaining contents of his mug with suspicion.

'Bloody hell, sorry about that,' said the owner, hurriedly taking the mug from him. 'I'll do you another one, full cream milk, OK?'

As he poured the offending tea down the sink, Piggy leant across the table and hissed at Ally, 'Will you fucking behave? I'm hoping to get a spot of breakfast without you fucking things up. Just behave and we'll be on our way.'

Ally looked at Piggy with unadulterated scorn. 'You make my skin crawl, Piggy, you greedy fat scrote. You know I fucking hate coming here poncing food off that slag,' he whispered as he leant forward to go nose to nose with Piggy. 'He's a fucking villain and needs locking up.'

'A villain? What the fuck are you on about?'

'Jesus Christ, Piggy, where the fuck have you been? He's a fence, one of the busiest on the Division. How many of those arseholes who've been leaving since we got here do you think were here to refresh themselves? They were here to buy and sell bent gear.'

Piggy looked at him in amazement. 'Derek, a fence?' he finally gasped. 'How do you know?'

Ally rolled his eyes to the ceiling and leant back in his chair. 'His name's Reggie, Reggie Dawes. Not Derek. Never has been, you twat. He's been in the frame as a fence for years. Have you ever bothered to read any of the stuff coming out of the collator's office? All those fags whizzed out of that bonded warehouse at Bandley last month apparently came through this shithole.'

Piggy continued to look thunderstruck. 'Derek? Are you sure?' he managed.

'Reggie. Reggie Dawes. Yes, as sure as anyone can be. I clocked at least three faces out front that I know.'

'Fucking hell, Ally, what do you think we should do? Fuck off, d'you think?' Piggy looked desperately towards the back door and the sound of Doreen's phlegm sizzling in the pan.

'Now we're here we might as well take advantage and have a nose round,' said Ally. 'If nothing else we can scare the shit out of the slag.'

At the sink Dawes could hear the two officers whispering and had to assume they were talking about him. He wished he'd blanked them when they'd arrived but he was going to have to brave it out now. The greedy fat bastard wasn't going to be a problem. He could lay a trail of buns back to their panda car for him, but that pint-sized Jock was a different proposition. He poured Ally another cup of tea, minus the long life milk, and walked back to the table with it.

'Here you go. Sorry about that,' he said weakly.

Ally kept his hands in his pockets and looked darkly at the mug and then at Dawes. 'How the fuck do you keep this dive going? It's a toilet – look at the fucking state of it. Don't the Health people ever pay you a visit?'

Dawes swallowed hard and felt a bead of sweat unconnected with his sweaty trade run down the back of his neck. He knew this bastard was going to start pushing him. He would have to be very careful with him.

'We got a clean bill of health only three weeks ago,' he said, trying to sound indignant and failing to mention that it had been achieved with the help of a bent, top-of-the-range car stereo system. 'Never had a problem with the council,' he added, and immediately regretted saying it.

'I'll bet you fucking haven't. Who you bunging to get the green light here then?'

'Bunging? You're having a fucking laugh,' said Dawes, a tad quickly.

He was saved, albeit temporarily, by Doreen who shuffled towards them with two cooked breakfasts which she banged down in front of Piggy and Ally. Piggy immediately dived into his spiked meal and soon had egg yolk running down his chin. He didn't appear to draw breath as he shovelled the food into his constantly opening and closing mouth. Ally still kept his hands in his pockets and peered closely at the greasy offering.

'What the fuck is this?' he shouted, and reached on to his plate to remove a pubic hair with his thumb and forefinger. He held it high in the air, his face a picture of disgust.

'It's a fucking fuse wire, you dirty bitch,' he bellowed at Doreen, who was now standing next to her husband bitterly regretting the additions to the meal. Dawes looked at her with undisguised fury. He knew very well what she'd done to the meals. She always did when the Old Bill ate there, but he couldn't believe she hadn't hidden the hair in the fried potatoes. Piggy had stopped eating mid-mouthful and sat with puffed-out cheeks resembling a bloated hamster, looking down at his plate, then to the hair in Ally's fingers, and then at Doreen.

'You dirty cow,' continued Ally. 'You've been raking about in your rat's pelt, haven't you, and dumped your fucking fuse wires in the food. What else is in here, you fucking slag?'

Piggy felt his gills getting chalky and spat what was in his mouth on to the kitchen floor. He took a swig of his tea to clean his mouth.

'Careful, Piggy. Fuck only knows what's in there. Had a piss in that, did you, Dawes?'

Piggy spat the tea on to the floor and then threw his mug at Dawes and his wife. 'You pair of cunts,' he screamed. He could take most things, but messing with his feeding ritual was too much. He grabbed the end of the table and upended it, scattering plates, mugs, knives and forks and the filthy plastic tablecloth on to the floor. The table bounced on its end towards the Daweses who backed away in terror. Piggy was on a mission. He advanced on them with his fists clenched, intending to beat them both to a pulp.

'Well, would you just have a look at this little lot,' he heard Ally say from behind him. He stopped, snapped out of his blood lust and turned towards Ally who was standing with his arms folded, smiling at a pile of boxes that had been concealed under the table. Piggy looked back at the Daweses, then back to the boxes. A smile broke out on his face.

'What's in the boxes, Derek? No, no, don't tell me, let me guess,' he mocked. 'This is a café, so my money's on tinned potatoes, peas or carrots. What about you, Ally?'

'Difficult one this, Piggy, but unless Panasonic have recently gone into the catering business I'm going to risk everything and have a little dash at stereos or video recorders. Who's right, Dawes?'

Dawes groaned and said nothing.

'Where'd you get the boxes?' Ally continued.

'I'm looking after them for a friend.'

'What's in them?'

'No idea. He just left them with me and I stashed them under the table.'

'Hid them away, you mean.'

'No, just put them away safe. You can't be too careful these days.'

'What d'you think's in them?'

'Fuck knows. He didn't say and I didn't ask.'

'Not very clever, that. Got to be bent gear, hasn't it?'

'Has it? I know fuck all about that.'

'What's this friend's name?'

'Can't remember.'

Ally bent down to one of the boxes and tore away the packing tape. He opened the top, peered in and stood up triumphantly.

'Oh dear, the fuck-up fairy's been to visit you, Dawes. Stereos,' he announced to Piggy.

'You two are fucking nicked,' shouted Piggy with glee. 'Whilst we're at it, we'll have a look round. Anything else you're looking after for a friend?'

Dawes and his wife remained silent as Piggy and Ally ransacked the café but failed to add to their haul of forty car stereo systems. They sat miserably in the kitchen as transport was arranged to get the gear back to Horse's Arse, before they were unceremoniously bundled into the back of the panda car.

'Christ, I'm fucking starving,' announced Piggy as they drove away, leaving the café unsupervised and at the mercy of the remaining patrons who were unlikely to look a gift horse in the mouth.

\*

The Brothers had been parked up with the engine running for about ten minutes without speaking. They watched the wipers clearing the windscreen, listened to the sporadic radio transmissions and occasionally glanced out of the windows, but they kept their thoughts to themselves. H closed his eyes and settled lower into his seat. He was exhausted and it showed in his pale, lined face and the dark rings under his eyes. He sighed deeply and Jim glanced at him.

'You look like shit, H. Why don't you have a kip for a while? I'll watch things; you get your head down.'

H smiled and without opening his eyes said, 'I'm fine, Jim. I just need to rest my eyes for a while.'

'Bollocks. What you need is some decent sleep. How long is it since you slept properly?'

H didn't reply. Jim sighed, shook his head and looked out of his window. He was right. H desperately needed to sleep, but he couldn't – he daren't. If he went to sleep he knew 'the Dream' would come and crucify him as it had done for the last three months, every time he fell asleep, every day since he had taken that call on his own when Jim had a day's leave.

During his eight years' service, H had seen most things – murder victims, horrific traffic accidents, bizarre suicides, industrial accidents. He had taken them all in his stride, considering himself to be immune to the horror and grief. Until he took that call.

Three months earlier, on a Sunday Early Turn, he had arrived in the muster room to be told that Jim had been granted a day's leave overnight to deal with a domestic matter (his father-in-law's death, as it transpired). H had declined to let Pizza crew Bravo Two Yankee One with him, and took the area car out on his own. Early Turn Sunday morning was the time for officers to catch up on paperwork, and H was parked up on the Park Royal estate writing up a speeding offence process book when the job was passed to him. A 999 call had been received from a hysterical woman who couldn't be understood by the operator. The call had been traced to an address in Abbots Grove, and, as the area car, H was assigned to an abandoned 999 call, nature of call unknown. In such cases, the crews had absolutely no idea what would confront them. It all added to the dubious fun of it.

H had responded quickly, and as he arrived outside the house shortly after 6.30 a.m. he could hear a woman screaming from inside. As he ran up the garden path towards the front door, he automatically and subconsciously noted things that were significant to him. The grass was neatly cut. The windows were freshly painted and the panes clean. The front door had new, bright brass fixtures and the doorbell worked as he pushed hard on it. From within the house he heard footsteps flying down the stairs and the door was flung open by a man wearing only a pair of underpants. His skin was the colour of parchment and H saw stark horror in his staring eyes. The screaming from upstairs was deafening. He thought she was screaming 'No' but the sound was so drawn out and distorted he couldn't be sure. The man said nothing but indicated upstairs with his eyes. As H ran up the stairs he mentally recorded the decent carpets, carefully hung wallpaper, pictures on the walls and fresh flowers in a vase on the landing. The screaming was coming from a bedroom at the back of the house and H barged through the door and into a nursery. Again the mental tape recorder noted care and order. The room smelt strongly of eucalyptus. Pink teddy bear wallpaper, mobiles hanging from the ceiling and an expensive cot in the corner of the room. His heart jumped into his throat, choking him, and his senses slowed. He knew what he was going to see. He seemed to go into slow motion and his hearing shut down. A woman knelt at the end of the cot, tearing at the wooden bars as if at the bars of a cell. Her hair was dishevelled, her face desperate and tear-streaked, and she turned and screamed at H but no sounds came to him. He saw her mouth open and close but heard nothing and began to walk like a man on the moon towards the cot. His head hummed and he could hear his racing heart beating. It was deafening. Already numbed, he approached the cot and saw something that utterly stunned him and rendered him unable to function for several moments. Lying on her back, quite serene, was a baby girl, her skin marble white with a blue tinge. Her eyes were closed and she was obviously dead.

Her bedding and pink Paddington Bear sleep suit were rumpled, probably by her mother's frenzied efforts to rouse her, but otherwise she looked like a much-loved, well-nourished and healthy child, fast asleep. H stared at her for several minutes as the seeds for his coming nightmare were sown.

The child was about six months old, probably the same age as his own adored daughter. It was more than possible that this child and his had been on the same ward together in Handstead Maternity Hospital. Perhaps their mothers had nursed them in adjacent beds. His throat was tightening to the extent that he thought he was going to suffocate and he stepped back from the cot and rubbed his Adam's apple hard. The slow motion world suddenly disappeared and he was back with harsh reality and the screaming woman. The man who had let H into the house was standing at the nursery door, shaking like a leaf, with tears streaming down his face, intermittently giving a loud, heart-rending sob.

'What's your name?' croaked H.

The man looked at him and tried to respond, but he was unable to form any words and gave up, looking down at the carpet with his tears falling one by one on to the deep pile.

'Listen, mate, I need you to help me. Can you get your missus out of here and calm her down a bit? I've got to speak to you both. Can you do that for me?'

The man didn't look up but continued to sob quietly.

'Help me,' shouted H.

The man raised his head and looked at H with red, watery, haunted eyes. 'OK,' he said softly, and went to the screaming woman. He knelt down beside her, put his arms round her heaving shoulders and forced her head into the crook of his neck. He began to talk quietly into her ear and gradually she quietened until she was completely still, the silence only occasionally broken by an involuntary sob. Feeling totally redundant, H walked to the couple, also knelt down and placed a hand on their shoulders. He spoke quietly and with a feeling he didn't recognise.

'I can only begin to imagine what you're going through and how you must be feeling. I promise you that I'll be here as long as you need me and that I'll look after her for you. But a lot of strange things have to happen now. Lots of people you've never seen before and will never see again will come into this room and look at her. They're going to ask you questions that you may find offensive and unnecessary. They're only doing their jobs and I'll be here to help you. Can I get you anything now? Do you want me to contact anyone?'

The man shook his head.

'I've got to get things rolling now. I'm going to have to ask you both to come downstairs with me. I need to get some details from you. Come on,' H said gently.

The man and woman got very slowly to their feet and stumbled past H out of the room. They were empty shells. H followed them downstairs, and once he'd got them settled in the kitchen he went out into the back garden to use his personal radio. He took several deep breaths before transmitting to be sure his voice was steady and businesslike when he spoke.

The day was nightmarish. As was normal in such a case, a police doctor attended to pronounce life extinct, CID officers interviewed the parents to rule out foul play, a Scenes of Crime Officer took photographs of the child in her cot and of the nursery in general, and finally undertakers arrived to remove her to the morgue to prepare her for the inevitable post-mortem. Neighbours alerted to the tragedy by the comings and goings began to arrive at the front door, well meaning perhaps, but only adding to the turmoil. H dealt with them all, fulfilling his promise to the parents to look after them and their dead child.

He returned to the station long after the rest of the Relief had gone home and sat alone in the report-writing room with his head buried in his hands as the image of the distraught parents saying goodbye to their child in the hospital's chapel of rest constantly replayed in his mind. He completed the double-sided Sudden Death report, underlining the heading 'No Suspicious Circumstances', posted it in the coroner's officer's pigeon hole and went home, absolutely shattered and close to tears. His daughter was asleep on his arrival, but he stood alongside her cot in her quiet, dark nursery for a long time, watching her breathe and occasionally touching her face with his trembling fingers. He went to bed without talking to his wife. The Dream came that night.

He was lying naked on a bed, spread-eagled on his back. It was dark and he was bathed in sweat. He was listening to hugely amplified breathing which filled his head. He knew he was listening to his daughter. As he listened the breathing became laboured and short, and after a while stopped. He knew his daughter was dying and went to rise from the bed to help her but couldn't move. He was paralysed, only able to raise his head. He tried to call and shout out, but no sound would come out. He began to thrash his head from side to side as he desperately tried to free himself from the invisible force holding him back, but to no avail. He could hear his daughter dying and could do nothing about it. He threw his head back and screamed silently to the heavens as his eyes bulged and every muscle and sinew in his body strained with the effort. It was the same every time he went to sleep. He feared sleep.

# Chapter Five

Bovril had been hanging around in a lay-by for nearly half an hour before he saw the greengrocer's van pass him on his way to his shop, nearly an hour away. Bovril hoped he'd overslept and wasn't running late because he'd had an early morning shag. It was one thing to shag another bloke's bird; quite another to stir his rice pudding.

He waited until the van was well out of sight before driving the short distance to the vicinity of the greengrocer's house. He parked up a street away and walked quickly to the back gate. He paused to make sure no one was around and no curtains were twitching before hurrying up the garden path to open the unlocked kitchen door. He stepped into the dark kitchen and stood waiting for his eyes to adjust to the gloom. As he waited he heard footsteps upstairs and a woman's voice called out, 'Alan, is that you?'

Bovril smiled, walked into the hall and called up, 'I saw him hotfooting it along the Manchester road a few minutes ago. This is your friendly milkman come to get payment in kind.'

The girl laughed and hurried down the stairs to greet him. 'His alarm didn't go off,' she said, to his enormous relief. She was about twenty, very pretty with short dark hair and a dazzling smile. Her dressing gown parted slightly as she ran, showing her firm breasts briefly. She gathered the dressing gown together and threw her arms round Bovril's neck as she stood on the bottom step. She kissed his lips and neck hungrily as Bovril's hands stroked her back and buttocks. Bovril could feel himself begin to swell and harden as her firm, lithe body pressed against him.

'I thought about you all night, David. I was so worried you weren't going to come today,' she whispered into his ear.

'I've been thinking about you too, darling,' he replied, holding her away to look at her. 'God, you're beautiful. I get horny just thinking about you.'

'Oh yes? How horny?' said the girl, reaching down to his groin to stroke his penis, which reacted immediately to her touch. Bovril groaned and buried his lips in the side of her neck. 'You feel huge,' she laughed.

'It's going to fucking burst if you don't do something about it,' he pleaded.

She didn't answer, but dropped down on to her haunches, pushed up his waterproof jacket and began to tug at his trouser belt. She unbuckled it, slowly pulled the zip down and allowed the weight of the belt to drop his trousers

to below his knees. Bovril's penis was now thrusting above
the elastic waist of his underpants and she gently pushed it
flat against his stomach as she tugged his pants down to his
trousers. Bovril held the banister firmly with one hand and
braced the other flat against the wall as she began to slowly
roll his foreskin back and forth over the bulging tip. She
then gently pushed his penis down to her mouth and flicked
her tongue around the end. Bovril began to roll his head and
closed his eyes.

'Is that good, David?' she asked, looking up at him with
big blue doe eyes.

Bovril didn't speak, but groaned in response. He began
to slowly thrust his hips back and forth to encourage her to
take all of him. She needed no further persuasion. Guiding
him deep into her mouth, she began to move her head back
and forth in time with his thrusting. Bovril took his hand
off the wall and gently held the back of her head as she blew
his socks off. She cupped his balls with her hand, and her
forefinger went further between his legs to the velvet spot
behind his scrotum. Christ, this girl could suck a golf ball
through a straw, thought Bovril. He began to feel the
telltale tingle and knew he was close to coming. Too soon,
too soon, he told himself. He looked down at her bobbing
head.

'Slow down, honey. I'm very close. I don't want to come
yet. My turn now,' he said breathlessly.

The girl looked up, hot and flushed and with a sparkle in

her eyes. She kept a firm hold on the object of her desire. 'Oh, yes, please,' she said smiling at him.

Bovril helped her to her feet and pulled her close. He tugged her dressing gown open, reached inside and ran his hands over her hips and flat stomach. She pushed closer as he cupped her buttocks, gently lifting and parting the cheeks. Her breathing quickened as he brought one hand back to her stomach and began to trace circles with his fingers. He allowed a finger to lightly brush over her soft, downy pubic hair, tantalisingly close to where she desperately wanted to feel it. She opened her legs slightly to encourage him but Bovril wasn't ready yet. He slowly pushed her back up the stairs until she was several steps above him and sat her down. Throwing the dressing gown wide open, he gently parted her legs and began to run his tongue along her calf, behind her knee and up her inner thigh. She grabbed his hair as his mouth passed across her lips, which were moist and swollen. She felt his hot breath on them and gasped as he continued across to the other thigh and then down to her calf. She dug her nails into his scalp as she felt his mouth returning to her core and gave a low cry as his tongue flicked at her moist rose. She began to try to thrust at his tongue and caught her breath as his tongue found her little trigger. Bovril began to force his tongue up and down her lips and as deep inside her as he could. She screamed as her first orgasm racked her whole body and he felt the warm gush against his mouth.

'I need you inside me, David, I need you inside,' she said, urgent and wide-eyed.

Bovril remained where he was for several moments, sucking gently on her soaking lips and flicking his tongue inside. Then he put his forefinger at the opening and she began to moan quietly and grabbed at his hand to force his finger in. He pushed it in slowly to the knuckle and felt her pelvic bone. She screamed again as another huge orgasm gripped her.

'Come on,' said Bovril, reaching down to take her hand and helping her unsteadily to her feet. 'In the kitchen.'

As she walked quickly to the kitchen, with Bovril waddling behind like a penguin with his trousers round his ankles, he removed her dressing gown. As he hurriedly tore his jacket off and dragged his trousers over his shoes, she turned to face him.

'Where?'

Bovril led her to the breakfast bar and faced her towards it. Then he lifted her right knee on to the tabletop, pushing her upper half flat on to the surface. She felt his fingers probing her exposed moistness and spread her arms wide and flattened her face against the worktop. She felt his iron hardness against her lips and orgasmed again as the tip easily slipped into her, and then she felt all of him slide deep inside her. He moved slowly, holding her hips gently, and then began to push her up and thrust faster into her. She was moaning with pleasure as the thrusts got deeper and quicker, and then he stopped pushing, leaving the tip poised at her lips.

'Tell me what you want,' he whispered, gently rubbing and squeezing her writhing buttocks.

'Fuck me! Fuck me hard,' she shouted.

'Do you want me to fuck you really hard?' he teased.

'Oh, fuck me hard, fuck me, hurt me, just fuck me,' she pleaded.

Bovril thrust himself deep inside and she shuddered and whimpered as she came again. He kept up the long, deep strokes, moving slightly from side to side to change his angle of entry.

'Oh, David, I'm coming again. Stop, no more, I'm coming again,' she gasped.

'I'm close too, honey,' he said, increasing the tempo as he sensed his second swelling and he felt as hard as steel. At the point of no return, he stopped moving and clamped himself deep inside, firm against her buttocks as he spasmed and then exploded. He shouted involuntarily and she screamed aloud as she felt him flood into her. His head slumped into the small of her back as he shook and trembled as his orgasm spent itself.

'Jesus H Christ,' he whispered, 'my fucking heart nearly stopped. That was unbelievable.'

After a few minutes during which neither spoke, but stayed gasping for breath with racing pulses, he withdrew from her and stood upright. His legs were still trembling and beads of sweat shone on his forehead. She lifted herself from the breakfast bar, turned, and buried her head in his chest as he held her tight.

'Oh, David, that was wonderful. I can't tell you how much I needed that. I thought I was never going to stop coming.'

'It was good, wasn't it?' agreed Bovril, who was beginning to feel something for this girl that made him slightly uncomfortable. It wasn't just the sex, which was the best he'd ever experienced; there was something else about her that was different from all the other women he'd known. He dismissed it from his mind; just post-shag euphoria, he reasoned. They stood holding each other for a while before he kissed the top of her head.

'I'm going to have to make a move, darling,' he said softly.

She looked up at him watery-eyed and whispered, 'OK.'

He realised that he didn't want to go. He'd happily spend the rest of the day with her, and the night, and the next day . . . Jesus Christ, what's happening to me, he thought. He'd only ever been to visit her when he was on duty and it occurred to him that he had only ever seen her in a dressing gown. They'd met when he'd taken an early morning call to her house to deal with overnight damage to her boyfriend's van, and now he wondered what she looked like when she went out: how she dressed, what she liked to do, where she worked, what her last name was.

'Listen, Lisa,' he began hesitantly, 'I'd like to do something different next time we get together.'

'Oh yes?' she said naughtily.

He laughed. 'No, not like that. I'd like to spend some time with you. You know, go out for a drink or a meal or something like that. Anything really, just spend some time together, get to know each other properly. Do you want to do that? Could you get away in the evenings?'

She didn't reply immediately, but looked at him, searching his face.

'I'm sorry, I shouldn't have asked you that. I'm getting ahead of myself,' he said apologetically. He began to get dressed and she retrieved her dressing gown.

'Are you being serious?' she said finally.

'Forget it, it doesn't matter. I was out of order.' Bovril fastened his belt.

'It does. I just need to know that you're not taking me for a ride. I know I'm not the first girl you've had. For all I know you may be off to visit another one now. But yes, I'd like to do that as well. I can get away in the evenings.'

Bovril paused. 'I can't explain how or why I feel the way I do about you. I only know that I want more. Much, much more.'

'Alan spends most of his evenings getting drunk with his mates at the snooker club,' she said. 'Tell me when and I'll be ready.'

'Deal,' said Bovril. 'I really want to see you again, and away from here.'

'OK.' She smiled, straightening his jacket and clip-on tie. 'Call me soon.'

He held her close and whispered, 'I will, I promise.'

They walked in silence to the kitchen door, which she opened slightly so she could peek out. 'Seems all clear.'

He kissed her on the forehead. 'Soon,' he said and began to walk down the path.

'David,' she called quietly. He turned back and raised his eyebrows questioningly. 'Nothing,' she said hesitantly. 'Just take care, OK?'

'I will, I promise,' he said again, before turning and hurrying away down the path.

# Chapter Six

Psycho Sean was one of the last of the Relief to leave the nick. Straight after Muster he had raced up to the third floor and the corridor occupied by the sub-divisional commander and his deputy. The main man, Chief Inspector Pat Gillard, was a coiffured, bone idle, permatanned old fart who wanted a quiet life and dreamt of his retirement, which he had only postponed until a cushier, better paid job in civvy street turned up. His interest in his job amounted to a big fat zero, and he delegated pretty much everything to his deputy, Inspector Hilary Bott. She was a different proposition altogether, and in Psycho's eyes epitomised everything that was wrong with the job. For a start she was a woman, hopelessly over-promoted and looking to make a name for herself. Hilary Bott was an extraordinarily unattractive woman in her late forties. She was chubbily overweight with pasty, blotchy white skin and teeth resembling polished plywood tombstones. She cut her mousy blond hair herself with a manly side parting and consequently bore an uncanny resemblance to Rosa Klebb of *From Russia With Love* fame. She had the sex appeal of a pile of damp towels. She had been sent to Horse's Arse on promotion, having spent the absolute minimum of time on operational duties, and with a brief from the hierarchy to throw her not inconsiderable weight around. Hard enough to do with a few years under your belt, but virtually impossible if you hadn't a clue how police officers operated on a day to day basis, especially at Horse's Arse.

She'd got off to a shocking start during her first week when she'd rebuked Sergeant Tucker, a grizzled thirty-year veteran, who'd failed to rise from a chair and show due deference to her rank. He'd put an arm round her shoulders and said firmly, 'Listen, darling, as long as you've got a hole in your arse, I'm only ever going to regard you as a fucking nuisance.' She'd reported him to Gillard who'd promised to deal with him and then promptly put the incident from his mind. He had far more important things to do, like arranging his retirement cruise. Tucker continued to make her life a misery, constantly referring to her as 'Cupcake' whenever he saw her. She vowed to get her revenge on the horrible old bastard. Unfortunately she hadn't a clue how to.

Psycho had taken an instant dislike to her. She had an emasculated husband tucked away at home, but Psycho was convinced that was merely a cover for her true sexual preference. 'She's got to be a fucking lesbian. How could

anyone fuck anything that ugly?' he regularly asked. Even
Bovril had to admit that she was on a list of five women he
could never shag. She was third behind Golda Meir and
Piggy's wife. Psycho had begun to wage a psychological war
against her, starting by defacing the stream of pompous
memos emanating from her office and graduating to
circulating a totally bogus one demanding that all male
officers expose their genitals to her instead of saluting when
they met her on the rare occasions she was out patrolling the
ground. Psycho had also noticed the similarity with Rosa
Klebb of SPECTRE and produced some surprisingly
professional 'Wanted' posters of Klebb with Bott's head
superimposed which had appeared around the nick. Klebb's
memorable and sinister words 'He seems fit enough' soon
began to appear added to all her memos, real and bogus, and
became a catch phrase amongst officers at the nick who
would greet each other with it. So popular did it become
that Gillard had begun to try to slip it into any conversation
he had with her as a bit of a personal challenge.

For the last two mornings, Psycho had crept into her
office using the spare key from Enquiries, and had a huge,
smelly crap in her toilet, which he didn't flush. Bott had
nearly vomited on entering the room yesterday. She'd rushed
into Gillard's office and dragged him back to show him.

'Jesus Christ, Hilary,' Gillard had said, his eyes watering,
'you'd better see a doctor. That thing's got veins in it.'

'I didn't do it, you fucking cretin,' she screeched. 'Those

bastards downstairs did it. If you don't sort this out, I'm going to take it up with the Chief Constable,' and she stormed out of the office. The outcome had been a collector's item of a memo from Gillard, reminding all officers that senior officers' toilets were for their exclusive use only – except in an emergency when care should be taken to ensure that they were flushed thoroughly.

Having fouled her toilet for the second morning running, Psycho hurried back downstairs and put the spare key back in the enquiry office safe.

'I hope you washed your hands,' said the Blister, hardly glancing up from the magazine she was reading. She'd seen it all before. Psycho cackled insanely and ran out to the back yard to get his car and be as far from the scene of the crime as he could be when the shit hit the fan, quite literally.

The Blister continued to read until she heard the front doors to the enquiry office open. She looked up to see Rosie, one of the local tramps, peering balefully through the reinforced glass window that separated the public area from the office itself. Rosie was about sixty, completely bald and toothless, wearing four layers of clothing and accompanied by her ever-present shopping bag on wheels. She was also hugely incontinent and generally had an exclusion zone of several feet around her that only the unwary dared to violate. She'd spent last night in a shop doorway and was particularly ripe this morning. The Blister detected the smell through the glass and wrinkled her nose.

'Morning, Rosie, what can I do for you?' she asked without getting up.

'Any chance of a cup of tea? I'm fucking freezing,' gummed the old woman. She knew the Blister was a bit of a soft touch, unlike most of the male officers who generally hurled abuse at her before hoofing her out of the nick on the end of a boot.

'Yeah, sure, but outside, OK?' said the Blister, getting to her feet and going into the telephone room where all the tea-making stuff was kept. Rosie obediently shuffled out on to the steps at the front of the nick and settled down. By the time the Blister brought out a polystyrene cup of tea to her, she had pissed herself again and a stream of urine ran gently down the steps on to the pavement. The smell was overpowering and Blister gasped as she handed over the cup.

'Jesus Christ, will you control yourself, Rosie. Drink that up and get on your way, preferably to have a bath somewhere.' She hurried back to her magazine, but looked up again a few minutes later when she heard the doors open and saw Rosie standing at the glass.

'More tea,' the woman demanded, holding her cup out.

'Bollocks. On your way, Rosie.'

'More tea or I'll shit myself here.' Blister knew bloody well that the horrible old witch was perfectly capable of carrying out her threat and capitulated immediately.

'OK, OK, go on, outside, I'll bring you another one,' she

said urgently, grabbing the cup under the glass partition. Rosie shuffled away as before.

Half an hour later, six cups of tea had passed straight through Rosie's decrepit insides and now ran down the steps in a torrent. The front of the nick was awash, the stench overpowering. Blister was beginning to panic as she realised that shortly she would have no option but to actually take hold of Rosie in order to get rid of her.

'Time you were on your way, Rosie,' she called unconvincingly from inside the front doors, holding her nose against the smell.

'Fuck off,' muttered Rosie, getting to her feet, hoisting her filthy, tattered skirts and shitting against the wall. Blister gagged and hurried back to her office. She'd pretend she knew nothing about Rosie, despite the smell, which was now infiltrating the nick. She tried to engross herself in her magazine, but was disturbed by the sound of a man shouting and swearing outside. An irate Chief Inspector Gillard then barged in through the front doors. He had decided on an early start to spend as much time as he could without Bott to annoy him, and as he hurried along the pavement had failed to notice either the liquid or the smell coming from the front steps of the nick. At the sight of a toothless old hag emptying her bowels on the upper steps, he had reeled and then lost his footing altogether, falling back into an ever-increasing puddle of piss. He was drenched, and, even worse, some of it had splashed into his hair. Now he stood dripping in the front office, glaring at the Blister with the veins in his temples standing out.

'What the fuck is that old bitch doing on my front steps?' he roared.

'What old bitch?' said the Blister innocently, getting to her feet.

'The one that's pissed and shit all over them, you stupid cow. What the fuck's the matter with you, have you no sense of smell?'

'Sorry, guv, I've got a shocking cold. Is there someone out there then?'

'Jesus fucking Christ,' screamed Gillard hysterically, 'look at the fucking state of me. Get rid of the old bitch now.' He squelched to the doors giving access to the nick and waited for the Blister to use the buzzer. She was craning her neck trying to see the scat she knew nothing about outside. 'Door,' bellowed Gillard.

'Sorry, guv,' she said, reaching below the desk to the buzzer. The door opened and Gillard stamped across the corridor to the stairs, leaving a trail of wet footprints behind him. Blister considered her options, which were not good. She didn't fancy ignoring Gillard's pretty concise instructions, but the thought of manhandling Rosie off the steps was not appealing. The smell that had followed Gillard in was worse than ever, and she was going to have to do something about it.

Salvation arrived in the form of Sergeant Tucker, who

had also arrived early for duty as court sergeant and now materialised from the nether regions of the nick. He stood ramrod straight, as befitted a former Guards drill instructor, and wrinkled his nose as he looked suspiciously at the Blister.

'What the fuck is that?' he asked.

'Some old scat's pissed all over the steps apparently. Gillard went arse over tit in it.'

'Have they now?' he barked, and marched out into the front office and opened the front doors. He took a step back as the full horror assaulted his senses.

'God's teeth,' he yelled, before marching back into the nick, propping open the internal doors, and disappearing down the corridor. The Blister watched with mounting anticipation. He reappeared a few moments later, dragging a firehose, which he carried out into the front office. Opening the front doors, he released the hose valve and directed the powerful jet of water at the source of the problem. The jet hit Rosie in the side of the head, flinging her like a rag doll down the steps.

'Bugger off, you filthy old slag,' roared Tucker with a manic light in his eyes. He continued to direct the jet at Rosie, rolling her across the pavement and into the road. Early morning passers-by couldn't quite believe what they were seeing, but this being Horse's Arse they continued on their way. Having hosed Rosie out, Tucker was about to kick her shopping trolley after her when he thought better of soiling his glass-polished shoes, and hosed it after her. He then directed his attentions to the wall and steps before shutting off the valve and vanishing back into the nick.

Rosie sat dripping next to her shopping trolley at the side of the road, shouting obscenities at the nick as passing cars hooted her. Gillard had returned downstairs to ensure that the Blister had complied with his instructions, and had seen Rosie disappear like so much flotsam. He promised himself that he'd look after Tucker; that bitch Bott could poke her complaints up her arse. He glared at the Blister again, who looked up, flushed, and quickly went out to make herself a cup of tea. Gillard staggered back to his office to change and wash before Bott arrived and completely fucked his day up.

'Why couldn't she have fallen in that piss?' he muttered to himself.

Pizza was soaked and freezing after half an hour's aimless wandering around the virtually deserted town centre. Large numbers of the shops were unoccupied, boarded up with 'To Let' signs peeling off outside, more in hope than expectation of a letting. He decided to try to ponce a cup of tea from the baker's shop on the other side of the market place, and quickened his pace as he passed through the rows of empty stalls. The drizzle had intensified and large drops were falling from the peak of his sodden, ill-fitting helmet.

Pizza had quickly lost the feeling of finding his vocation in life and was worried that he'd made a dreadful mistake.

His job was pointless, he felt he achieved virtually nothing, and, worse, no one seemed to give a fuck, either about the job or about him. He was ignored by his supervisors and colleagues, and despite his best efforts to ingratiate himself they regarded him with icy contempt. He took it very personally, unaware that he was undergoing a rite of passage that all police officers were subjected to, and endured, before they were accepted as a member of a group. It was nothing personal. Newcomers couldn't be trusted until they'd been thoroughly tested by their peers. Once you were in, you were in for life, but if you were out you were fucked. Pizza felt well fucked.

The lights from the baker's shop pierced the damp gloom, and he felt a surge of well-being as he pushed open the door and stepped into the yeasty warmth. He took off his helmet and shook his overcoat, sending a shower of water on to the floor. He smiled at the young girl watching him from behind the counter. She had a richer crop of spots than he did, and he began to feel even better.

'What a poxy morning. Cup of tea, please,' he said pleasantly. Wordlessly she filled a mug and placed it on the counter. He picked it up and began to sip the tea.

'20p,' she said, holding out her hand.

'20p?'

'Yeah, 20p. You didn't think you were getting it for nothing, did you?'

Pizza was speechless. This had never happened to him

before when he'd been out with the others under instruction. He put the mug down and began to desperately search his sodden trouser pockets. He began to redden as he realised he was skint. The girl took the mug from the counter and threw the tea into the sink.

'Come back when you've got some money.'

'Yeah, right,' said the crushed Pizza, putting his helmet back on and slinking back out into the drizzle. His eyes began to fill with tears as the feeling that absolutely everyone hated him began to consume him. He stood for a moment to compose himself before walking slowly towards the nearby Grant Flowers tower blocks. He was sure he'd recover a nicked motor or two there. Give him a chance to show the others that he was a grafter. Whilst they were all cosseted in nice, warm, dry cars, he was out there on the cobbles in the rain, doing what real coppers had been doing for over a hundred years. Showing the flag, getting amongst them, getting his hands dirty, looking them in the eye. At least he would if there was anyone about; the little slag in the baker's shop who'd just slaughtered him didn't count.

The tower blocks loomed out of the gloom in front of him like a modern Stonehenge but with none of the mystery or magnificence. They oozed silent malevolence. Thirty storeys high, they resembled a child's neglected Lego construction. They had vast, subterranean garage blocks that had long been abandoned by car owners, and their unlit, vandalised depths were now home to the drug addicts and glue sniffers whose tools of trade littered the permanently damp floors. It was a favourite dumping ground for nicked motors, which were stripped and invariably torched.

He remembered his first visit to the flats with Ally, who gave him some salutary advice that had stuck with him. 'Keep away from the building line, keep looking up and never use the lifts,' he'd said simply. Not using the lifts was obvious enough, but why keep away from the building line and keep looking up? 'Because the rodents that live here have the habit of dropping fridges and tellies out of their windows on to people they don't like the look of,' had been the reply. Pizza would never forget that conversation. Amid the mind-numbing, parrot-like learning of definitions of offences and powers of arrest, this was the sort of thing he really needed to know about. It had begun to dawn on him that there was absolutely no substitute for experience.

As Pizza entered the first of the garage blocks, he took out his torch and shone it into the forbidding darkness. The weak beam landed on the rusting, burnt-out shell of a car at the back of the block, and he began to walk slowly along the rows of garages, all without their doors and resembling huge, gaping tooth cavities, his boots crunching on discarded syringes. His breath hung in large clouds as he walked, shining his torch into the dark. He could hear the relentless dripping of condensation from the low ceiling, and felt his childhood fear of the dark begin to wrap its icy arms round his shoulders. The abandoned garages were full of rubbish of every description, and stank of human excrement. Discarded condoms in most of them evidenced another activity popular down there, and he wondered what sort of person chose to have sex in such a place. There was little of interest in the garages on the right-hand side and he began to walk back along the other side, back towards the distant, weak light of the entrance. The first few garages contained nothing to merit further examination, but halfway along, his torchlight fell on a pile of rubbish that appeared to have only recently been dumped and arranged so as to conceal something within it. Very slowly, he walked into the garage, checking from side to side before he began to gingerly move the rubbish to one side with his boot. Under the pile was a large, black, bulging bin liner. Putting on his gloves, which he'd been trying to dry in his pockets, he pulled the top of the bag open and shone his torch inside. He could see what appeared to be clothing. Intrigued, he pulled the bag free from the surrounding rubbish and noticed that attempts had been made to set fire to it. It was so damp that it had barely smouldered. He carried the bag back to the entrance of the garage block and emptied the contents on to the ground. Inside were three pairs of jeans, a pair of brown trousers, two pairs of Doc Marten's boots, a red and a checked shirt, a pair of trainers and a blue denim jacket. All were covered in what appeared to be dried bloodstains. Now he felt he was doing something worthwhile. This was interesting, proper police work. What was the story behind this little lot? Now the others would take some notice of him. This could be a quality job. He pulled his radio out of his inside jacket pocket and called Handstead Control.

'What d'you want, Pizza?' answered the operator, who shared his colleagues' disdain for him.

'I'm down at the Grant Flowers garage blocks,' started Pizza, 'and I've found a bag of clothing.'

'Does any of it fit you?'

'What? No, no, I've found a load of clothing covered in blood.'

'Very interesting, Pizza. And?'

Pizza was speechless for the second time that morning.

'And?' repeated the disinterested, indolent operator.

'Well, what should I do with it?' queried the rapidly deflating Pizza.

'You could take it to a launderette,' offered the operator.

Several miles away on the used car forecourt, the Brothers were listening attentively to Pizza's radio message. It sounded as though he had stumbled on something that might be of interest later. And whilst they had little time for him, they had even less time for the operator.

'He's a useless idle bastard,' snarled Jim, grabbing his radio and transmitting without identifying himself. 'Get it back to the nick and book it in,' he shouted in his unmistakable accent.

Pizza heard the advice, replaced everything in the bag, slung it over his shoulder, and headed back towards the nick. If nothing else, he could kill an hour or so out of the rain booking it in. He might even be able to spin it out until breakfast.

It took him ten minutes to get back. When he walked into the front office the Blister was still engrossed in her magazine. She buzzed him in and only glanced up when he dropped the bag on the floor next to her.

'What's in there?'

'A load of bloodstained clothes and boots; what's that smell?'

'Rosie pissed herself earlier. I hope you don't think I'm booking it in. You brought it in, you book it in.'

'OK, I didn't expect you to,' said Pizza, trying to sound aggrieved. 'Which register should I put it in?'

'Miscellaneous Property,' said the Blister, imperiously waving a finger at a rack of registers and files above the front desk. Pizza located the register he needed, picked up the bag and began to walk down the corridor towards the report-writing room.

Sergeant Jones was in the corridor sniffing the air as Rosie's aroma filled the nick. 'What the fuck is that smell, and what are you doing in?' he demanded of Pizza, determined to improve his day by making someone else's a misery.

'Rosie the scat pissed herself earlier, apparently, and I've brought in a bag of bloodstained clothing.'

'What for?'

'She can't control her bladder, or her arse, apparently.'

'The fucking clothes, not Rosie. Why have you brought them in?'

Pizza was about to reply, 'Because someone shouted over the radio to do it,' but thought better of it. He considered the question again.

'Well?' said Jones testily.

'It's covered in blood and had been hidden away,' replied Pizza, finding inspiration, 'and I think that merits a little investigation.' Jones bridled at the perceived insolence and tried to think of a suitable response.

'For fuck's sake,' was all he could manage before he hurried towards the toilets for the third time that morning.

Pizza hung his soaking coat over a radiator and sat himself down at a desk to start logging the contents of the bin liner. 'Please let this be a decent job,' he said quietly to himself.

'Hope Pizza's got something decent,' said Jim quietly to H, who still had his eyes closed. 'First time for everything, I suppose.'

# Chapter Seven

Frankie Turner rolled out of bed shortly before 9 a.m., lit a cigarette and sat on the edge of the mattress smoking. He could hear the bitch downstairs with the kids and decided to wait until she took them out before he did anything. He lay back on the bed, flicking his ash on to the floor, listening to the clamour downstairs. He was bored shitless with her, had no time for his children who were unplanned and unloved, and promised himself for the hundredth time that he'd bugger off soon. Only one thing had stopped him going before, the fact that he was an idle bastard incapable of looking after himself. He'd considered going back to live with his mother, but he hated her only marginally less than the bitch. He was stuck and he'd have to make the best of it. Still, today wouldn't be too bad. Pick up his dole; meet the boys at the pub, good drink, game of cards, pool. Who knows?

He looked at his watch as he heard the front door open

and slam shut. Nine o'clock. Best get ready; want to be there when they open up. Stubbing his cigarette out in an overflowing ashtray by the bed, he hurried into the bathroom, splashed some cold water on to his face and pulled on the smoky clothes he'd worn the night before and had thrown on to the floor when he undressed. He smelt dreadful, but that wasn't something that had ever bothered Frankie.

Hurrying downstairs, he eased on his trainers and went into the kitchen in search of his car keys. They were nowhere to be seen. He was sure he'd left them on top of the fridge, but they weren't there now.

'That fucking woman,' he shouted, opening and slamming drawers and cupboards in an increasingly frantic search for them. Slamming a drawer shut, he stood with his hands on his hips looking round.

'Fuck it, fuck it,' he shouted. The town centre was only two miles away, but there was no way he was going to walk it, certainly not in this weather. The bus service was shit, and still involved a walk. He was going to have to make other arrangements.

A few hundred yards away, the cause of his anguish gurgled contentedly as he sucked on the nice leather key fob his mum had given him, and stared at the nice shiny keys. Had his mum been aware of the chain of events she had unwittingly put into motion, she couldn't have been happier.

The Brothers were both now sitting upright waiting for

Frankie, wide awake and eager for what they hoped would happen. If they were really lucky, he'd play up after they'd let him run and then they'd get to beat the crap out of him. Fingers crossed. They were watching every vehicle passing from their right intently, even though they knew which car Frankie had been using. They were taking nothing for granted and hadn't ruled out the possibility that he had another car stashed somewhere. What they hadn't bargained on, though, was what he had under a tarpaulin at the bottom of his overgrown back garden.

Frankie had found the single, worn key in a drawer in the bedroom, and ran to the bottom of the garden. He pulled the tarpaulin away and briefly admired the motorcycle he'd had tucked away for an emergency. Rolling it off its centre stand, he straddled it, put the key in and began to jump on the kick-start.

'Start, you fucker, fucking start,' he shouted as the engine coughed and spluttered. He began to leap in the air as he kicked harder and harder, and at last the engine fired. He revved it hard until the whole frame shook and the garden filled with acrid blue and white smoke. He kept the engine screaming for several minutes before he was sure it had warmed sufficiently to be allowed to idle. He put it into gear and rode slowly through the long grass and up to the side of the house, slipping the clutch and keeping the revs high. He didn't have a crash helmet and he paused briefly as he considered the likelihood of a pull from the Old Bill. It was only a short ride; the odds were good. The Old Bill would be keeping out of the rain, he reasoned. He'd be fine. He stamped the bike back into first gear, accelerated down the path and across the pavement, and turned left towards the town centre.

The drizzle had soaked him completely and his hair was now plastered to his head. He kept his eyes screwed tight against the rain and rode past the used car forecourt, completely missing Bravo Two Yankee One in amongst the cars for sale. H saw the helmetless motorcycle rider first, bent forward over the handlebars trying to coax more speed from the ancient machine.

'Look at this prick,' he said. 'Can you fucking believe it? Any day but today.'

As the bike passed them in a cloud of smoke, the Brothers leant forward to better see the rider and the numberplate.

'Fuck me, it's Frankie,' shouted H, selecting first gear and moving quickly off the forecourt.

'Are you sure?' asked Jim. 'It didn't look anything like him to me.'

'It's Frankie, Jim. Do a check on the number, will you?'

Unconvinced, Jim picked up the main channel handset and spoke quickly. 'Delta Hotel, this is Bravo Two Yankee One, moving vehicle check please, Bolton Road, Hotel Alpha,' and reeled off the registration number which was just visible through the choking smoke. There was a brief pause before the operator spoke.

'Yankee One, that comes back to a lost or stolen from Hotel Alpha since May last year. Your location now please?'

'Bingo! The wanker's on a nicked bike,' yelled Jim, before speaking calmly into the handset again. 'Yankee One, we're still Bolton Road, towards Liverpool Road crossroads, speed forty m.p.h.'

'Thank you, Yankee One. All units Hotel Alpha, be advised Yankee One has a lost or stolen red Honda five hundred cc motorcycle, on the move in Bolton Road towards the Liverpool Road crossroads. No assistance required at this time.'

The radio traffic increased tenfold as other vehicles responded, giving their locations and intended intercept points.

'Fuck off, you bastards, he's ours,' roared H. 'We don't want anyone else getting in the way.'

'Yankee One, commence commentary please,' said the operator calmly.

'Yankee One, we're now left, left at the crossroads into Stockport Road. Passing Chamberlain Grove, speed still forty m.p.h. Solo rider not wearing a crash helmet, white male, early thirties, wearing blue jeans and a green jacket. Don't think he's clocked us yet. Now passing Abbots Grove towards Hotel Alpha town centre.'

The bike didn't have wing mirrors, but something made Frankie glance over his shoulder, where to his horror he saw Yankee One about fifty yards behind him. H flashed the front lights at him and waved. Jim picked up the handset and flicked the public address button. His voice boomed out.

'Yoo hoo, Frankie. You're fucked.'

Frankie faced forward again, cursing his luck. How the fuck did they know who he was? Jesus Christ, how had they got to him so quickly? He didn't recognise the two coppers. If he had, he'd probably have pulled over and got into the back of their car unassisted, but he decided to make a run for it. He opened the throttle up and powered the bike away.

'He's off,' yelled H. 'Fuck me, that's a fiver I owe you, Jim.'

'Easiest money I ever earned,' said Jim, resuming his commentary. 'Yankee One, he's off and running. Speed now sixty-five m.p.h, still Stockport Road towards the town centre. Traffic's light both directions. Now passing the Gables, speed is seventy m.p.h.' He released the transmit button. 'Fuck me, H, he's giving it loads.'

'We're with him, Jim. He'll make a mistake soon.'

Jim continued his commentary as H kept Yankee One purring in third gear, waiting for Frankie to get it all wrong. They normally did. Then Frankie decided to use the only advantage he had and mounted the pavement, barely reducing his speed, and rode up on to the grass verge and into a play area.

'Bollocks,' swore H. He quickly spotted a gap between two parked cars, and powered Yankee One after the bike.

Jim punched the blue light and airhorn buttons and the surrounding area began to resound to the thrill of the chase.

As he crossed the grassed play area, Frankie began to feel the back end of the bike go as the power through the rear wheel proved too much for the virtually non-existent tread on the muddy ground. Barely managing to remain upright, he reduced his speed, allowing Yankee One to close.

'Yankee One, he's left, left across the pavement on to a play area, speed fifty m.p.h. plus and accelerating towards . . .' Jim released the transmit button. 'Where the fuck are we going?'

'Grosvenor Park.'

'. . . into Grosvenor Park, still accelerating, no pedestrians, speed sixty-five m.p.h.'

Around the town, the crews of other cars swore and made hurried recalculations, executed swift three-point or handbrake turns, and headed towards new projected intercept points.

Frankie glanced over his shoulder again and briefly saw the two emotionless faces in the police car, which was getting closer and closer. The passenger was making cutting motions across his throat. H floored the accelerator and moved Yankee One to within inches of the spinning rear wheel of the bike, which was slipping from side to side as Frankie kept the power on.

'Just to let him know we're here,' said H quietly and nudged the bumper against the tyre. Frankie felt the contact, which bounced him two feet clear, and his stomach leapt.

Jesus Christ, these bastards are going to take me out, he thought. He continued across the grass and saw a tarmac path running across the park ahead of him. He steered to the right, hit the tarmac and felt the bike become more stable. He opened the throttle right out, sending the rev counter into the red.

'Yankee One, he's turned right, right along a path, speed is eighty m.p.h plus, headed towards the swimming pool, still no sign of stopping.'

H put Yankee One into fourth gear and kept the front of the vehicle just a few feet behind the bike. 'The mad bastard's going to kill someone like this,' he remarked casually, ignoring the fact that he was right up Frankie's arse, giving him no quarter or margin for error. Jim smiled as he paused his commentary.

'How long are you going to let him take the piss out of you, H? He's going to lose us at this rate.'

'Fuck off,' exploded H, 'he's going nowhere. He can't ride it except in straight lines. Look at him.'

Frankie had clipped the verge and again nearly lost it. His lack of control took him back on to the grass and he began to reverse his route.

'Yankee One, he's left, left off the path back on to the grass and heading back towards Stockport Road. Speed sixty m.p.h. plus, he's all over the place but still refusing to stop.'

The operator had left the channel open to allow everyone else to listen to the chase and only spoke briefly.

'Thank you, Yankee One. Lost or stolen motorcycle is still in Grosvenor Park back towards Stockport Road.' A cacophony of voices followed as other units responded again to the change of direction.

'Fucking hell, H, some other bastard's going to have him away soon. Take him out, for fuck's sake,' said Jim urgently.

'Not yet. He'll make a mistake soon. Stop worrying.'

Jim wasn't convinced, but said no more and resumed his commentary. Frankie continued along the grass and back on to the path and was now very seriously worried. He knew he was in Grosvenor Park, but had no idea which way he was going or how he could get out of the park. The last time he'd been there was as a child when an aunt had taken him to the small boating lake where he'd spent the time stoning the ducks. He saw the lake up ahead and decided to head towards it, simply because he recognised it. Swerving back on to the grass, he continued at the same speed.

'Yankee One, he's right, right off the path towards the boating lake, speed still sixty m.p.h. plus,' said Jim in a calm, businesslike manner.

The boating lake was a desolate concrete circle of black, rubbish-strewn water, surrounded by a rusting iron fence intended to keep the local dogs from fouling the area. Neglected since it was erected, the fence had lost numerous rods over the years, and like the rest of the park the boating lake area was awash with dog shit. Locals remarked that the changes in the seasons could be gauged by the smell of freshly mown dog shit from Grosvenor Park. Frankie spotted a small gap in the fence, and, beyond that, the narrow path that bisected the lake and gave pedestrian (and motorbike) access to the main road. He could just get through the gap; the bastards behind him could either wreck their motor or go round. Either way, he was home free.

H had spotted the gap slightly before Frankie. 'He's going for that gap, Jim. Hold tight – time to finish things.'

Jim understood, nodded, and sat further back in his seat as he continued his commentary. H dropped Yankee One into third gear, again floored the accelerator and moved closer and closer to the bike's back wheel. He knew Frankie's mistake was imminent.

Almost subconsciously, Frankie had been aiming the bike either side of the piles of dog shit on the grass, and about thirty feet from the gap he did so for the last time. Having avoided the deposit of what appeared to be an elephant, he suddenly realised he was off line for the gap, panicked, came off the throttle and hit the footbrake. The bike slowed dramatically and skidded and H floored Yankee One. From where he sat, the decrease in the bike's speed and the increase in Yankee One's had the effect of making the bike seem to go into reverse. Yankee One's bumper touched the rear wheel, catapulting the bike forward and throwing

Frankie back, his hands coming off the handlebars. He remained on board until the bike disintegrated against the iron fence and he was thrown high into the air. H brought Yankee One slithering sideways and undamaged to a halt, and the Brothers watched dispassionately as Frankie flew in slow motion, end over end, across the fence, landing with a sickening thud on the concrete surround.

'Yankee One, he's come to grief big time at the boating lake. Request an ambulance on the hurry up and supervisory for a vicinity only POLAC,' Jim said into the handset, using the recognised code for Police Vehicle Accident. 'We are uninjured, vehicle undamaged,' he added matter-of-factly as he replaced the handset. 'Nice one, H. I think he's dead,' he said, opening his door. H didn't reply, but couldn't see how Frankie could have survived the accident.

The Brothers walked over to the fence, through the gap that was to have been Frankie's salvation and over to his crumpled body. His trainers had come off during his flight, and his jeans and jacket were torn from his landing. A pool of blood was forming under his head. His eyes were closed and he lay very pale and still.

'Hmm, he looks well fucked,' said Jim, poking Frankie's back with his boot. Frankie groaned and the Brothers took a step back.

'Fuck me, he's alive,' said H in amazement. 'Keep an eye on him, Jim. I'm going to check the motor.' He walked back to Yankee One, knelt down at the front bumper and examined it closely. The contacts with Frankie's back wheel had not marked it at all and he smiled for the first time since the chase had started.

'Not a mark,' he called to Jim as he walked back to join him at the boating lake. 'How's he doing?'

'You bastard, you tried to kill me,' whispered Frankie.

'He's fine,' said Jim. 'By the way, Frankie, you're fucking nicked, and you owe me a fiver, H.'

Benson and Clarke stood impatiently at the back of the custody sergeant's office as Collins finished charging and bailing one of the other overnight prisoners. They'd destroyed Morgan and thrown him back into his cell where he now lay shaking and crying, still naked, on the floor. Clarke held the pages of the interview on which now appeared Morgan's shaky signature. As the prisoner was led out of the door, Collins looked up at the two detectives.

'How'd it go?'

'Brilliant. Got the lot, Andy,' said Clarke, indicating his papers. 'We've got the rest of the team in the frame and an address for them.'

'And a cough from him?'

'Oh, yeah. He can be charged whenever you like. We'll get him to court this afternoon and get him banged up. With a bit of luck we can get them all by the end of the day.'

'Result. Where are the others?'

'All crashing at Alan Baker's flat at the Grant Flowers. They should all be there, according to Morgan. We need to get a team together to put the door in. Who's patrol skipper today?'

'Mick Jones,' replied Collins.

'Who, Mick Jones? Who's he?' queried Benson.

'Yeah, fresh meat just got here from Alpha Sierra,' said Collins. 'He should be floating around somewhere. Have a word with him and see who he can lay his hands on.'

'Thanks, Andy. We'll sort out a warrant and get a team together. Can we leave Morgan to you?'

'Yeah, sure. But what about the other Mafia?'

'We'll be back for them later. They'll all be no comment interviews so they can fucking stew. By the way, Morgan's going to need a new suit,' said Clarke.

'OK, I'll deal with him in a minute. Let me know if you're going to be bringing bodies in and I'll clear some cells out.'

'We'll keep in touch,' said Benson as he and Clarke left the room.

They walked quickly back up the stairs, pausing only to comment on the strong smell of piss in the corridor, and back into the CID office. Two other officers were at their desks.

'I'll sort out the warrant, Bob,' said Benson, opening a drawer in his desk, replacing the rubber bands and taking out a black hardback book. He looked at his watch. Nine thirty: the colonel should be awake by now. He opened the book, found what he was looking for and dialled a number. The phone was answered quickly.

'Good morning. This is DC John Benson from Handstead police station. Could I speak to Colonel Mortimer please?' He paused and shortly spoke again. 'Morning, Colonel, John Benson from Handstead.'

'Good morning, John. How are you?'

'Ticking over, Colonel. You know how it is.'

The colonel laughed. 'What can I do for you, John?'

'The Mafia went on the rampage last night and GBH'd a pub landlord. We've got some of them banged up here, but the others are all in a flat at the Grant Flowers flats. I'm after a warrant to go and pay them an unexpected visit.'

'How soon do you need it?'

'Ideally, now, Colonel. I can pop straight over if it's convenient.'

'Can you be here in ten minutes, John? I need to go out this morning.'

'I'm leaving now,' said Benson. 'I'll be with you in five.'

'Fine. The kettle's on,' said the colonel, putting down the phone. Benson turned to Clarke.

'Just nipping out to get the warrant sorted, Bob. Be about half an hour,' he said.

'Thanks, John. I'll get a team together. As soon as you're back we'll make a start.'

Benson grabbed a set of car keys from a row of hooks by

the office door and hurried down the stairs to the back yard. Clarke picked up his phone and dialled the sergeant's office downstairs. It rang for several minutes before an out-of-breath voice answered it.

'Sergeant Jones.'

'Hello, sarge. Bob Clarke from the CID. Andy Collins tells me you're patrol today.'

'That's right,' said Jones, slumping into a chair as he recovered from yet another dash to the toilet. 'What's up?'

'We need to go out shortly to lift the other Mafia involved in the GBH on the landlord. We're going to need some of your finest. How many can you let me have?'

Jones hadn't a clue how many officers he had working that morning, or about the job that Clarke was referring to. His muster had been a nightmare he was trying to forget and he could only vaguely remember reading their names out, never mind their numbers.

He paused. 'We're a bit tucked up this morning. I think the area car's busy. Have you tried getting hold of the Patrol Group?'

'I need to do this on the hurry up,' said Clarke, quickly becoming exasperated. 'I can't wait for the Patrol Group to get here. You must have a few bodies spare. You can come along, can't you? There's one?'

Jones was horrified. Go out on a job? At his last nick the skippers shined their arses for eight hours before they went home. It hadn't even had a cell block where they could be gainfully employed. Go out on a job in Horse's Arse? This guy must be fucking joking.

'Oh, I don't know about that,' he stammered. 'I think you'd better speak to Inspector Greaves. He's the Early Turn guvner, and he might not want to take officers off the street. He's in his office, I think,' he added, trying to sound helpful.

'Wonderful. You've been a great help,' said Clarke curtly, slamming down the phone. At the other end, Jones stared briefly at his receiver before replacing it and hurrying off to the toilets again.

'Problems?' asked one of the other DCs in the office as Clarke banged the flats of his hands on his desk.

'The fucking woodentops are being awkward again,' he snapped. 'I need a hand to lift some of the Mafia and I get some arsehole skipper telling me they're too busy.'

'If you need a hand, Bob, I'm about most of the morning,' said the DC.

'Appreciate it,' said Clarke, picking up a station directory to find the number for the duty inspector's office.

Jeff Greaves lay back in his chair in the inspector's office and closed his eyes. His soaked slippers and socks were drying on the radiator behind him and he had a huge grin on his face. He'd locked the door to avoid being visited unexpectedly and to give him time to prepare if necessary.

Greaves had been a career detective who'd fallen foul of a

previous Assistant Chief Constable who viewed the CID as a whole with grave suspicion. Not without reason, it had to be admitted, but when Greaves had appeared before a discipline board chaired by him, facing charges of falsehood and prevarication following the collapse of a robbery trial, there could be only one outcome. His return to uniform, but without loss of rank, was generally viewed as not a bad result; but the consequence that only the detectives in the Force took into account was the huge financial loss it meant to Greaves. As a DI he had earned vast sums in overtime alongside the occasional bung he took, as was the norm. Back in uniform, overtime for a divisional inspector was as rare as rocking-horse shit, and decent earners virtually non-existent. It was the loss of money that really hurt Greaves and he had resolved to make the Force pay. Very few people were aware of what he was up to.

His plans to be pensioned out of the Job on the grounds of ill health had been carefully discussed with his wife and a few chosen confidants. After eighteen months at Horse's Arse playing the part of a broken dribbler, his mental breakdown was well documented. It had been his wife's idea that he come to work in his slippers, and he had to admit it had been inspired. He'd noticed the odd glances and shakes of the head his appearance had prompted. He knew the story would be round the nick before lunch. 'Heard about that mad sod Greaves? Turned up for Early Turn in his slippers, absolutely pissed through.' He laughed quietly to himself. It was only a matter of time before Gillard sent him to see the Force doctor and he was confident he could do a number on him. Everything he now said and did was part of the master plan. His pièce de résistance was scheduled for next month when he was due to receive his Long Service and Good Conduct medal (despite his discipline record) from the Chief after twenty-two years' service. He would wear his light grey suit and wet himself as he and the Chief posed for photographs before bursting into tears. The assembled senior officers and members of the Police Committee would be horrified, and he'd be out of the door like a greyhound a few days later. He would be sorry to sacrifice his grey suit, but it would be worth it.

He settled deeper into his chair with his hands folded in his lap and his bare feet up on the desk. With luck, he'd be working with his brother Ian in a few months, doing a job not dissimilar to his old one. Ian, who was two years younger, was an ex-DS who had left the Force some years earlier as the fallout from a corruption inquiry touched on the Regional Crime Squad he had been an active member of. His involvement with a bent DI from Liverpool, who had been virtually running a team of blaggers, had surfaced during the inquiry. Whilst he had avoided criminal prosecution (the DI went to prison) he was left in no doubt as to where his future lay, or rather did not lie. He had resigned and now ran a private investigations business which had proved enormously profitable. He employed numerous serving police officers on an unofficial, casual, part-time basis, and had almost unlimited access to information and facilities through them. He got results and paid handsomely for them. His unofficial employees were looked after and they knew he would never let them down. For many of them, working for him had become their primary source of income. Greaves had done a couple of very profitable jobs for him, and when Ian had proposed that he join him as a partner, there really hadn't been much to think about. He had agreed to plough most of his retirement lump sum into his brother's business and the good times beckoned. First, though, he had to get out of this fucking job and into his index-linked pension.

He began to drift off as he listened to the rain driving against the office window and the elderly radiator gurgling and banging behind him. He was shaken from his slumber by the sound of the phone. He let it ring for a while as he composed himself and got into character.

'Hello?' he said timidly.

'Inspector Greaves?' said a firm voice at the other end.

'The shoes aren't mine and the spoons arrive tomorrow.'

'Fuck off, Jeff. It's Bob Clarke and I need your approval for something.'

Greaves relaxed and laughed. He and Clarke had been on the RCS together and Clarke was one of the few in the know.

'Hello, Bob. Sorry about that, but I can't be too careful.

What do you want from me then – me, just a fucking woodentop?'

Clarke laughed. 'Woodentops is about right. Fuck me, I've just been speaking to your Sergeant Jones about taking some of your boys out to nick the rest of the Mafia, and all I get is him giving me a load of bollocks about being too busy. Said I should speak to you.'

Greaves decided to prolong Clarke's annoyance. 'Oh, he's quite right, Bob,' he said. 'We've got motorists to fuck about and lost dogs to round up and you're whining about nicking villains. Dearie me, what are you thinking of? Where are your priorities?'

Clarke was momentarily stunned before both men began to laugh. 'OK, you loony bastard, sulk over. Can you help me out?'

'Sure, Bob. How many are you looking to nick?'

'Could be as many as seven.'

'Fuck me. Seven addresses to do?'

'No, no, they should all be in a flat at the Grant Flowers.'

'That makes things easier, but you're still going to need a few, aren't you? I can take it they'll play up?'

'Not much doubt about that.' Clarke began to read from the interview he had in front of him. 'Alan Baker – it's his flat – Danny and Cliff Reilly, Bobby Driscoll, Peter Thomas, Des Anderson and that mad slag Myra Baldwin. Quite a collection.'

Greaves whistled softly. 'Fuck me. A full house, and

pretty much their hard core. Be a right result to take the whole team out, wouldn't it? How many you got locked up at the moment?'

'Eight. We've interviewed one and got these names from him. The others won't give us the time of day, but this soft little shit gave us everything. If we get all fifteen we'll have pretty much sorted the Mafia.'

'Yeah, you're right, Bob. You can have whatever you need. Tell that wanker Jones I've given you a blank cheque. If he fucks you about get hold of me on the hurry up. Let me know how it goes, won't you?'

'Thanks, Jeff,' said Clarke. 'Why don't you come along? Could be fun.'

'Bob, I'm mad,' he replied, 'but not that mad.'


John Benson drove the unmarked CID car up the sweeping gravel drive to the front door of Colonel Mortimer's imposing detached house, which stood in its own grounds on the outskirts of Handstead. Quickly, he filled in the blank warrant he had brought with him, resting it on the vehicle's logbook. Tucking it into his jacket, he crunched up to the steps, which were flanked by two large, mildewed dragons.

He rang the bell and waited for a few moments until the colonel himself opened it. He smiled when he saw Benson, extended a handshake and ushered him in. As he was led towards the study, Benson considered the magistrate he had come to see. A man the CID at Handstead had come to rely on, Mortimer was in his late fifties, a former Ordnance Corps bomb disposal officer, with ice water running through his veins. During his three years on the bench, he had become the scourge of the local villains. He dominated his colleagues, and in reality every verdict that was handed down was his verdict. Defence solicitors would move heaven and earth to get their cases shifted from his court, and God help the lawyer defending a client charged with assaulting a police officer. Peering over his half-moon spectacles, Mortimer would regularly interrupt defence submissions with gems like 'Are you seriously asking this court to believe such an unlikely event?' or 'Please, please, you are beginning to enter the realms of fantasy now.'

One memorable morning, a defence brief had been pleading on behalf of a client to pay a fine in 50p instalments. 'I imposed a fine on your client,' Mortimer had snapped, 'I did not invite him to join a book club,' before substituting the fine with a gaol sentence. He was a regular guest and speaker at police functions, and would take his lunch in the station canteen if he had a morning court. Over a convivial brandy at the bar after lunch, he regularly took the opportunity to discuss with CID officers cases that were likely to arrive before him in the future. He was a godsend, but the CID were careful not to take him for granted and occasionally bit the bullet and went to other magistrates.

Mortimer motioned Benson to a deep, green leather

chesterfield, and sat down opposite him. A large mahogany grandfather clock in the corner of the study chimed the quarter to the hour.

'What have you got for me then, John?' Mortimer asked. He liked Benson because he detected in him some of the hooligan that he had been as a young soldier.

'The landlord of the Hoop and Grapes had the living shit kicked out of him last night by fifteen Mafia. We captured eight at the scene; the other seven are in a flat at the Grant Flowers.'

'Where did you get that information from?'

'We interviewed one of the eight this morning. He made a full confession and volunteered the names of the others,' said Benson, smiling.

'Interviewed, was he?' said the colonel, his eyes sparkling. He remembered the interviews he'd conducted when he served in Aden and the admissions he'd obtained. 'Are you sure he's telling the truth?'

'As sure as I can be, Colonel. We've got him bang to rights with forensic and an admission to his involvement. I'd say he was telling the truth.'

'Good, good, John. Got something for me to sign?'

Benson reached into his jacket pocket and handed over the prepared search warrant. The colonel quickly read it and signed the bottom, then got to his feet and handed the warrant back. Shaking Benson's hand again, he led him back to the front door.

'I know I promised you a cup of tea, John, but I'm going to have to kick you out without one. I've got to be elsewhere at ten.'

'Don't worry about it, Colonel. I appreciate you seeing me so quickly. Perhaps another time, and maybe something stronger?'

'Definitely,' replied the colonel. 'By the way, I assume your miscreants will be at court some time today?'

'Not till after lunch, probably,' said Benson.

The colonel nodded. 'Excellent. I'm sitting this afternoon. I take it you'll be making applications to refuse bail in all cases?'

Benson laughed loudly. 'See you this afternoon then, colonel. Look after yourself.'

He got back into the car and drove away. Mortimer watched the car turn on to the main road and looked at his watch. He still had plenty of time to get to his stress-relieving massage appointment. Put him in a better mood to deal with that scum this afternoon. Especially if he got that damn fine little wog girl again. That reminded him of Aden as well.

# Chapter Eight

Pat Gillard was teasing his bouffant back into place in front of the mirror in his office when there was a single knock at his door and Hilary Bott flounced in. He had showered and changed and was once again fragrant; his mood had improved considerably, but he raised his eyes to the ceiling as Bott heaved into view and his spirits plunged. He hated it when she just walked in without waiting to be summoned. The woman was starting to drive him mad. She looked at the sodden, stinking pile of uniform by the door.

'Morning, sir. Problems?' she asked brightly.

He glared at her before walking to his desk and sitting down. 'Nothing I can't handle, thank you, Hilary. What can I do for you?' He couldn't hide the contempt and boredom in his voice.

'I thought you might like to know that the area car's taken out a motorcyclist in Grosvenor Park. The rider's on his way to hospital with two broken legs and a broken collarbone.'

'Grosvenor Park? What the fuck were they doing in Grosvenor Park?'

'Chasing the bike. It's a lost or stolen, apparently.'

'Thank fuck for that. Who was driving?'

'One of the Brothers,' said Bott darkly. Neither spoke for a moment as they held eye contact.

'It's all kosher, I take it?' said Gillard finally.

'Apparently,' replied Bott, 'but knowing those two I can't believe there isn't more to it. I believe the rider was a disqualified driver they'd been after for a while.'

'Are we dealing with it as a POLAC?' asked Gillard.

'They called it in as a vicinity only and asked for a supervisor to attend.'

'Who's gone down?'

'No one yet. They can't find the patrol sergeant so I suppose we'll have to send Jeff Greaves. He's Early Turn inspector.'

'Greaves? Are you mad, woman?' said Gillard, raising his voice. 'He's likely to turn up stark bollock naked, if he gets there at all. He's as mad as a March hare; I don't want him going anywhere near this.' Inspiration began to come to him. He could get rid of her for the day. 'No, I want you to take this on,' he continued. 'Get down to the scene and speak to the Brothers, and then on to the hospital to see the rider. Make sure you get a Traffic Accident investigator to the scene as well. You've obviously got a feel for this, Hilary, so I think you should deal. Anything else?'

Bott stood and stared open-mouthed at him. 'You want me to deal?' she spluttered finally.

'Yes I do,' said Gillard firmly. 'You do know what to do, don't you?'

'Of course I do,' she blustered. 'It's just that I am your deputy here, and—'

He interrupted her. 'Precisely. My deputy, and I want you to deal with the Brothers' POLAC. I'd like an interim report on my desk by close of play today. Don't forget the telex to Headquarters. Let me know if you need any help. Thank you, Hilary,' he said dismissively, looking down at a suddenly important piece of paper. She continued to stare at him for a moment before turning on her heels and hurrying out of the office. As the door slammed shut behind her, Gillard punched the air in triumph.

'Fuck you, you stupid bitch,' he said quietly to her imaginary back. He chuckled at the thought of the merry dance the Brothers would lead her. She hadn't a chance. They were a punchy pair of bastards, but what he wouldn't give for a nick full of Brothers, especially in a toilet like Horse's Arse. He had a very good idea of what had happened and was confident that they'd be completely exonerated after the investigation. After all, Bott's report would have to come through him for final action. If need be, he'd simply lose it.

He picked up his phone and dialled the front office. It took the Blister a while to answer.

'You took your time,' he barked.

She recognised his voice straight away. 'Sorry, guv, I was dealing with someone at the counter,' she lied.

'Are you sure they haven't had a shit whilst they were there?' he said, and continued before she could reply, 'What do you know about Yankee One's POLAC?'

'Not much, other than it all finished at the boating lake in Grosvenor Park. They picked the bike up in Bolton Road and the rider's gone to Handstead General. Broken legs, I think.'

'Let the Brothers know that Mrs Bott is on her way to deal,' he said curtly, before putting down the phone. He knew they'd cope with her, but forewarned was forearmed. He shuffled the papers around on his desk and found what he was looking for. The cruise to the Norwegian fjords looked good, but Mrs Gillard fancied a bit of sun on her back. He supposed it would have to be the Caribbean. He sighed and searched for that brochure. Decisions, decisions.

Back at the boating lake, the Brothers had watched as Frankie was loaded into an ambulance, cursing and swearing.

'I suppose one of you will be coming with us?' said an ambulanceman as he shut the back doors. 'Seeing as he's under arrest.'

'Nah, we'll hang on here, mate,' said H. 'Besides, he's hardly likely to have it away on those toes, is he?' He and Jim began to roar with laughter, whilst the ambulanceman merely smiled and got back into his vehicle. He knew the Brothers of old. Pair of mad bastards, but very handy when things got out of hand in the casualty department at the weekends. At least there, the recipients of their violence didn't have far to travel for treatment.

As the ambulance pulled away, Jim's personal radio hissed into life.

'Yankee One, Yankee One from Hotel Alpha.'

'Go ahead, Hotel Alpha,' he replied.

'Yankee One, be advised Inspector Bott is en route to deal with your POLAC,' said the Blister.

'Thank you, Hotel Alpha,' said Jim, and the Brothers looked at each other.

'Bott?' said H incredulously. 'She's got a root growing out of her arse into her chair. What's she coming for?'

'Two guesses, H, and we can discount the one about her coming to do us any favours. Have another look at the motor – I'll check the bike.'

As H returned to Yankee One, Jim went to the wrecked bike and knelt down to examine it closely. He spun the buckled rear wheel until he found the telltale signs of contact, but otherwise there was nothing on the bike to indicate their direct involvement in the crash.

H was kneeling at the bumper of Yankee One, again

looking closely for damage, when he heard a loud 'whoosh' from behind him. He turned to see Frankie's bike enveloped in flames and a large plume of black smoke heading heavenwards. Jim was walking back towards him with a big grin on his face.

'Fuck knows how that happened,' he said innocently. 'Lucky I wasn't standing too close. I might have got hurt.'

'Electrics must have shorted and ignited all that petrol,' offered H helpfully.

'Must have, yeah,' said Jim, turning to watch the blaze as he pocketed his lighter.

'Better call the Brigade in a minute,' said H.

'Yeah, in a minute,' said Jim. 'Motor all right?'

'Not a mark that I can see. Have a look, will you?'

Jim knelt down, and after careful examination agreed. 'Fine. All we need to do now is keep the story straight and simple. Frankie got the line wrong, went too fast and fucked himself.'

'Agreed. We kept well back and he made a terrible mistake. Happens all the time. Christ, I'm soaking. Let's get back in the dry until Bott gets here.'

The Brothers got back into Yankee One and awaited the arrival of Gillard's Chosen One, completely unaware of the forces working on their behalf. It was significant that they always referred to 'us' and 'we' in their discussions. There was never a suggestion that as the driver, only H might be in the firing line. They accepted joint responsibility for everything without question.

As the blaze took hold, Jim reported a sudden fire and requested the attendance of the fire brigade. On arrival they surveyed the smouldering wreck and departed without even using a hand-held extinguisher. A surly, disinterested Traffic Accident Investigation Unit sergeant arrived shortly afterwards, announced there was nothing for him to look at, took some cursory measurements and departed after confirming that his very short report should go to Bott. She arrived some time after he had gone, having had a devil of a job finding the boating lake.

'Well, what happened, then?' she demanded of the Brothers, who had left their vehicle and were standing, arms folded, eyeing her warily.

'He got his line wrong, was going too fast and piled it into the fence, ma'am,' said H.

'How did it catch fire?' she asked suspiciously.

'Not sure. Probably the electrics shorted and ignited the tank. Brigade have been and gone; nothing for them.'

'Any damage to your vehicle?' she continued, peering at the front of Yankee One.

'No, nothing. There shouldn't be, either. We didn't touch him,' said H indignantly.

'I'll be the judge of that, and the Accident Investigation Unit,' she said pompously.

'He's been and gone, said there was fuck all for him.'

Bott began to get flustered. 'Who was it? I'll want to speak to them personally.'

'Don't know his name. Traffic skipper, but he knows you're dealing.'

'Right. I'll need statements from both of you. Who was driving?'

'Me,' said H.

'I'm suspending you from all driving duties until I've completed my inquiries. Your colleague can take over behind the wheel.'

'What?' exploded H. 'I never touched him. You're having a laugh, aren't you?'

'I've never been more serious. Get yourselves back to the station and make a start on your statements. I'll see you when I get back from the hospital.'

She stalked back to her vehicle as Jim laid a restraining hand on H's shoulder.

'Leave it, H,' he said quietly. 'She's going nowhere and you'll have your permit back in a couple of days.'

H was breathing deeply as he struggled to keep his composure. 'I can't fucking believe she's done that, Jim. She's suspended me,' he said desperately.

'Relax – it'll only be for a few days. Come on, let's get back and do our statements before the stupid cow finishes at the hospital.' He guided H to the passenger door of Yankee One, took the keys from him and settled himself in the driver's seat. H was seething. Jim looked at him sympathetically.

'H, forget it,' he said firmly. 'We've had a fucking good result. Whatever Frankie says, it's his word against ours. He's a disqualified driver riding a nicked motorcycle. Where's it going to go?' He started Yankee One up and drove slowly across the grass, over the path and back towards the play area they had first crossed.

Bott's visit to the hospital was a waste of time. Frankie had been taken straight into the crash room where a doctor adamantly refused to allow her to see him. He'd then gone to X-ray which confirmed his collarbone and both legs were broken, and a rib had punctured his left lung. Before she left, he'd been transferred to the Intensive Care Unit. The hospital eventually provided her with his personal details and she decided to inform his next of kin of what had happened.

Fifteen minutes later she arrived at his shabby house and looked distastefully at the overgrown garden as she knocked at the front door. The Bitch answered it and glared at Bott.

'Yes?' she said aggressively, folding her arms and leaning against the doorframe.

'Are you Mrs Turner?'

'No.'

'Oh, well, do you know Frankie Turner?' continued Bott, immediately unsure of how to deal with this appalling, unkempt woman.

'Yes.'

'I'm afraid I've got some bad news for you. Can I come in?'

'Is he dead?' hissed the Bitch.

'No, but—'

'Fuck it, then I don't want to hear about it. Fuck off, you toffee-nosed bitch.' She turned her back and slammed the door in Bott's face. Bott stood on the doorstep, speechless. These people were savages. How on earth do you reason with them? She bent down to the letterbox and pushed it open.

'He's in Handstead General after a road accident,' she called. 'Why don't you let me in and I can fill you in with the details over a cup of tea?' She remembered reading somewhere that the relatives of accident victims often reacted strangely to the news and a cup of tea never failed to remedy the situation. The reply was a blast from an air-freshener aerosol that caught her full in the face, causing her to stagger backwards, coughing and spluttering. As she stood, bent double on the path trying to recover her breath and her senses, the front door opened and the Bitch appeared holding a very soiled baby's nappy.

'If you're not out of that gate in five seconds, you'll be eating this,' she shouted. 'Now fuck off.'

Bott beat a hasty retreat to her car and sped off coughing like a sixty-a-day navvy, her eyes watering. The Bitch threw the nappy into the long grass and slammed the door.

*

Bott drove quickly back to Horse's Arse and tried to get into her office unseen. Gillard however spotted her creeping up the stairs and shouted from behind his desk: 'Here a minute, Hilary. I need a word.'

Scowling, and with her eyes still watering, she stood in front of him like an errant convent girl up before the Mother Superior.

'How'd it go?' he asked, looking up from his brochure.

'Fine. Everything's in hand. Rider's in intensive care but not likely to die. The Brothers should be in doing their statements and I've suspended Walsh from driving.'

'What the fuck for?' yelled Gillard, forgetting the door was open and attracting the attention of two passing clerical workers. He got up, slammed the door shut, and repeated the question.

'Well, because it's a serious accident,' replied Bott.

'I know that, but is there any suggestion that they caused it?' he asked testily.

'No, not really, not at the moment, but I haven't finished my inquiries,' she replied nervously.

'Did you examine both vehicles?'

'The motorcycle was burnt out.'

'What about Yankee One?'

'Undamaged,' she said flatly.

'Any skid marks to look at?' Gillard pressed.

'No. The fire brigade and ambulance had churned

everything to mud. Accident Investigation apparently found nothing either.'

'Did you breathalyse Walsh?'

'Um, no, no I didn't. Why?' she stammered, licking her lips. Gillard saw the chink in her armour.

'Force Orders are quite clear on this matter, Hilary. Officers involved in road accidents are to be breathalysed. But you didn't. I thought you said you knew how to deal with this,' he said crushingly.

She didn't reply, but hung her head and began to bite her lower lip.

'Still,' continued Gillard, 'I suppose I should be grateful that you followed Road Traffic Act procedure at the hospital. You did do that, didn't you, Hilary, with the rider? Asked the doctor to take a blood sample and all that?'

'No.'

'Jesus fucking Christ, Hilary,' he said, shaking his head and clasping his hands in front of him, 'you've completely fucked this up. I hope you realise it'll be going nowhere now. Let me have your interim report in an hour and I'll do my best to keep your head above the shit line. Thank you, Hilary,' he finished dismissively, pursing his lips and sighing loudly. As she turned to leave and opened the door, he said loudly enough for passers-by to hear, 'That perfume you've got on is dreadful. Smells like you've spent the morning on the toilet.'

Bottom lip quivering, Bott slunk back to her adjacent

office, shut the door and burst into tears. Worse would follow shortly when she went into her radioactive toilet to dry her eyes and wash her face.

In his office, Gillard heard her muffled sobs and smiled grimly to himself. 'That'll stop your farting in church, madam,' he said quietly, and went back to his brochures.

# Chapter Nine

Marjorie Wallis was the 58-year-old wife of an ICI director who perfectly reflected what she was. Portly, rather than overweight, she was made up to the nines, had dressed herself that morning in her latest Gucci trouser suit, overcoat and crocodile shoes, and liberally doused herself in her hideously expensive Chanel No.5 parfum.

Travelling through Handstead in her Mercedes sports convertible with personalised plates, she stood out like a sore thumb, but she rather enjoyed showing the cave dwellers how the other half lived. She was accustomed to getting her way and expected instant, due deference and respect from those she considered to be her social and evolutionary inferiors. That included just about anyone not related to an ICI director.

She excelled at bawling out waiters, and delighted in making her gardener's and maid's lives a daily misery. She was a pompous, arrogant old harridan.

Marjorie was on her way to pick up a girlfriend from the other side of town for a day at a health spa, and was now wishing she hadn't decided to travel through Handstead to get there. She was starting to get seriously pissed off with the driver of the battered old Ford Cortina in front of her, who kept missing his gear changes, was slow away from traffic lights, hadn't a clue how to negotiate a roundabout, and, when he was moving, did so at 20 m.p.h. in a cloud of filthy smoke. Try as she might, she couldn't get past him.

'Come on, you bloody idiot,' she bellowed, hitting the Merc's horn for the umpteenth time and flashing her lights. The elderly driver of the almost as elderly Cortina took not a blind bit of notice, and the car belched a blacker cloud of smoke in reply. She hit the horn again and kept it pressed down.

Psycho had parked up in a lay-by to kill time before breakfast and plot his further acts of psychological warfare against Bott. He heard the strident, blaring car horn coming from some distance away, and wound his window down to better judge its direction. Shortly afterwards, he saw the old Cortina pass from his right with a Merc convertible inches from its back bumper, lights flashing, and the fat woman driver banging the car horn with her hand as if she was going mad. She was purple with rage, and despite the distance between them he could just about make out that she was screaming at the top of her voice. He smiled contentedly to himself and pulled out into the traffic behind the Merc, slowing the driver behind with a raised hand out of the window. This could be fun, he thought.

Marjorie was blind with rage, and completely failed to notice the police car that had slipped in behind her. She kept her hand on the horn and only snapped out of her road rage when she heard a car hoot her from behind.

'Fuck off,' she yelled, briefly looking into her rear-view mirror. Psycho lip-read her request, hit his horn again and put on his vehicle's blue light.

'Foul-mouthed old slag,' he muttered to himself, and flashed his headlights.

Marjorie again glanced at her rear-view mirror and groaned. Just what she didn't need. Some jumped-up little oik in a uniform going to lecture her about her driving. This shouldn't take long. Soon send him on his way with his Neanderthal tail between his legs. She indicated left, pulled slowly over to the pavement and watched as the police car pulled in behind her and its occupant got out. This one is just out of the trees, she thought to herself, a real bottom feeder. She wasn't far off the mark, but failed completely to interpret the smile on the approaching officer's face. As he came alongside her car and knelt down, she wound the window down, looked him in the eye and said haughtily, 'Yes?'

Psycho's grin grew wider and his eyes twinkled. She was going to help him add to his legend.

'Morning, sweet buns,' he said pleasantly. 'You're a bit

old to be making all that noise, aren't you? This your grandson's motor?'

Marjorie was thunderstruck. What had he said? Were her ears deceiving her?

'What did you say?' she thundered. 'How dare you, you insolent oaf.'

Psycho continued to smile sweetly at her. 'You should know better at your age. Touch of PMT, or the menopause, do you think?'

'You bastard,' shouted Marjorie, 'I'll have your job. I want your number.' She began to free herself from her seatbelt. Psycho stood up and moved away from the door as she wrestled her plump little body out of the low-slung car and stood opposite him. Her eyes were blazing and she began to jab her finger into his chest as she berated him.

'You jumped up lowlife, how dare you speak to me like that? My husband knows most of your superior officers and I'll see to it that your feet don't touch the ground. You're a disgrace—' Psycho had grabbed the jabbing finger and the smile had been replaced with an icy mask.

'You do that again, Grandma, and I'll snap your little pinky off and stuff it up your arse.'

The smile returned. The wind had been completely taken out of her sails and she now stood, apparently holding hands, staring in awe at the uniformed hooligan before her.

'I bet you've flattened a bit of grass in your time,' Psycho leered, winking at her.

Marjorie continued to stare at him. 'I – I . . .' she started.

'Always had a soft spot for birds a bit older and plumper,' Psycho continued conversationally, holding her hand tighter and pulling her closer to him. 'Always found them really grateful for what they could get.' He began to raise and lower his eyebrows in classic 'How about it?' mode. It had been several decades since Marjorie had been referred to as a 'bird', and almost as long since her henpecked husband had winched up a boner and pleasured her. The thought of being ravished by this monster in front of her was both appalling and dangerously appealing.

A small crowd of passing pedestrians had gathered as Marjorie's diatribe had increased in volume, and now waited expectantly for the outcome. Psycho spoke very loudly for their benefit.

'This is the last time I'm going to warn you. Prostitution is a very serious offence and next time I find you hanging around the transport café you're going to get nicked. Now on your way, you old whore.' He released her hand and gave her bottom a playful but resounding smack that snapped her out of her fantasy.

Marjorie was speechless and stood staring, open-mouthed, at the beaming Psycho. She grabbed his hand to steady herself in case she passed out.

'Come on, darling,' he said pleasantly, 'no need to suck my dick in exchange for a caution *this time*.' He had raised his voice as he spoke, and now freed himself again from her grip. 'You get yourself off home to your grandchildren before they end up in care again.'

'Thank you, officer,' she mumbled almost incoherently as she stumbled back into her car, 'thank you very much.'

Psycho strolled back to his car, smiling at the dispersing crowd who had begun to catcall Marjorie as she desperately tried to start her Merc and escape this nightmare. Some of them had made a note of her registration number in case they should meet her in the future and she fancied earning a few extra bob. It would be some hours before she recovered sufficiently to make a formal complaint and add another chapter to the Psycho legend. He'd simply deny that it had happened like that and let someone try to prove it. Not a chance. He picked his moments carefully.

He pulled out behind Marjorie's Merc and followed her for a few hundred yards, before he turned right and headed through the Ashwell estate back towards the town centre and the nick for breakfast. God, he'd enjoyed that little encounter. It'd put him in the mood for a bit more fun. The drizzle hadn't let up at all and he noticed that not many of the oncoming vehicles had their headlights on. Drizzle constituted inclement weather, and the law required the use of dipped headlights at such a time. He decided he had time for a quickie.

He pulled over into a bus stop, put on his overcoat and went to the boot of the car. Rummaging among the traffic cones and accident signs, he found the large polythene bag he always kept there, and tucked it under his arm. Then he took up position at the kerbside watching the traffic coming towards him. Again, he picked his target with care.

The first half a dozen vehicles to pass him without their lights on had at least one passenger on board, so he contented himself with pointing at the vehicle as it approached and shouting 'Lights' very loudly. The seventh, however, was driven by a lone male who was evidently looking for a turning off the road. Psycho could see him craning his neck left and right as he sought to read the road names. Obviously not a local, thought Psycho happily, so more likely to make a complaint and add to his reputation.

The driver saw the policeman standing by a police car on the verge up ahead and decided he'd better start concentrating on his driving. He knew roughly where he was and had no need to ask directions. As he got closer, he saw the policeman take a large piece of card out of a plastic bag and hold it out in front of him with both hands. Intrigued, he slowed and peered intently through his windscreen to read what was written in large black capital letters. He came alongside the policeman, slowed even more, and screwed his eyes up to read the words. He spoke them to himself as they became visible. 'Lights – you cunt,' he murmured to himself. He drove on past the policeman for several yards before he stopped in a state of complete shock. No, it couldn't have said that. Could it? He turned round in his seat, looked out of the back window and saw the police car disappearing in the opposite direction. He shook his head. It didn't really say LIGHTS – YOU CUNT, did it? No, it had to have been something else. Didn't it? Still shaking his head, he put his headlights on and drove on, still looking for his turning.

Psycho was still chuckling to himself as he parked his vehicle in the back yard. What a blinding morning so far. He'd done Bott, sorted out the fat bitch in the Merc and had his sign out. What a start. The rest of the day was likely to be pretty mundane; he'd peaked too early. Bovril was parking up at the same time and held the back door, waiting for Psycho who jogged across the yard when he saw him.

'Thanks, Bovril. You been up to much? What a fucking morning.'

Bovril could have said that he'd spent the last hour or so thinking about Lisa, as he'd never thought about another woman before. He could have said that he was worried about the extraordinary feeling in his stomach and the fact that he felt light-headed. He might even have told him that he'd met the woman he wanted to spend the rest of his life with. But he didn't. He wondered what she was doing now. In fact, she was standing in her dressing gown in her kitchen, drinking a cup of coffee, thinking about him. Her drab life was changing more quickly than she had thought possible.

'Nah, just catching up with some paperwork. Thought I

might get a piece of the Brothers' chase but never got near it. Sounds like they've been up to their usual tricks,' he said, smiling.

Psycho grinned. 'Put money on it.'

'What you been up to?' asked Bovril, as they walked down to the report-writing room to hang their coats and caps up before breakfast.

'Fuck all really. Didn't get near the chase, like you, had a bit of sport with a stroppy old cow in a Merc and did a short lighting awareness campaign before grub. Not much, really. Oh, by the way, I've brought my pictures in.'

'What pictures?'

'You know, *the* pictures. I told you about them.'

Bovril furrowed his brow. 'When? What pictures are you talking about?'

'The pictures of the women I've shagged,' said Psycho slowly and deliberately, as if he was talking to an idiot. They had reached the report-writing room, and Pizza, who had finished logging his property, deposited it in the Property Store, and returned to hide himself away until breakfast, was listening intently.

'Pictures of women you've shagged?' said Bovril incredulously.

'Yeah. I told you. I've brought them in.'

Bovril racked his memory and, finally, vaguely recalled a drunken conversation with Psycho at his last party.

'Oh yeah, I remember now. Pictures of women you've

shagged. What are they, head and shoulders shots or ones you've cut out of your porn mags?' he jeered.

'Fuck off,' said Psycho indignantly. 'They're my own Polaroids, full meat shots, the works.'

'Full meat shots?' queried Pizza, who was absolutely enthralled.

'Fucking right,' said Psycho, without explaining. 'I'll bring them up for breakfast.' He hurried off to the locker room.

'Full meat shots?' said Pizza to Bovril. Bovril shook his head disdainfully and walked out without speaking. Pizza hurried after him and they walked in silence up the three flights of stairs to the top floor where the bar area and canteen were situated. Piggy and Ally had already booked Dawes and his wife into custody, and were now sitting at a table. Ally was drinking a mug of tea, watching in undisguised horror as Piggy devoured a fried breakfast large enough for a family of five. Bovril and Pizza went to the counter, placed their orders with the canteen ladies and returned to the table.

'Got a couple in, then?' said Bovril.

'Dawes and his missus,' replied Ally. 'Found a load of nicked stereos under his table. That fucking bitch tried to poison us with her pubes in the breakfast. Fuck knows what he'd done to the tea.'

Piggy had stopped eating and spoke with his cheeks bulging. 'Will you fucking stop it,' he snapped, spraying half-chewed food in all directions. 'I'm trying to forget all about it.' That said, he resumed the relentless transfer of food to his constantly opening and closing mouth.

'It's disgusting isn't it?' said Ally dispassionately as the three of them watched him, and Piggy wiped a piece of bacon rind off his face. 'It's something of a miracle that they ever get the cutlery back.'

Bovril and Pizza didn't have to wait long for their breakfasts and were soon eating their considerably smaller meals. As they started, the Brothers walked into the canteen.

'Nice one, boys,' called Bovril. 'How's the rider?' The four men at the table laughed.

'He'll live,' said H sourly. 'That bitch Bott's suspended me from driving.'

'Routine, H, that's all,' said Ally reassuringly.

'That's what I told him,' called Jim from the counter, 'but he's sulked all the way back. Anyone want a cup of tea?'

'Me, me,' said Piggy, quickly draining the full mug in front of him. H, Bovril and Pizza also accepted the offer, and soon all six of them were around the table.

'Psycho's gone to get his porn pictures,' said Bovril mysteriously.

'What porn pictures?' said Ally.

'Full meat shots,' offered Pizza knowingly.

'What porn pictures?' repeated Ally.

'Mad bastard says he's got pictures of all the women he's shagged. Polaroids. He's bringing them up now.'

'You're fucking joking, aren't you?' said H through a mouthful of tea. Before Bovril could reply, Psycho walked up holding a blue plastic photograph album. They stared at him, then at the album, but no one spoke. Psycho pulled a chair over from an adjacent table and sat at the end of theirs, placing the album in front of him. He patted it proudly.

'There it is, boys, as promised: my life of debauchery in glorious Technicolor.'

'You've got pictures of the women you've shagged in there?' said H slowly. 'They just let you take a picture with your Polaroid?'

'Full meat shots?' asked Pizza.

'Yup,' said Psycho matter-of-factly.

Without a word, H pulled the album towards him and opened it. The others left their chairs and gathered round his shoulders.

'Jesus Christ,' said H quietly. Psycho had been telling the truth. The first two pages each contained four Polaroid photographs, apparently of the same girl, taken in what the group recognised as Psycho's bedroom. Fairly routine nude poses, in what she and Psycho clearly felt was the more upmarket men's magazine mould, progressed to one of her using a truncheon on herself, another of her sucking his cock, taken looking down over his huge, hairy belly, and finally one of her on her back, legs wide open.

'Full meat shots,' gasped Pizza, finally understanding.

The next two pages also contained eight photographs of

different girls in virtually identical poses. No one said a word. However, the last page caused ructions. It contained four photographs of the same fat woman; in two she had her face strategically turned away from the camera. The third was taken from behind with her on her hands and knees, but the fourth showed her on her back, legs wide apart, holding her lips open for the camera, and her head raised with a big smile for David Bailey. She looked shitfaced.

'Oh my God, it's the Blood Blister,' whispered Ally. Psycho pushed his way to the front of the mêlée and looked over H's shoulder.

'Oh, bollocks. I forgot those were in there. For fuck's sake, keep it quiet, will you, lads?'

'Looks like a black cat with its throat cut,' said Jim finally. 'I didn't know you'd shagged the Blister.'

'Yeah, after my last party,' said Psycho unapologetically. 'It was on offer and I never turn down a freebie.'

'I feel ill,' said Piggy, moving away from the gathering and heading towards the toilets. He'd seen enough pubic hair that morning to stuff a mattress. Psycho grabbed his album.

'That'll do, boys. I'm counting on you not to say anything to anyone, especially the Blister. She'll go fucking mental if she finds out I've shown you them.'

'You can count on us, Psycho,' said Ally, with not a hint of sarcasm.

Psycho hurried away to hide his album, bitterly regretting showing it to the others. The bastards are bound to say something, he thought. The only consolation was that it was most unlikely that the Blister would make a formal complaint.

Piggy rejoined the others at the table. 'That made me feel very queasy,' he announced. 'I'm not touching another kebab as long as I live.'

# Chapter Ten

Following his conversation with Greaves, Clarke had again telephoned Sergeant Jones and relayed his message. Well, most of it.

'Take who you want,' said Jones mournfully. 'Some of them will be in for grub now – you can have them. Let me know who you've got, will you?'

'Will do, sarge,' said Clarke brightly, 'and thanks again for all your help.'

'You're welcome,' replied Jones, completely missing the sarcasm in Clarke's voice and sounding more and more like Eeyore from *Winnie-the-Pooh*.

Clarke replaced his phone and hurried up to the canteen in search of uniforms eating. He saw a group of seven huddled over something at one of the tables, but decided not to interrupt them just yet. He recognised all but the young, spotty one. He went to the counter and ordered himself a cup of tea. As he waited for it, he used the phone on the wall to dial the CID office, and spoke to the DC who had previously offered his help.

'It's Bob. I'm in the canteen. I think I could do with your help later. I'll have seven uniforms, and with you, me and John we should have enough. Is John back yet?'

'No, not yet – when you planning to go out?'

Clarke looked at his watch: 10.30 a.m. 'As soon as possible,' he replied. 'When John gets back, why don't you pop upstairs and we'll do the briefing here?'

'Yeah, fine, Bob. Steve Lloyd's in and offering, OK if he comes along as well?'

'More the merrier, Dave. We're not proud.' Clarke laughed, replaced the phone, picked up his mug of tea and walked over to the uniforms' table. Psycho had gone and he heard the fat one called Piggy telling the others that he felt unwell.

'Not too ill, I hope,' he interrupted. 'I've got a little job for you and the others.'

It was an unintentional and unfortunate statement that immediately had the uniforms' hackles up.

'Is that fucking right?' said Ally, getting to his feet. 'Not for me you fucking haven't. Piggy and I have got bodies locked up. Come on, Piggy. Best we go and deal with them before the CID find something useful for the woodos to do.'

Piggy had also taken umbrage at Clarke's perceived arrogance and quickly cleared his plate. 'Sorry, things to do,' he said, wiping his hand across his mouth and following Ally out of the canteen. 'Fucking CID.'

'Hold on, lads,' called Clarke plaintively. 'I've spoken to Mr Greaves and he's OK'd it. For fuck's sake, what's up with them?' He turned to the others, who'd remained seated.

'You're going to have to work on your communication skills, aren't you, Bob?' said H quietly. 'You've got the unfortunate habit of letting us woodentops know you're about to fuck us.'

'Christ, I didn't mean anything like that,' said Clarke, sitting down. 'Fact is I really need some help from all of you to lift a load of Mafia. I cleared it with Jeff Greaves before I came upstairs.'

'That's what I mean, Bob,' said H. 'You've got a decent job for us but you fuck it up straight away by coming on like a fucking headmistress. You should know by now how easily Ally gets the hump when the suits start lording it.'

Clarke shook his head: 'I'll square it with him and Piggy. Can you four give me a hand?'

The Brothers, Bovril and Pizza all indicated in the affirmative.

'Is this connected with the GBH at the Hoop and Grapes?' asked Pizza.

'Yeah. The seven Mafia we're after are all in a flat at the Grant Flowers. We're just getting the warrant sorted and we'll be off. Can you all be in the muster room in fifteen minutes? I'll go and placate Ally and Piggy and bring them along. Any idea where Psycho went?'

'Locker room,' said Jim. 'Putting some gear away.'

'If you see him before me, can you tell him I'm looking for him? Nicely, please,' he added, laughing.

He got up and went back to the phone on the wall. He spoke again to his office, confirmed that Benson was not yet back and cancelled the briefing in the canteen. 'Make it the muster room in fifteen,' he said. 'I'm having a few problems getting everyone together.'

Clarke then hurried down to the cell block where he found Ally and Piggy waiting to speak to Collins. 'Can I have a word, boys?' he said. 'There's been a bit of a misunderstanding here.'

Ally and Piggy looked suspiciously at each other, and then walked to one side with Clarke so as to be out of earshot of the prisoners.

'Listen, lads, I'm sorry if you've got the hump with me, but I really didn't mean anything. I need your help to nick some Mafia and I was going to put some action your way, that's all. Honestly, I wasn't trying to take the piss. Can you give me a hand? I need all the help I can get. I've got seven to nick.'

Ally spoke first, offering a handshake. 'Forget it, Bob. Yeah, we'll be there, won't we, Piggy?'

'Suppose so,' said Piggy glumly, not relishing the thought of more activity.

'We'll let Andy Collins know we'll be back to deal with Dawes and his missus later,' continued Ally. 'A bit longer in the pokey won't do either of them any harm. Where's the briefing?'

'Muster room, ten minutes,' called Clarke as he hurried out of the custody area in search of Psycho. Jim had mentioned the locker room, so he walked down the main corridor and opened the locker room door at the far end. 'Psycho,' he called loudly.

There was no reply and he paused briefly before he stepped back into the corridor. Before the door shut, he heard a voice from the locker room say, 'Who's that?' and put his head back round the door.

'Psycho?' he called again.

'Who's that?' repeated the voice from the other end of the locker room.

'Bob Clarke. Psycho, is that you?'

Psycho appeared from behind the lockers at the far end and grinned. 'Hello, Bob. What's up?' He looked relieved.

'What the fuck are you up to, Psycho?' said Clarke, walking up to him. Psycho didn't reply, but moved to one side to allow Clarke to squeeze past him. On the bench seat by Psycho's locker was a shoebox that Clarke could see contained half a dozen thunder flashes. They had been carefully taped together, and their fuses wound into one. Clarke turned and stared at Psycho. His face asked the question.

'Relax,' said Psycho. 'They're for that bitch Bott. Either

under her car or under her toilet door, I haven't decided which yet.'

Clarke shook his head. 'You're a fucking loony, Psycho, and getting worse. Listen, I don't want to know about that, but I could use you on a little job of mine. Can you give us a hand to take out some of the Mafia? Briefing's in ten minutes in the muster room. Should be fun, Psycho. You could really let your hair down.'

Psycho considered the offer. Clarke was right: he could really indulge himself with the Mafia, but the down side was that none of them would complain about him. He'd have to perform to an audience.

'Yeah, sounds like one not to miss, Bob. I'll be there,' he replied finally.

'Thanks, Psycho,' said Clarke, quickly leaving the locker room, and, as he would one day be known, the Handstead Khazi Bomber.

The Brothers, Bovril and Pizza had left the canteen together and wandered downstairs. As they strolled along the corridor towards the muster room, Bovril suddenly branched off into the report-writing room.

'Just got to make a quick phone call. I'll see you in there,' he called to the others. He was relieved to find the room empty, and picked up the phone on the desk in the corner. He dialled Lisa's number and became anxious when she didn't reply after a few rings. At last he heard her voice.

'Hello, darling. It's only me,' he said softly.

'David,' she said, sounding pleasantly surprised. 'I've been thinking about you ever since you left.'

'I've been thinking about you too,' he said. And he meant it. But how to tell her without sounding a complete twat? How could he tell her that she was the only person in the world who called him David, and he loved her for it?

'How are you, honey?'

'Lonely and neglected.' There was a teasing pout in her voice. 'I wish you were here now. I really need a big cuddle.' He felt himself begin to harden as she continued to whisper to him. 'You make me feel like a different woman, David. You do things to me that I've never experienced before. You make me feel special. I never want that to stop.'

'Please, please, I'm going to do myself an injury like this. I've got a briefing to go to,' he protested, laughing.

'Briefing? What's that about?' she said, suddenly sounding a little anxious.

'We're going out with the CID shortly to nick some of the Mafia. Should be a bit of fun. Listen, can we meet tonight?'

She had heard about the Mafia from him before. Her tone changed. 'David, please be careful. I don't want anything to happen to you. Promise me you'll be careful.'

'Honey, honey,' he said reassuringly, 'of course I will, I promise. It's no big deal, honestly. I can tell you all about it tonight if you can get away. Do you think you can?'

She didn't reply immediately – something was bothering her.

'Honey, you still there?'

'Yes, I'm still here. Sorry. Look, why don't you ring me when you finish and we'll sort something out?'

'OK, sure,' said Bovril, a little confused. 'Is everything all right?'

'Everything's fine, David,' she said, brightening. 'Promise me you'll ring later?'

'I promise, darling.' He paused and summoned the courage to continue, 'Lisa, I really feel something different about you. I just can't explain it to you very well. You're very, very important to me. I hope you understand that.'

'I think I recognise the feeling as well, David,' she said softly. Neither spoke for a moment.

'I'd better go, honey. I'll ring you when I get back, OK?'

'You'd better,' she replied, 'or there'll be trouble. Promise me you'll take care.'

'I promise, I really do. Don't worry, I'll ring you as soon as I get back.'

'Speak to you later then, David. I love you,' she said, and put down the phone. Bovril held the buzzing receiver to his ear as her parting words ricocheted around his head. She loved him. She loved him. She'd plucked up the courage and told him. He loved her but couldn't bring himself to tell her.

'You wanker,' he told himself, putting down the phone. As he walked to the muster room, he resolved to tell her everything when they got back. He felt euphoric, and when he slumped into a chair next to Ally he put his head back, closed his eyes and smiled happily.

'What're you so fucking happy about?' growled Ally. 'You're going to be up to your elbows in shit shortly.'

'Ally, life is good, God is in his heaven, day follows night, Uncle Percy has a ginger moustache,' he replied dreamily.

'He's fucking mad,' said Ally to Piggy. 'Been poking his knob where he shouldn't. I told you you'd catch something,' he said loudly. Bovril laughed and remained as he was.

The Brothers were sitting behind him with Pizza a respectful two seats from them. The six of them were joined shortly after by John Benson, Bob Clarke and two other DCs, Dave Thompson and Steve Lloyd. Clarke perched himself on the desk at the front, whilst the others pulled up chairs.

'I'll be as quick as I can, lads; we need to be off as soon as possible,' he began. 'As you know, the Mafia tried to run the Hoop and Grapes last night and GBH'd the landlord. Eight are currently locked up; the other seven we're after are probably in a flat at the Grant Flowers. We've got a warrant for flat 612, Alan Baker's place. Sixth floor, so we don't have to worry about anyone going out of the back window.'

'Who're you expecting to be in?' asked Jim.

'The hard core,' replied Clarke, reading from his piece of paper. 'Baker obviously, Thomas, Driscoll, the Reillys and

Des Anderson, and last but not least, that evil bitch Baldwin.'

'Oh, very nasty,' said Jim. 'Can't see any of that lot surrendering quietly.'

'Not a chance,' said H. 'It's got to be a case of sticks out and ask questions later.'

'Agreed,' said Clarke, 'but just a few reminders about what we need when we're in there. We'll get fuck all in interview, so we need some forensic. Seize any clothing and footwear and make sure you can attribute it to someone. Steve's going to be the exhibits officer, so get everything to him and make sure it's logged. Don't just leave it with him and assume he knows where it's from.'

He paused as he noticed the very odd looks he was getting from the uniforms.

'You're doing it again, Bob. We have done this before, you know,' said H.

'Sorry, lads. I'm not trying to teach you how to suck eggs, I just can't emphasise enough how important some tight forensic evidence is going to be. When we get in,' he continued, 'take a prisoner each, if possible, subdue them if you have to, cuff them and search them. If they give you loads of verbal, try to remember it. You never know, one of them might fuck up. Once we've got them tied down, we'll search the place systematically. Don't let them move around, keep them where you nick them. Any questions at all?'

'What about weapons?' asked Psycho.

'You can't take any,' said Clarke.

'Not me, you twat,' said Psycho to loud laughter, 'them.'

'Can't discount them, can we?' said Clarke. 'They used fists and boots and a bottle on the landlord. Nothing else as far as we know, but most of them have got form for carrying.'

'Carrying what?' said H.

'Knives, pickaxe handles, bicycle chains and the usual home-made stuff.'

'What about shooters?' asked H. There was a loud, heavy silence in the room as they all waited for an answer. It hadn't happened to any of them yet, but they all accepted that one day they would be confronted by someone with a gun. They all hoped that they'd do the right thing, whatever that was.

'No. Why do you ask that?' said Clarke. 'None of them has got any previous involving shooters. Have you heard something then, H?'

'No, but it's only a matter of time before we see one. This bunch of nutters are top of my list to start using them. Do you think it might be a good idea to take an AFO with us?' The other uniforms murmured their agreement. An authorised firearms officer might be very helpful.

'We'd never get it authorised, H. We've got no information or good suspicion that they've got access to a shooter, have we?'

'No, I suppose not,' admitted H. 'Still, I'd feel a lot

happier shoving the barrel of a shooter up their noses first,' he added to more laughter.

'Wouldn't we all?' Clarke laughed. He looked at his watch – 10.50 a.m. 'Let's make a move and meet outside the Grant Flowers front door. We'll put the flat door in as soon after eleven a.m. as we can.'

They all got to their feet and began to filter out of the room.

'Can I ride with you, Bovril? I was on foot this morning,' said Pizza.

Bovril was full of the joys of spring. 'Pizza, it'd be a pleasure to work with you. Grab your stuff and meet me in the yard,' he replied. He strode purposefully down the corridor feeling benevolent and at peace with the world. Pizza was momentarily taken aback by the unexpected welcome, but didn't need to be told twice and trotted off to collect his overcoat and helmet. Bovril was a decent bloke and he promised himself he'd not let him down at the flat. They'd be there as partners. It would be a first for Pizza.

# Chapter Eleven

In her office, Hilary Bott dabbed at her eyes with a handkerchief and tried hard to pull herself together. Gradually the sobs subsided and she sat quietly contemplating the wreckage of her career. Things had gone wrong the moment she arrived at this hellhole and had continued to get worse. What had happened this morning was that Gillard had finally shown his true colours and torn away the pretence of supporting her. She shook her head as she remembered her humiliation. It wasn't really her fault. As a PC she'd done the bare minimum and had never dealt with a traffic accident on her own. She'd always relied on someone else to help. Unfortunately, her innate inability to admit any shortcoming or lack of knowledge or experience had led her to blunder into the Brothers' POLAC and get it completely wrong. She was prepared to admit that to herself now, but to no one else, certainly not that bastard Gillard. She would learn from today though. *Lesson One.*

*You're on your own, girl,* she said to herself.

She felt slightly better and got up from her chair and walked towards the toilet door. As she neared it, a familiar stench assaulted her nostrils. Oh, God, not again, she thought. Surely not.

She took a deep breath, cautiously opened the door and peered in. The room was in darkness, so she reached round the doorframe, found the light cord and pulled the light on. Everything seemed in order. Still holding her breath, she walked to her toilet, which had the lid down. She was fast running out of air, but was determined to check her toilet. Lifting the lid slowly she peered underneath.

What she saw made her gasp, drop the lid and cry out in horror, which in turn caused her to gag and retch as the stench attacked her nervous system. She began to stagger and wave both her arms in the air as though she could somehow push the smell away. Her eyes were streaming and she turned to find the door, which had begun to shut after she had entered the room. It had snagged against the carpet and was half open, edge on to the staggering Bott. She blundered away from the horror in the bowl and straight into the edge of the door with a crack like a perfectly hit cricket shot. Unconscious, she slumped to the floor. The door freed itself from the carpet and closed quietly.

Gillard had heard the single, blood-chilling scream from her office and stopped leafing through his Caribbean cruise brochure. Spider or something, he'd thought. However, the more he thought about it, the more he realised that it wasn't a spidery sort of scream; more a scream of extreme shock. Christ knows what the bloody woman is up to now, he thought bitterly as he got to his feet and went to her office to investigate. As he knocked at her door, he was joined by the DI who had an office further up the corridor.

'Did you hear that?' asked Barry Evans.

'Yeah,' said Gillard wearily, knocking again. There was no answer. He opened the door slightly and put his head into the office.

'Hilary, you all right?' he called. He and Evans walked in and stood sniffing the air.

'What the fuck is that?' said Evans. Gillard noticed the light shining under the toilet door and motioned to him.

'In there,' he said, walking to the door and knocking on it. 'Hilary, are you OK in there?' he called, with his ear pressed to the door panel. There was still no reply. He looked quizzically at Evans. 'I suppose we'd better have a look,' he said, 'just in case.'

'Just in case of what?' replied Evans. 'If she's having a dump she's going to go fucking mental. By the smell of it I'm not surprised she can't speak.'

Gillard pushed the door open and peered into the room. He winced and held his nose with his fingers as he took the full force. Looking down to his right he saw the prostrate Bott on the floor.

'Better call an ambulance, Barry,' he called over his shoulder. 'She's passed out.'

Evans pushed past him and went over to the toilet bowl, also holding his nose. He lifted the lid and peered in.

'I'm not fucking surprised she's out cold. Is she still breathing? This thing's big enough to be making contributions to the pension fund.'

He made a hurried exit to the main office to telephone for an ambulance as Gillard went to see for himself before kneeling down next to Bott and patting her face. 'Hilary, Hilary,' he called softly.' 'It's me, Pat Gillard. Can you hear me?'

She began to murmur and move her head from side to side, but her eyes remained shut.

Evans returned to the room. 'Ambulance is on its way,' he said, and began to flush the toilet. After four goes it was finally clear. As Gillard continued to speak quietly to Bott, he located an air-freshener can under the sink and began to liberally spray the room. The spray fell on to Bott's face and she slowly opened her eyes. As her vision cleared, she saw Gillard kneeling next to her, patting her hand, and Barry Evans standing alongside him.

'What happened?' she croaked. 'What are you doing in here?'

'Don't worry about it, Hilary,' said Evans cheerfully. 'I've clubbed it to death; it was a bastard to flush away, though.'

'What?' said Bott. 'What are you talking about?'

'Listen, Hilary,' said Gillard, 'next time you need to take a shit, let me know and I'll make sure there's a midwife on standby.'

'Or a seal trainer,' added Evans.

'What?' repeated Bott, before the terrible realisation of what these two morons were on about dawned on her. 'No, you don't understand . . .' she began.

'Forget it, Hilary,' said Gillard soothingly. 'We understand. Women's problems and that sort of thing. It's happened before, hasn't it? You're going to have to speak to a doctor about it though, aren't you? I did wonder why the Japanese whaling fleet was moored outside,' he added, warming to his task and taking a lead from Evans.

'No, I walked into the door. It was already in there,' she said hysterically.

'Calm down, calm down,' said Gillard, before looking up at Evans and saying, 'She's starting to hallucinate, Barry. It could have done some damage internally.'

'It was already there,' screamed Bott, trying to free her hand from Gillard's and get up off the floor.

'You stay where you are, Hilary,' he said firmly. 'It's done more damage than you think.'

She began to struggle violently and shouted, 'Let go of me, you fucking idiot. Let me go.'

'Give us a hand, Barry,' said Gillard. 'She's lost it completely.' Evans knelt down on the other side of her, and both men held her to the floor as they waited for an ambulance crew. 'Must have been fucking agony,' said the Chief Inspector, sounding genuinely sympathetic as Bott thrashed around underneath them.

Psycho was walking past the door when he saw the ambulance crew in the front office with their casualty chair, waiting to be buzzed in. He opened the door from the corridor and held it open as they bundled the chair in.

'You here for us?' he asked. 'Something up?'

'Got a call to the first floor, an Inspector Bott's office, report of a female collapsed.'

Psycho was temporarily speechless. Surely nothing to do with his handiwork?

'Can you lead the way, mate?' said an ambulanceman.

'Yeah, of course,' he replied slowly, and led them to the stairwell. As they climbed the stairs they could hear Bott screaming.

'She's conscious, then,' said Psycho. 'Can't be too bad.'

He took the two ambulancemen into Bott's office, where they paused as they caught sight of Gillard and Evans struggling on the toilet floor with Bott. The ambulancemen hurried to help, leaving Psycho with their chair.

'What happened?' asked one of them.

'Passed out after a huge shit,' replied a perspiring Gillard. 'She's started to hallucinate and become hysterical.'

'It was a fucking monster,' added Evans. Psycho glowed with pride as he listened from the door.

'OK, we'll take over,' said the other ambulanceman,

opening his kitbag and removing a syringe. He plunged the needle into a small glass phial containing a clear liquid, squirted some of the liquid into the air and flicked the syringe with a finger. Bott had stopped struggling and was watching him, wide-eyed.

'What are you doing?' she shouted.

'Just relax, darling, this'll help you no end,' he said without looking at her. He then addressed Gillard, Evans and his colleague. 'Turn her over for me, lads. I'm going to need plenty of flesh for this one.'

'You're not fucking putting that in me, you bastards,' shrieked Bott. 'I banged my head, I'm fine, it was already there. Fuck off . . .' She trailed off as they unceremoniously turned her on to her front.

'Incoming . . .' muttered the ambulanceman as he hauled her skirt up, exposing her huge wobbling bottom encased in a suspiciously grey pair of shapeless knickers. The group pulled lemon-sucking faces at the spectacle, and glanced at each other. The unspoken question 'How could anyone fuck that?' passed between them. Psycho, who had the morals of a tomcat (if it moved, he shagged it; if it didn't he pissed on it), quickly assessed her as at least a fifteen pinter. Even after that copious alcohol intake it would still be a toss-up as to whether he'd rather shag the horrible old lesbian or stick pins in his eyes. Perhaps a shag would put her back on the straight and narrow. He'd have to think about it.

'Fire in the hole,' shouted Psycho from the door as the needle was thrust into her buttock.

The result was almost immediate as Bott completely relaxed and seemed to sink into the floor with a loud sigh. Her eyes glazed over and a stream of spittle ran from the corner of her mouth as she slurred, 'You bastards . . .'

The ambulanceman pulled her skirt down as his colleague went to fetch the chair. Gillard and Evans helped to load her into it and a blanket was wrapped around her, tucked up under her chin. They lifted her down the stairs, preceded by Psycho who opened the front office doors for them again.

The rest of the Grant Flowers raiding party were in the corridor as he did so, and watched in astonished silence as the gibbering Bott was wheeled out into the front office.

'I banged my head,' she drooled. 'It was already in there . . .'

Psycho tapped the side of his head as he looked at the others. 'Gone mad after a massive shit apparently,' he said in his best diagnostic manner.

Evans had stayed upstairs to let the first floor know all about Bott's predicament whilst Gillard had followed her downstairs and then outside. He watched as she was loaded into the back of the ambulance. He'd give her husband a ring shortly to tell the poor sap of her plight. He looked up at the front of the nick to see a mass of smiling faces at every window. She'd endeared herself to everyone in such a short space of time.

'I always thought she was full of it,' he muttered as he walked back to his office, 'but Christ, that must have hurt.'

Psycho loitered around the front office long enough for the Blister to confirm in her own mind that Bott's departure to hospital had everything to do with him. She sidled up to him as he peered out at the departing ambulance.

'You've excelled yourself this time, haven't you? What on earth did you do to her?'

'Nothing,' replied Psycho, entirely unconvincingly.

'So your visit to her office this morning was to leave her a bunch of flowers, was it? Or chocolates perhaps?'

'Leave it out, for fuck's sake,' hissed Psycho. Only the Blister knew he'd been up there earlier and he wanted it kept that way. 'I'll tell you all about it later if you like. Why don't you pop over after work?' It had occurred to him that he might be able to buy her silence with another shag, perhaps two or three. It had also occurred to him that if those bastards mentioned the Polaroids to her, he was dead. He hadn't for a moment envisaged an outcome like this. The success of his campaign had exceeded his wildest dreams, but the fly in the ointment was the Blister. She could put him away in style if she had a mind to. He'd have to speak to the lads again about keeping quiet.

'Yeah, OK,' said the Blister, who like Psycho never

looked a gift horse in the mouth. Spending the evening being pumped up by Psycho was marginally better than listening to her elderly mother complain about the queue in the post office. 'I'll be over about six.'

'Great, look forward to it,' Psycho lied. God, the sacrifices he had to make for his art. He walked out into the yard where the rest of the raiding party were standing.

'Psycho, you're single crewed today, aren't you?' said Clarke.

'Yeah, why?'

'Can you take the van for us? It'll be better for getting bodies and property back. Is that OK?'

'Sure, no problems,' he replied and went back into the nick to collect the keys for the divisional van from the control room.

'The van' was a battered old Ford Transit with bench seats running down either side in the back. It was used to collect the drunk and dirty prisoners and, despite regular washes with industrial-strength disinfectant, stank. Night Duty officers had abandoned it in the far corner of the yard, reversed up to the far wall of the cell block, with its exhaust pipe hard against a ventilation brick. Having collected the keys, Psycho settled into the driver's seat, opened the manual choke wide and fired the engine. It coughed into life and was soon roaring merrily, pumping noxious exhaust fumes through the ventilation brick and into the cells occupied by the Mafia. Psycho kept the revs high for several minutes before moving off, completely unaware of the havoc about to ensue in the cell block.

For the last two hours, the Mafia prisoners had been really performing, shouting and hammering at their cell doors, demanding to see solicitors and generally abusing Collins and his gaoler. He'd decked a couple of them through their inspection hatches, but it hadn't led to a lull in the din. After a while, Collins had ceased to notice it. What he did eventually notice was the silence. Puzzled, he called out to his gaoler.

'Go and have a look at that lot, will you, make sure they haven't escaped,' he said, only half joking. He'd never lost a prisoner during his years as a custody sergeant, and he didn't want to break his duck by losing one, or all, of the Mafia prisoners. He'd never hear the end of it.

The gaoler smiled and ambled into the cell corridor, jangling his bunch of keys. He rushed back very soon, ashen-faced and coughing. Collins looked up at him from his desk.

'What's up?' he asked worriedly. 'They're all there, aren't they?'

'Oh yeah, they're still in their cells, sarge, but you'd better come and have a look,' the gaoler replied between coughs and splutters. Grabbing his keys, Collins followed him into the cell corridor, and immediately noticed a strong smell of petrol. A blanket of wispy smoke hung across the corridor at about head height.

'What the fuck is this?' He coughed.

'Smells like exhaust fumes,' spluttered the gaoler. 'Have a look in the cells, sarge.'

Collins went to the first cell, flung open the inspection hatch and peered in. Deep amid the billowing yellow fog inside, he could vaguely make out the shape of a body on the floor. 'Fucking hell,' he yelled, unlocking the cell door and running inside. He grabbed an arm and pulled the body out into the corridor. He looked down at Peter Jeffries, one of the Mafia, and couldn't detect any sign of life.

'Get the others out quickly,' he shouted to the gaoler, and dragged Jeffries out into the main custody reception area. 'Blister,' he bellowed. She appeared from the front office quickly. 'Call for some ambulances. All the fucking prisoners have been gassed. Let Gillard know we're in deep shit.'

'Gassed?' asked the Blister incredulously. 'How'd that happen?'

'Never mind that,' roared Collins, 'get on the fucking phone on the hurry up.' Blister hurried back to the front office as Collins began to slap Jeffries about the face and was relieved to see his eyelids flutter as he began to regain consciousness. 'Thank fuck for that,' he muttered as the gaoler dragged two more prisoners into the room, pulling them along the floor by their shirt collars. 'How many more down there?'

'Seven,' coughed the gaoler. 'They're down the far end.'

'Get the windows and doors in here open,' commanded Collins. 'Look after these three and I'll get the others.'

Holding a handkerchief to his nose and mouth, he disappeared back into the poisonous fog and a few minutes later had all his prisoners laid out in the reception area. All were gradually recovering, but lay where they were, coughing and moaning.

'What the fuck happened?' asked the gaoler, who was leaning out of the window gulping the fresh air.

Collins shook his head. 'Christ knows,' he said quietly. 'Jesus, that was close. Too bloody close. Get me the custody records, will you? We'd better make sure all the visits are up to date, and make sure the Blister's called for some ambulances, will you?'

He slumped into his chair and gave silent thanks to the patron saint of custody sergeants. Leafing through the custody records, he was relieved to see that his gaoler had been on the ball and all the prisoners were shown as 'visited and all correct' shortly before they'd been found unconscious. As long as none of them died, it was unlikely that anyone would look too closely at the timings of the visits. Collins pushed the papers to one side and waited for the inevitable shitstorm. It wasn't long in arriving.

Gillard could scarcely believe his ears as he listened to what the Blister had to tell him. She had to repeat herself twice.

'All the prisoners have been gassed?' he said very slowly to ensure he'd got it right. 'Are they dead?'

'No idea, guv. Sergeant Collins didn't say,' she replied calmly. Gillard slammed his phone back on to its cradle and put his forehead on his desk.

'Jesus fucking Christ, what is it with this place?' he asked his blotting pad. 'One thing after another. It doesn't happen anywhere else, only here. Every fucking time the shit rolls downhill it ends up here.'

He picked up his phone again and dialled the custody office. Collins let it ring twice before answering. Before he could speak, Gillard was off and running.

'What the fuck happened, Andy? How bad are they, any of them likely to die, whose fault is it?'

Collins pondered the questions put to him and smiled as he considered who might have been at fault.

'Difficult to say what happened, guv, but it looks like a vehicle in the yard filled the cells with exhaust fumes. It wouldn't be the first time; you'll probably remember the memo I sent you last year concerning the problem we had then. I recommended that the ventilation bricks were blocked up and extractor fans fitted.'

There was silence from the other end as Gillard frantically racked his memory. Christ, yes, he did vaguely remember the memo, but what the hell had he done with it?

'I can't say I do, Andy,' he lied finally. 'More to the point, how are the prisoners?'

'Recovering nicely, I think, but they're all going to need medical attention. We're going to have to arrange escorts and guards in hospital.'

'I'll be down in a minute,' said Gillard, putting down his phone. He began to rummage through his desk drawers before he finally sat back holding a sheet of paper in his hand. 'Fuck,' he said quietly. It was Collins's memo, and other than a date stamp showing it had reached him the previous November, nothing had been written on it. He pondered his predicament for a few minutes before he smiled broadly and began to write. Under the existing date stamp, he wrote, 'Inspector Bott to deal and report ASAP. This is a serious issue that needs resolving.' He then altered the date on his desk stamp and stamped his instructions for two days after he had received the memo. Quickly, he went to Bott's empty office and began to go through the files she kept in one of the desk drawers. He found one labelled 'Memos – Outstanding', and another, 'Memos – To Deal'. He opened the 'To Deal' file and found a draft proposal for a crime prevention initiative in the summer. He slipped the offending memo in amongst the draft and replaced the file. He was back in his office seconds later. He'd covered his arse very nicely, and ensured that Bott would take any blame if it came to it. Things were working out quite nicely on the whole. She was in hospital gibbering like an idiot, and if she ever got back to work the memo would be ticking like a time bomb in her desk. Yes, all in all, things could be worse, he assured himself as he went downstairs to the cell block.

He breezed into the custody reception area and almost tripped over one of the prostrate prisoners who was coughing and spluttering on the floor. Stepping gingerly over him and the others, he went to Collins's desk.

'I do remember your memo, Andy. I passed it to Mrs Bott to deal. I take it you heard no more about it, then?'

'Not a thing, guv.'

Gillard shook his head and tutted. 'Oh well, I'm sure she's looking into it. Not the sort of thing you'd want to sit on, is it?'

'Not now the shit's hit the fan, guv,' said Collins slowly, looking suspiciously at the Chief Inspector. He knew him of old. Gillard was a slimy, devious old bastard, and a little voice was telling Collins that Big Chief speaks with forked tongue. However, he kept his suspicions to himself.

'This is going to fuck up the CID's inquiries,' said Gillard, looking at the wheezing prisoners. 'They won't be able to speak to this shower for days.'

'No great loss,' replied Collins. 'None of them would have said a thing. Those two' – he indicated Dawes and his wife – 'are in for handling. They've not been interviewed yet either.' He deliberately made no mention of Morgan's interview.

'Who's dealing with them?'

'Stewart and Malone. They've gone out with the CID to

nick the other Mafia,' he said, keeping his voice down for the benefit of the prisoners on the floor. 'Thinking about it, I'd better let them and Control know that we're closed for a while. I'll send all prisoners to Alpha Tango if that's OK.'

'Yeah, fine, Andy,' agreed Gillard. 'I'll let Division know what's happened. Is everything tidy on the paperwork front before I do that?'

'No problems, thanks, guv.'

Gillard picked his way out of Custody and retreated to the sanctuary of his office. He rarely gave a moment's thought to what the officers under his command did on a daily basis, or how they coped, but seeing Collins downstairs, barely keeping his head above water, made him grateful that promotion had lifted him out of the swamp. He knew what Collins would, in all likelihood, now face. The lizards from Complaints and Discipline would be all over him like a rash, looking for any minor indiscretion to confront him with. Collins was good at his job; he knew his stuff and Gillard genuinely hoped that he was as watertight as he seemed to think he was. But any mistakes and those bastards would find them.

He phoned Division to speak to the Chief Superintendent and spoil his day. That phone call sparked a forest fire chain reaction. Within a few hours, Horse's Arse would be visited by more senior officers than it had seen over the last decade. Even the Chief Constable himself announced that he would venture from his ivory tower and mingle with the infidels. Gillard got the phone call from the Chief's staff officer and felt his blood chill. The place was in danger of imminent meltdown, his deputy was drooling in hospital and now the Chief was coming to visit. He knew he wouldn't be coming to shake hands and slap backs. He'd have all sorts of fucking stupid questions about use of resources and deployment strategies. Gillard briefly considered leaving the building, but knew the staff officer would drop him in it. The other alternative was a huge heart attack, and he felt that probably wasn't far away. He decided to make sure that the i's had been dotted and the t's crossed on the fiasco in the cell block, and got on the phone to Collins again.

At Headquarters, Chief Constable Robert Daniells, QPM, sat in his large, sumptuous office on the sixth floor, reading for the third time a telex message received from Chief Superintendent 'B' Division. Perhaps sumptuous was too grand a description of the office. Although larger than most senior officers' offices, it was still furnished with the same spartan 1960s Home Office furniture. Glass-fronted bookcases filled with legal tomes unopened since their distant publication, high-backed, foam-filled chairs for his visitors, and a low coffee table littered with copies of the Force's annual report. He had a large desk with drawers on either side and the whole ensemble was in the same polished, beech finish. The only concession to his rank was his reclining padded leather chair and the carpet and wallpaper that at his insistence had not come from the Force housing department's catalogue. Their drab samples would not have looked out of place in a Moscow housing development and he had put his foot down. A youthful Queen Elizabeth surveyed the bureaucratic lack of taste with barely concealed disdain from her frame on the wall behind his desk.

He leant his portly, six-foot frame back into his chair and let out a large sigh as he glanced around at the numerous group photographs on the walls. He pushed the telex message back across the desk to his staff officer. Inspector Kevin Curtis picked it up and looked quizzically at him.

'What the hell is going on at Hotel Alpha, Kevin?' the Chief asked. He knew bloody well what was going on down there, but he enjoyed watching his ridiculous staff officer jump through fiery hoops. Daniells had spent his entire thirty-four years' service with the same Force, almost unique amongst chief officers. He'd got his hands dirty as he rose through the ranks on merit alone, and had served at Horse's Arse as a DI. That had been some years ago, before the town came to resemble a war zone, but he had always recognised the potential for serious trouble there. His predecessors in the top job had handed him a poisoned chalice by never getting to grips with the place, and since his appointment two years ago he had been wrestling with the problem. He suspected, quite rightly, that the crux of the problem lay in a complete lack of leadership. It had been his idea to send

Hilary Bott there to sort things out. The telex informed him, amongst other things, that she was now in hospital following complications whilst passing a stool. He shook his head.

His obsequious, 25-year-old staff officer drew on his non-existent experience and launched into a lengthy explanation of simmering social discontent and inappropriate policing methods that required immediate addressing through open meetings with the discontented locals. Curtis was a classic 'Bramshill Flyer', fast-tracking through promotion on the back of a degree in archaeology from Cambridge. His operational experience was limited to two years as a probationary constable when he was wrapped in cotton wool at a quiet rural nick, followed by promotion into the training department. He hadn't set foot out of Headquarters for five years. He knew his Greek and Roman ruins, but he knew the square root of nothing when it came to real policing.

'Complete bollocks, Kevin. The place has gone to rat shit, pure and simple,' said Daniells, leaning forward in his chair and glaring at him. 'What are we going to do about it?'

'Encourage dialogue?' said Curtis timidly.

'Dialogue? Are you fucking mad?' barked Daniells. 'Dialogue be fucked. We're going to send the Patrol Group in there for a couple of weeks and kick shit out of the place. What d'you think about that?'

Curtis stared open-mouthed at his Chief. He was never

sure if he was joking. His Bramshill instructors were nothing like him.

He hated his current job, but viewed it as a necessary evil to achieve his next goal, promotion to Chief Inspector. There wasn't a back he wouldn't stab to achieve it, but he knew the Chief had little time for either him or the system that had promoted him so quickly. 'Bringing through a bunch of limp-wristed cocksuckers,' he'd shouted at him one day when he'd reminded him of a seminar he was due to attend at Bramshill.

His role as staff officer was a 24-hour one, with regular overnight stops away from Force with the Chief when he attended conferences and the like. Curtis's wife was beginning to tire of his long days and regular absences, and life at home had become distinctly awkward.

'The Patrol Group, sir? Is that wise? You know what they're like. They could inflame things badly.'

You complete knob, thought the Chief to himself, and taking a deep breath, 'How could things get any worse, Kevin?' he said aloud. 'What have we got to lose? We need a new commander in there to support Hilary; a couple of weeks of the Patrol Group on a long leash and things will quieten down. The place is a complete shithole, but I'm buggered if a group of young thugs is going to be allowed to terrorise the few decent folk there whilst we organise group meetings to discuss the problem. The problem's clear enough. Arses need kicking on both sides of the fence.'

'If you say so, sir. Are you sure?' stammered Curtis.

'As sure as I can be. Have you told that imbecile Gillard that I'm going to pay him a visit?'

'Yes, yes I did, sir,' replied Curtis, immediately regretting the phone call which had been no more than a professional courtesy.

'Wish you hadn't. Never mind, though; it'll give him time to work himself into a real lather. Maybe bring on that huge thrombo he's due. When are we going?'

'Any time you like, sir. Your car's downstairs.'

'Fine, let's do it now,' said Daniells, grabbing his cap and coat from a hatstand in the corner and striding purposefully out of the office, followed at a respectful distance by his bag carrier. The office enjoyed views across playing fields to Heston Lakes, and only four miles beyond them Horse's Arse. Daniells could see the Grant Flowers tower block from the office and he glanced briefly in that direction as he left. As he did so, the raiding party neared the flats.

# Chapter Twelve

The Patrol Group that Daniells saw as part of the answer to the problems at Horse's Arse comprised three mobile units that covered the whole county with a brief to make short, sharp visits to divisions with a specific problem. Each unit consisted of a sergeant and ten constables, and for the most part they patrolled in liveried Ford Transit vans fitted with grilles on all the windows and heavy rubber skirts around the wheel arches. Their speciality was public disorder and each vehicle carried riot shields and NATO helmets which they liked to utilise as often as possible. A two-year attachment to the group was viewed as a major achievement and generally officers only got on to it having proved themselves elsewhere as a good thief-taker and handy in a punch-up.

The rivalry between the three units sometimes manifested itself in fistfights during the monthly training day when the entire Patrol Group got together. They would practise deployment from their vans with shields, storming buildings, riot control – when petrol bombs were thrown at them – and, bizarrely, huge exposure to CS gas in a hut on a disused airfield. They were all trained in the use of .38 Smith and Wesson handguns and Remington pump-action shotguns and were regularly deployed, fully armed, at high security trials at the local Crown court.

The units built up close camaraderie and proved enormously successful wherever they went. They were responsible for huge numbers of crime arrests and had recently begun to take on responsibility for drug offence investigations around the county. They wore their hair slightly longer than divisional officers, Jack Regan sideboards were 'de rigueur', and their caps were usually worn at a jaunty angle on the back of the head. The real 'hotdogs' preferred slashed peaks rendering normal vision virtually impossible. They were issued with overcoats that were exclusive to the group and revelled in their reputation.

Above all, they had a reputation for violence. Officers on the Patrol Group accounted for two thirds of all complaints currently under investigation by Complaints and Discipline. Unit Three, which covered 'B' Division and Horse's Arse, had worked hard to cultivate their reputation as mad, bad motherfuckers, and with four officers on their complement who had served at Horse's Arse it was not one they would lose in a hurry.

Unit Three were based at, and run from, County Headquarters, but had offices at the stations they covered where they would retire after an operation to get their evidence sorted. This morning they were at their Divisional HQ at Alpha Tango, writing up their pocketbooks about a drugs raid they had undertaken the night before. They'd had a good result: six prisoners including the main dealer, several pounds of cannabis resin seized, and nearly forty wraps of white powder which was due to go to the lab for analysis later that morning. The dealer had received the kicking of his life before he'd given them the whereabouts of his stash, and now his car lay in pieces in the back yard as two officers systematically dismantled it looking for more drugs.

Six other officers were at their desks, talking quietly and writing their pocketbook entries, all carefully corroborating each arrest, seizure of drugs and report of admissions. Their sergeant, John Frost, was in the small adjoining kitchen making tea when the phone in the main office rang. He left the kettle to boil, went into the office and picked up the receiver.

'Patrol Group,' he said abruptly.

The voice at the other end belonged to the inspector who ran the Patrol Group from County Headquarters.

'Hello, John. Nice result last night, I hear.'

'Yeah, very nice, guv. Six bodies and quite a bit of gear recovered.'

'I take it your boys are still writing it up. Any idea how long you'll be? I've got a job for you that's right up your street.'

'Couple of hours, that's all, guv. Why, what you got for us?'

'Things have gone tits up at Horse's Arse again. The Mafia went on the rampage last night and the Chief's decided to stamp on them. He wants to put a unit in there for a couple of weeks with a blank cheque to sort things out. If you're tucked up I can use Unit Two – they're only doing some shoplifting operation at the moment.'

'No, don't do that, guv,' said Frost urgently. 'We'll finish up here on the hurry up and be with you as soon as we can. We'll deal. Unit Two don't know Horse's Arse. We do.'

'OK, John. Let me know when you're on your way. I'll have more details by then.'

'Thanks, guv. See you later,' said Frost, hanging up the phone, ignoring the boiling kettle and going out to the office where his boys were still writing.

'Listen up, lads, good news,' he said. They stopped and looked up at him. 'Horse's Arse needs another visit from us,' he continued. 'The Mafia's been playing silly buggers and the Chief wants it sorted. No questions asked. We need to finish up here and get back to HQ as soon as we can.'

The group of writers erupted in joyous whoops and shouts and resumed their scribing with renewed urgency. Frost went out into the yard to speak to the officers stripping the dealer's car and received an identical response. He then wandered over to their van and began to check that they had everything they'd need for their visit. He loved his job and regarded his boys with paternal affection. Satisfied that the shields, helmets and pickaxe handles were all in place, he busied himself checking fuel, oil and water. They'd be on their way soon enough, back into Horse's Arse where they really belonged.

As Morgan had told the two detectives, the other Mafia were indeed at Alan Baker's flat, and still fast asleep. After their escape from the pub, they'd burgled an off-licence and drunk until the early hours of the morning, smoking huge spliffs and generally whooping it up. They were the kings of their squalid universe and confident of their invincibility despite the capture of eight of their number. The Mafia's code of conduct demanded complete non-cooperation with the police and it was strictly enforced with brutal beatings of those suspected of even slight deviation from the path. There was no way that those locked up at Horse's Arse would tell the Old Bill anything. Not a chance. Not even the youngest and newest member. No fucking way. Morgan had been discussed during the piss-up and despite some reservations all had eventually agreed that he knew what was best for him. 'He'd fucking better,' Alan Baker had growled, 'if he wants to keep eating solids.'

Baker was a vicious, tattooed young thug whose appetite for violence had propelled him into the upper echelons of the Mafia, second only to Bobby Driscoll. A true psychopath, Driscoll ran the Mafia like a feudal warlord, utilising the less intelligent Baker to enforce his perverted will. Driscoll and Baker were a formidable duo. Driscoll, full of animal cunning, was an accomplished manipulator. He operated a Stalinist 'divide and rule' doctrine, keeping the Mafia at each other's throats with snide innuendoes and insinuations. Even Baker, his right-hand man, was not spared. From time to time, Driscoll would identify another member of the Mafia to him as having indicated that they fancied moving into his place. All complete rubbish, of course, but sufficient to goad the mentally unstable Baker to administer a brutal attack on his perceived challenger and maintain the air of brutalised instability that Driscoll thrived on like a malodorous baboon pack leader.

Driscoll was something of an oddity amongst the group he led in that he had stayed at school until he was seventeen and was relatively well educated. However, Adolf Hitler's observation that 'knowledge is ruin to my young men' was never truer than in his case. Physically no match for most of his group, he had discovered at school that the ability to bullshit soon had the bullet-heads furrowing their brows and looking at him with lower jaws sagging. His hardcore, original Mafia had all been at school with him from an early age. They had run as an unruly pack in junior school, but it was not until they entered the local comprehensive that the group of about twenty, all resident on the Park Royal estate, came under his sinister spell and gelled into what became known as the Mafia. The original

Mafia were now all in their early twenties and liked to keep themselves apart from the younger, newer recruits like Morgan. Including the newer recruits, Driscoll had at his disposal around forty aggressive young hoodlums, though in reality it was rare for as many as half of that number to be together at any one time. The fifteen that had tried to run the Hoop and Grapes had been an exceptional turnout. Losing eight to the Old Bill was quite a setback, but he was confident none of them would tell them anything. Not even Morgan.

There was a lot riding on Morgan's keeping his nerve, not just the liberty of those who had escaped capture at the Hoop and Grapes. Driscoll had brought him into the 'senior' Mafia against the wishes of some of the others, Baker included, and during the piss-up he was acutely aware that the doubts expressed about Morgan were indirectly aimed at him. His warped intellect and contrived rage eventually brought grudging agreement that Morgan would keep quiet, but Driscoll could see cracks appearing. He knew he'd have to get them fighting amongst themselves again very soon, but first he had to get Baker back onside, which wouldn't be difficult. That was where Myra Baldwin, the only female in the Mafia, would come in useful. Her primary task was to provide Driscoll with sex as and when it was required and she obliged without question. She was Driscoll's to use and abuse as he pleased.

As the stolen drink and the drugs began to take hold of

them all, Driscoll had called Baldwin to him, taken her by the arm and led her to Baker's bedroom. Pushing her into the room, he turned back to the rest of the group and summoned Baker to join them. Puzzled, but with his light-bulb brain beginning to glow, Baker had hurried to join Driscoll and Baldwin. The others returned to their revelries without comment. They had a very good idea of what was going to happen, even if Myra didn't. She was Driscoll's property and it was clear to them that he was going to share her with Baker. Theirs was not to reason why. In the bedroom, Myra had her arms round Driscoll's neck when she heard the bedroom door shut and turned to see Baker leering at her.

'Fuck off, retard,' she snapped dismissively before gazing adoringly into the face of the man she worshipped. 'Tell him to fuck off, Bobby.'

'I promised him he could watch,' Driscoll whispered into her ear, 'give the twat a bit of a treat.'

She pulled back from him and looked questioningly at him. 'Watch? Why?'

'Don't worry, it'll be fine,' he breathed into her ear, his tongue flicking around the lobe. She trusted him and relaxed into him. Over her shoulder, Driscoll grinned like a wolf and winked at Baker.

The group had finally passed out around 5 a.m., lying on the floor and slumped across chairs, blissfully unaware of the gathering storm and strangely confident. They knew they could expect a pull from the Old Bill in due course, but Bobby had taken care of things. They'd be all right.

The Chief's vehicle swept into the back yard at Horse's Arse just as the cast of Ben Hur hurried out through the front. As news of the impending visit had spread, suddenly everyone had urgent inquiries elsewhere. Gillard saw them go and again considered mingling with the crowd and vanishing. He watched the Chief and his staff officer get out of the rear of the vehicle and saw the Chief speak briefly to his driver before walking to the back doors. He had in fact told his driver to remain with the vehicle at all times to prevent its ending up on bricks minus its wheels. Running his trembling hands through his bouffant hair, Gillard took a deep breath and hurried downstairs to meet him. The Chief was still waiting outside the back doors when he got there, with a face like a slapped arse. His repeated pressing of the buzzer had brought no response from the control-room operator who was busy on the phone telling a colleague at Alpha Tango of the shitstorm enveloping Horse's Arse. Gillard opened the door and proffered a handshake, which was pointedly ignored.

'Chief Constable, good to—'

'What in hell's name is going on here, Mr Gillard?' said the Chief, pushing past him, followed by Curtis. Curtis smirked as he entered. He was never happier than when the shit hit the fan and none of it was likely to land on him.

'Little prick,' muttered Gillard as he followed them into the custody area. Daniells stopped in his tracks when he entered and saw the prostrate prisoners, now being tended to by the crews of three ambulances that had parked at the front of the nick. Collins rose to his feet as Daniells entered and acknowledged him with a simple 'Sir'.

'What happened, Sergeant?'

Collins offered the same explanation he had given Gillard but diplomatically avoided mentioning the previous incident.

'Has it happened before?' barked the Chief, rendering his diplomacy redundant.

'Um, yes, I'm afraid it has, sir, late last year. Same thing but only one prisoner affected.'

'Were you on duty then?'

'Yes I was, sir.'

'What did you do about it?'

There was nothing Collins could do but mention his memo. 'Brought it to the attention of the powers that be that day, sir.'

'You mean Mr Gillard, do you, Sergeant?' said the Chief, looking at Gillard, who looked as if he'd just had a pineapple stuffed up his arse.

'Yes, yes, that's quite correct, Chief. I remember the memo well. I passed it to Mrs Bott to deal. I'm not sure how far she's got with resolving the problem,' Gillard said quickly, wringing his hands.

'Fucking nowhere by the looks of this fiasco,' shouted Daniells, causing the ambulance crew to look up at him. 'Where's Mrs Bott now?'

'Handstead General in an observation ward, sir. She had to be sedated to get her out.'

'Jesus Christ. Mr Curtis, get hold of Superintendent Grainger at Complaints. Tell him to drop whatever he's doing and get over here now. I want this mess examined today, understand?'

'Understood, Chief,' said Curtis joyously, before hurrying out to find a telephone.

'What's happening with the inquiry into the attack on the landlord? I understand prisoners are outstanding?' the Chief continued.

Collins came to Gillard's rescue, realising that he'd have little idea of what was going on. 'Eight nicked last night, sir, amongst this lot. CID and some of the Early Turn have gone out to nick the others. Could be as many as seven more.'

'They won't be coming back here, I take it?'

'No, sir. They'll all be going to Alpha Tango. I've warned Custody over there to expect them and the CID have been told the good news.'

'And what about this lot?'

One of the ambulance crew answered the question for him. 'They're all suffering various stages of carbon monoxide poisoning. It's not life threatening because your lads got them out in time, but they're going to need to be kept under observation for at least twenty-four hours.'

'And under guard,' said the Chief. 'Have you sorted that out, Mr Gillard?'

'All in hand, sir,' he replied, looking desperately and hopefully at Collins, who discreetly nodded in the affirmative.

'I've got a unit of the Patrol Group coming over to get stuck into this toilet, Mr Gillard. I'd like a detailed breakdown from you on where they can concentrate their efforts by this afternoon. Understood?'

'Perfectly, sir,' the Chief Inspector answered meekly, resolving that the second piece of paper he presented his superior with would be the notice of his retirement. Fuck this for a game of soldiers.

'Why's this one naked?' asked Daniells, pointing at Morgan who lay shivering, barely covered under a blanket, amongst the group of prisoners. The Chief Constable noticed the livid purple welts on his lower back but decided not to pursue it.

'Vomited earlier, sir,' replied Collins quickly. 'I was on my way down to him to give him a fresh suit when I found what had happened.'

Daniells still looked puzzled.

'He's one of the Mafia, sir. We seized all his clothing for forensic,' explained Collins.

Satisfied, but not convinced, Daniells turned on his heel

and left Custody, followed by Gillard. The less he knew the better.

'We'll use Mrs Bott's office for the time being,' he said over his shoulder as they climbed the stairs to the first floor. As they walked, he noticed the slightly less strong smell of piss but said nothing until he had seated himself behind Hilary Bott's desk. There was an overpowering smell of cheap air freshener in the room. Gillard noticed his twitching nostrils.

'Mrs Bott's accident, sir – it was rather unpleasant,' he offered.

The Chief said nothing but looked Gillard straight in the eyes. He'd spotted Collins digging him out of the shit in Custody, and his years as a detective had alerted a sixth sense about his response to the memo concerning the ventilation problems in the cells.

'Go and find Mr Curtis and tell him to meet me here, and then find out which unit of the Patrol Group are on their way,' he said, without expression.

'Sir,' said Gillard, hurrying from the office. He expected the Chief to start looking for the memo but was not unduly worried. He'd taken care of things.

As soon as the office door shut, Daniells began to go through the drawers in Bott's desk, carefully examining each piece of paper and replacing everything in the same order. After just a few minutes he found what he was looking for and leant back in the chair to read Collins's memo. Dated

23 November 1975, it was detailed and to the point and ended with two recommendations. First, that vehicles should be prohibited from reversing towards the cell block when parking up, despite the drawbacks when it came to achieving fast exits from the yard, and second that the ventilation bricks be covered over and extractor fans fitted in the cell block to provide ventilation. The memo ended with the observation that they had been lucky to avoid a tragedy. Under Collins's signature was a date stamp reading Sub-Divisional Commander's Office 25 November 1975, indicating that it had taken two days for the memo to travel one flight of stairs to Gillard. There then followed Gillard's instructions to Hilary Bott to deal, concluding with what the Chief thought the typically pompous observation that this was a serious matter. Those instructions had then been stamped Sub-Divisional Commander's Office 27 November 1976. It was too pat; he knew Hilary Bott would never have sat on her hands for two months without doing anything about the matter. Something was wrong and he read the memo again. And then he smiled, pushed the memo on to the desk and waited, arms folded, for Gillard to return.

Gillard had eventually found Curtis in the sergeant's office speaking to Complaints on the phone.

'. . . he says tell him to drop everything and get his arse over here on the hurry up,' he heard the staff officer say as he walked in. 'The place is in uproar . . .' Curtis trailed off and replaced the phone when he saw Gillard glaring at him.

'Chief wants you in Bott's office now, Inspector,' he said harshly. 'And find out which unit of the Patrol Group are on their way over.'

Curtis didn't reply, but picked up the phone and dialled HQ switchboard. He asked to be put through to the Patrol Group admin office, spoke briefly and replaced the phone.

'Unit Three, briefing first at HQ, then due here within the hour,' he said. 'Shall we join the Chief?' He pushed past Gillard and made his way back to the first floor, closely followed by the Chief Inspector, who was determined not to miss anything that passed between him and Daniells. He need not have worried. When he entered Bott's office, hot on the staff officer's heels, he was surprised to find the Chief beaming merrily.

'Everything OK, sir?' asked Curtis.

'Couldn't be better, Kevin,' he replied cheerfully. 'I found Sergeant Collins's memo, Mr Gillard,' he said, leaning forward and pushing it towards the Chief Inspector.

'Oh, good,' said Gillard awkwardly, glancing at it but not picking it up. 'Had she made any progress with it?'

'Absolutely none at all, Mr Gillard,' said the Chief mournfully, shaking his head, 'but then that's not altogether surprising as she's never set her eyes on the fucking thing, is it?' he finished with real venom in his voice.

'What – what do you mean?' said Gillard, swallowing hard as his mouth began to dry out.

'Have a look for yourself, man,' replied Daniells.

Hands trembling, Gillard picked up the memo, and having read it looked blankly at the Chief. 'My instructions are quite clear, sir . . .' he began.

'Yes they are,' interrupted Daniells, 'but she won't get those instructions until later this year, will she? Look at the date.'

Beginning to shake, Gillard focused hard on the stamp he had recently added to the memo. The colour drained from his face and he felt faint. He'd changed the day and the month, but not the year. He threw the memo back on to the desk and thought he was about to be sick.

'You're finished, Mr Gillard,' said Daniells quietly as Curtis stared open-mouthed. 'Get out of here and remain in your office. Mr Grainger will interview you as soon as I've briefed him. Don't bother to submit any papers to retire just yet, will you? There are a few matters to sort out before you creep off to the sun. Once Mr Grainger has seen you, you may take whatever leave you're still owed, or go sick if necessary, but you are not, under any circumstances, to set foot in this station after today. Do I make myself clear?'

Gillard nodded. Seeing nothing, he turned and shuffled out of the office a broken man. He returned to his office and slumped in his chair, staring at a wall.

Back in Bott's office, Daniells located an A4 plastic wallet and carefully placed the incriminating memo in it. 'I don't think we'll need it,' he told Curtis, 'but a pound a penny to a pinch of shit, the fingerprints on there won't belong to Hilary Bott.'

'Unit Three will be here within the hour, sir,' the flabbergasted Curtis said eventually. He'd just witnessed the end of the career of a senior officer who'd tried to ensure that a subordinate took the can for an incident that had enormous ramifications for the Force. He still couldn't quite believe what he had witnessed. He couldn't wait to tell his wife. There was going to be a vacancy for a Chief Inspector, albeit at Horse's Arse. Right man in the right place at the right time and all that. But at Horse's Arse? He'd speak to Mrs Curtis, if she'd speak to him at all.

'Let's get a cup of tea, Kevin,' said the Chief, getting up from the chair and handing him the memo to look after. 'I'm as dry as a nun's cunt after that. And contact Oscar One for me,' he added, naming the main Force control-room inspector, 'to divert the Patrol Group direct to the Grant Flowers flats. The CID officers there can do the briefing. No point them coming here.'

Curtis blushed profusely and scurried after the Chief. He just could not get used to his profanities, which usually came thick and fast when they were alone together. In the company of other senior officers Daniells generally managed to act in an appropriate manner, but the rough edges were still there and endeared him to the junior ranks who knew he'd been there, done it and got the T-shirt.

\*

Clarke, Benson, Lloyd and Thompson were sitting in their unmarked Ford Escort behind the Grant Flowers tower block in complete silence. The Brothers, Bovril, Pizza, Ally and Piggy were parked up behind them, still waiting for Psycho to arrive in the van. All had heard the message directed to the CID officers. Oscar One had contacted them on the main radio set with nothing but bad news. Their prisoners were en route to hospital under guard and out of reach for at least twenty-four hours, and the Chief Constable himself had directed that they were not to take any further action until a unit of the Patrol Group arrived at their location. The only half-decent news was that it was Unit Three on the way and their ETA was only fifteen minutes. Clarke had acknowledged the message with a simple 'Understood, standing by' and was silent for a few moments.

'Something's gone seriously pear-shaped,' he said finally. 'I mean, how often does the Chief get involved in poxy little jobs like this?'

'Best we get it spot on then,' remarked Benson. 'We're struggling without some forensic with these bastards.'

They all expected Morgan to retract his statement once he got anywhere near a solicitor. Whilst they were confident they'd got enough on him anyway, they really wanted the rest of the hardcore Mafia. They couldn't rely on identification parades as their witnesses were bound to be got at.

'I'm worried about those mad fuckers we've got with us,' Benson continued, indicating the marked vehicles parked behind them. 'I can see what's going to happen, Bob. They're going to batter the bastards senseless and we'll end up with claret everywhere.'

'I hope not,' said Clarke with a sigh. 'They know what we need, but you can't really blame them for wanting to do a number on them. They deal with this shit all day, every day. When we get to them they've usually had some of the shite kicked out of them.'

Benson nodded in agreement. He sympathised with the uniforms at Horse's Arse but sometimes wished they'd be a little more discriminating with the violence they administered. There were other ways to get what you needed, as he knew only too well.

None of them was aware of what had happened back at Horse's Arse, or of Daniell's decision to hammer the Mafia as of today. He wanted the Patrol Group in for the first cull and was already drafting a press release with Curtis which referred to an operation involving 'local officers assisted by the Force's elite Patrol Group against a gang of dangerous local criminals who posed a serious threat to the decent, law-abiding citizens of Handstead'. Such citizens were something of a minority in Handstead, but the real message would be sent to the Mafia and other like-minded hoodlums.

'At least it's Unit Three,' remarked Jim to H, 'but there

aren't going to be enough prisoners to go round at this rate. We'll have to tell Bob that we go in first and the Patrol Group can have what's left.'

H nodded his agreement and Jim got out of Yankee One and went over to the CID car. He knelt at Clarke's window, had a brief conversation and returned with a smile and a thumbs-up for H.

'It's Horse's Arse's job. They're only here as back-up,' he said as he got back in and slammed the door.

Unit Three had completed their paperwork at Alpha Tango and had been racing to the briefing at HQ when Oscar One had diverted them directly to Horse's Arse to liaise with CID officers at the Grant Flowers flats.

'It's starting early, lads,' Frost shouted excitedly from the front passenger seat as he struggled to make himself heard above the screaming engine and occasional blast of the sirens. 'Don't forget, we're taking out some nasty fuckers, so no fannying about. Lay them out first and worry about the rest later. Anything goes, the Chief said.' His boys smiled grimly and patted the weapons they'd selected for the job. This was going to be a real humdinger.

Bovril watched the rain running down the windscreen of his car. He'd left the engine running to keep warm, but turned the windscreen wipers off. Pizza could see virtually nothing and kept wishing Bovril would at least put the wipers on intermittent, but he said nothing, not wishing in any way to offend his new-found ally.

'What d'you think's up?' he asked finally.

'Christ knows,' replied Bovril, not taking his eyes off the rain-streaked windscreen, focused a thousand yards away on infinity. He slid down into his seat and pulled his overcoat closer around him. Despite the car's heater, he felt chilled to the bone and uneasy. He was desperate to get to a phone and make the most important phone call of his life. He had to tell Lisa, and was raging that he'd missed his opportunity earlier. He just wanted to get this bloody operation out of the way, keep on the periphery of the inevitable violence (there'd be plenty of willing volunteers), and tell her. He wondered where she was, what she was doing. Was she thinking about him, was she wondering how he felt about her? God, why hadn't he told her?

'What'll it be like when we get in there?' continued Pizza nervously. Bovril hardly heard the question and only answered when he realised that Pizza was looking hard at him.

'Sorry, Pizza. What'll it be like? A fucking bloodbath in all likelihood, but don't worry, you'll be fine if you stay close to me and don't get separated.' He looked at him and saw the apprehension in his face. The poor kid had never experienced real violence; it was unlikely he'd ever hit anyone before, seen a man's face split and bleed because he'd caused it to. Bovril laughed gently and patted his arm to comfort him. 'Stick with me, Pizza; do as I do and do as I say. We'll be fine, I promise you.'

Feeling better, but not wholly convinced, Pizza peered through the windscreen at Ally and Piggy's vehicle ahead of them.

'This is a fucking joke,' moaned Piggy, banging his hands on the steering wheel. 'We might as well fuck off if Batman and Robin are on the way. We've still got Dawes and his slag wife to sort out. I was hoping to get home sometime today, and I'm hungry,' he finished plaintively.

Ally had the passenger seat pushed back as far as it would go, and fully reclined. His cap was over his face as he tried to snooze.

'Shut the fuck up, Piggy. You're always hungry. You look like you've had a footpump stuck up your arse as it is. Dawes and his missus are going nowhere for a few days; CID'll want to speak to them anyway. This is the best chance we're going to get to really screw the Mafia.'

'Yeah, I know all that, but we're going to be tucked up for fucking ages.'

'And getting paid, you lazy fat bastard. Just shut the fuck up, will you,' snapped Ally, leaving little doubt that their conversation was at an end. He was thoroughly looking forward to getting to grips with the Mafia. Thomas particularly, whom he'd encountered for the first time not so long ago. He'd been amongst a small group of Mafia that

Ally had thrown out of a chip shop where they'd been abusing the Chinese owner. Not enough to nick them, but once Thomas had put sufficient distance between himself and Ally, he'd given him a mouthful of abuse concerning his shape, ancestry and lack of a father. The shop owner had identified Thomas to him and Ally had promised himself that one day he'd ram those insults down the little arsehole's throat. He was a great believer in JFK's enlightened observation: 'Don't get mad, get even.' Please God, let him be in the flat, he thought to himself. Piggy on the other hand, as he'd demonstrated earlier, needed a different motivation to inspire him to violence.

'You OK, Bovril? You seem miles away,' said Pizza, keen to break the silence.

'Yeah, I'm fine,' he replied without taking his eyes off the windscreen. 'I've fucked up, that's all.'

'Fucked up how?'

Bovril smiled. 'I should have told someone something important but I bottled out. I'll do it later, but I wish I'd done it before.'

'Anyone I know? Nothing really important, I hope?'

'No, no one you know, but it's important to me and I should have told her.'

'Her?'

'Leave it, Pizza, just leave it', said Bovril, and Pizza understood that the topic was now closed. He kept quiet and wished Bovril would put the wipers on so he could see what was going on.

Psycho arrived at the rendezvous at the same time as the Patrol Group. He remained in the van and watched as John Frost got out of the unit's vehicle and hurried over to the CID car, turning his collar up against the drizzle. He knocked at the passenger window, which was wound down by Bob Clarke.

'Hi. John Frost, Patrol Group, Unit 3. Understand you need a hand here.'

'Not really, sarge. Something's gone tits up and the Chief's decided to get you lot involved. We've got plenty of local lads here, but I suppose a couple of yours would always come in handy. Have you got a couple of horrors on board? Then you can give us a hand to get the bodies back to AT.'

'No problems. Got a couple of ex-Horse's Arse head-bangers on board positively foaming at the mouth. What's the job?'

'The Mafia kicked the living shit out of a pub landlord last night and we're going to take the hard core out here now. We're expecting seven more in the flat, all nasty bastards, so tell your boys to get their revenge in first. More importantly, sarge, we're light on forensic, so we're looking for bloodstained clothes, shoes, the usual really.'

'Understood,' said Frost. 'I'll speak to my lads now. When do you anticipate going in?'

'Soon as they're ready.'

Frost ran back to his van and quickly briefed the two lucky candidates in the back. Whilst the others complained loudly, like children denied an ice cream, the chosen two selected their pickaxe handles and stepped out into the rain as the CID officers got out of their vehicle. Taking their cue, the Brothers, Bovril, Pizza, Piggy and Ally joined the huddle by the CID car. They all recognised the Patrol Group officers, nodded in acknowledgement, but said nothing.

'All ready then?' said Clarke. 'The Patrol Group lads are along for the ride. It's our job and the prisoners are ours, understood?' he said pointedly to the Patrol Group officers. They nodded in agreement. No problem at all. They'd get to beat the crap out of some of the Mafia and have none of the paperwork to worry about.

'Come on then,' continued Clarke, leading the way to the front door of the flats. 'We'll take the stairs. No way I want us all stuck in the lift in this fucking shithole.'

Pizza observed happily that, without exception, they all kept looking up until they were through the doors.

The walk up the graffiti-scarred, urine-stinking stairs to the sixth floor took five minutes, and once on the landing the group paused to draw breath. The corpulent Piggy was breathing through his arse and slumped against the wall for support. Clarke spoke again, this time in a whisper.

'That's the one, 612,' he said, indicating a peeling red door on the far side of the silent, rubbish-strewn landing.

They could hear nothing from any of the flats and edged quietly to the door. Clarke put his ear to the paintwork and listened intently. He then knelt down, gingerly opened the letterbox and peered into the darkened flat. He could see down a corridor to the main living room where he could just about make out a number of motionless, prostrate bodies on the floor and a battered old sofa. Two doors on either side of the corridor were closed, but the door to a small kitchen on the right was open. The unmistakable, sickly sweet smell of cannabis and alcohol began to seep through the letterbox. Shutting it carefully he stood up.

'They're in there and well out of it, lads; stoned out of their tiny minds by the smell of it,' he whispered. 'I think you're going to be a bit disappointed with the reception you're likely to receive.'

'We're not fussy,' hissed H, caressing the slim lead-filled mahogany truncheon he held in his right hand. 'Just like the Gurkhas, it's out and now it's got to be blooded.'

Clarke rolled his eyes to the ceiling as the rest of the uniforms sniggered and murmured their agreement. They were all carrying truncheons except Psycho who had a heavy yellow metal Bardic lamp and the two Patrol Group lads with their pickaxe handles. 'Where's your stick, Psycho? You won't need a lamp in there,' he said.

'This is my stick. My equaliser. Never let me down yet,' replied Psycho whose eyes were wide with excitement and anticipation. 'Come on, Bob, let's fucking get on with it.'

Shaking his head and now fearing the worst, Clarke again put his ear to the door. Satisfied that the occupants were still unaware of their presence he tapped silently on the door with his little finger.

'Police, we've got a warrant, open up or we'll put the door in,' he said, so quietly that the group behind him could barely hear him. 'No, refusing us entry,' he continued slightly louder. 'Put the door in, lads.'

The Brothers hurried forward as Clarke stepped to one side, eager to show their expertise. Jim had picked up one or two tricks in Ulster which he had passed on to H and they now used on a regular basis. H put his arms under Jim's armpits, linked his arms around his chest and braced his legs. Jim then jumped into the air and slammed both feet against the door lock. The flimsy frame splintered, the door crashed open against the far wall and the Brothers led the charge into the flat, Jim screaming at the top of his voice, 'You're fucking dead, you scumbags.'

# Chapter Thirteen

Myra Baldwin was lying naked on Baker's bed, alone under a filthy duvet, curled up in the foetal position. She had stopped crying, but her face was tear-streaked and the pillow wet from her tears. She was still in pain and gave the occasional sob as she winced, but otherwise she was calm. The pain wasn't the reason she had been crying. Her betrayal by the man she worshipped, and the only man she trusted, had been too much for a girl already teetering on the edge of the abyss of madness. Abandoned at birth in the toilet of the railway station, Myra was a classic product of the system in which she subsequently grew up. Educationally backward, she had been unfortunate enough to inherit her unknown mother's good looks and figure and as she reached adolescence had begun to be abused by her 'carers' and fellow inmates. She had her first abortion aged thirteen, the result of repeated rapes by the senior social worker at her home. Others followed. At the age of seventeen she had found herself booted out into the real world with a hatred of men that bordered on the psychotic.

She picked up a handful of convictions for petty crime, but really came to the notice of the local law with her last two, assaults on police officers that had left her victims shocked by the sudden, explosive, truly vicious attacks. The last officer to be attacked by her, during a disturbance outside the Park Royal pub, sagely observed as he nursed deep fingernail scratches under both eyes, 'That evil bitch is going to kill someone one day.' Myra couldn't explain, even to herself, why she would suddenly erupt, but she knew that she enjoyed the notoriety it inspired. That, coupled subsequently with her relationship with Driscoll, elevated her above the common herd in her own eyes. The derisory fines imposed by the local magistrates (she hadn't appeared before Colonel Mortimer) only served to reinforce her dangerous psychotic state.

Myra had been given a council flat on the Park Royal estate but had no idea how to live outside an institution. Quickly, she drifted towards the gutter. Driscoll had first come into her life one evening in the estate pub a few months after she arrived. He was different, an obvious leader, and, unlike all the other men she'd known, hadn't tried to screw her straight away. On the contrary, he talked to her at length, didn't lay a finger on her and left the entire running to her. His strategy was spot on and after a couple of weeks Myra was convinced that something was wrong with her. She pursued Driscoll with manic intensity, finally bedding him in her filthy flat and swearing lifelong loyalty to a man who made her feel differently about herself. She belonged to him and gave herself completely, body and soul. She was his property and as such became part of the Mafia, always at his side. She'd been alongside him as they'd laid into the landlord at the Hoop and Garapes last night and had allowed him to escape ahead of her before following through the window behind. He was her Messiah, she his disciple. But he had betrayed her. He was no better than the others. He had betrayed and deceived her.

At his bidding she had undressed and mounted him as he lay back on Baker's bed, to give Baker 'a bit of a treat'. After a few minutes, Driscoll had suddenly wrapped his arms round her and pulled her tightly against him. As she struggled to breathe she became aware of Baker moving closer behind her.

'What you doing, Bobby?' she gasped. 'You're hurting me. Let me go.'

'Relax, you stupid little bitch,' Driscoll hissed. 'You'll do as I tell you – you're mine. Take it and tell me you like it.'

'I don't like it. You're scaring me. Let me go, Bobby,' she pleaded as Baker began to caress her raised buttocks. Then she felt his erect penis pushing against her anus and she began to struggle violently. Both men restrained her as Baker viciously buggered her. She screamed at the ripping pain, but Driscoll held her head firmly against his chest, and vaguely she heard him saying repeatedly, 'You're mine, you bitch, tell me you like it.' Baker ejaculated inside her quickly and roughly withdrew, causing her to scream even louder, and Driscoll pushed her off him onto the bed. She curled into a defensive ball as he stood over her, masturbating.

'You fucking little slag, you enjoyed that, didn't you? You're mine and I can use you as I please. If I want to share you I will.'

She heard Baker laugh out loud as Driscoll ejaculated, and felt his warm semen splatter on to her hips and legs. As he pulled up his trousers and buckled his belt he turned to her.

'We'll be back for seconds later, Myra. Get yourself cleaned up, you lucky bitch.' He and Baker were laughing like hyenas as they left the room and she began to sob.

He had betrayed her as no one had ever betrayed or abused her before. Her warped and distorted version of life with Driscoll was all that she had to cling to, and now that had evaporated along with all the rest. Once again she peered into the pit and saw only the swirling darkness that billowed over the edge and covered her completely. The stunted emotions that left room for vulnerability began to shut down, and a veil was drawn across her face as her last tenuous grip on sanity made its apologies and departed. Ten minutes later, icy-faced and feeling nothing physically or emotionally, she kicked the duvet aside and began to search the room for something to clean herself up with. In the top drawer of the shabby little table by the bed she found two pairs of relatively clean underpants, one of which she used to wipe herself. She was bleeding slightly and pushed the second pair between her buttocks to stanch the flow. She felt no pain now. Opening the bottom drawer, she began to hurl the socks and T-shirts she found over her shoulder. Then she stopped and smiled strangely at what had been hidden underneath. The snub-nosed, gunmetal-grey model 10 .38 calibre Smith and Wesson handgun had been bought three weeks earlier in a pub in Hanstead by Baker for £75. He wasn't really sure why he'd bought it, and hadn't mentioned it to Driscoll, as he was unsure of his reaction. He'd toyed with the notion of robbing an off-licence in nearby Ashington, but dismissed the idea when he accepted that he could never operate independently of Driscoll. The gun had come with three rounds in the chamber and Baker had hidden it away for a rainy day when Driscoll might announce, 'I wish we had a shooter.' He contented himself with occasionally holding the weapon and quick-drawing in front of the bathroom mirror. One day Driscoll would congratulate him on his foresight and initiative.

Myra got back on to the bed, covered herself with the duvet, and was cradling the gun in her hands when she heard the front door come off its hinges as the Brothers led the charge into the flat. The alcohol and drugs had lost their hold as her freezing madness engulfed her. She lay wide-eyed, staring at the wall, waiting to kill the next man who came to abuse her, Driscoll, Baker, whoever. She had no idea whether the gun was loaded or not; if she had to she would beat him to death with it. She waited quietly, her breathing controlled and steady, like a lioness on the African veldt watching a zebra detach itself from the group.

Somewhere, deep in the dark recesses of his drug and alcohol-sodden subconscious, Baker heard the commotion and the animal instinct in him told him that it meant danger. He was lying on his back on the floor by the sofa, surrounded by empty lager cans and cigarette butts stubbed out on the ruined carpet. His lank black hair was plastered to his head where Driscoll had doused him with lager as they celebrated their attack on Myra. He stank like the wild beast he was. As the warning voices in his befuddled head got louder, he opened one eye, vaguely made out figures moving around him, and then felt his world erupt as H stamped on his testicles as hard as he could. The Brothers had spotted Baker as they rushed in, knew he was the most dangerous, and instinctively went for him together. As Baker lurched upright screaming, H and Jim hit him simultaneously with their sticks, H in the mouth and Jim in the back of the head. Baker slumped against the side of the sofa unconscious again, broken teeth falling from the side of his mouth, blood streaming from his nose. The danger man dealt with, the Brothers now turned their attention to Driscoll as the rest of the raiding party tore into the other sleeping Mafia members. Baker's scream had roused

Driscoll, who was now desperately trying to focus his eyes and get up from the sofa. Someone kept pushing him in the face, keeping him down.

'I'll fucking do you,' he slurred, eyes narrowed as he tried to identify his tormentor. He heard a voice say 'Hello, Bobby', and tried to place it. He was sure he recognised the accent. 'Who the fuck is it?' he said, rolling his head around. 'I can't see you.'

'You know us, Bobby,' said another voice quietly. Driscoll stopped rolling his head and raised his iron-heavy eyelids as his head slumped against his left shoulder. Yes, he recognised those voices, but from where? Two large figures swayed in and out of his vision and then finally the picture cleared like a 3D puzzle suddenly becoming obvious.

'Fucking hell,' he screamed as he recognised the grinning Brothers, who appeared as twin Grim Reapers to him. As he tried to get to his feet, H stooped down and hit him on the kneecap with his truncheon. As if shot, Driscoll grabbed his knee and fell screaming from the sofa on to the floor. As he thrashed about, Jim took careful aim and smashed the other kneecap with his stick. Driscoll vomited and passed out alongside his similarly unconscious enforcer.

Around the room, the other Mafia members were receiving similar treatment. Danny Reilly was beaten like an old carpet by the Patrol Group lads with their pickaxe handles until he seemed to burst like an overripe tomato. His younger brother Cliff had tried to help him and been instantly felled by a blow that Babe Ruth would have been proud of. The CID officers had remained in the hall as the uniforms played catch-up with the Mafia, and only now ventured into the living room.

'Holy fucking shit,' whispered Clarke, glancing from the unconscious Driscoll and Baker to where Psycho seemed intent on hammering Des Anderson's head through the floor into the flat below. His bardic lamp was covered in blood and sent sprays on to the wall behind him on the upstrokes.

'For fuck's sake, Psycho, stop it,' he shouted. 'You'll fucking kill him.' Psycho stopped with his arm raised and looked maniacally over at Clarke and then down at Anderson, who had been unconscious for some time. He shrugged, got off him and stood over him for a few seconds before wandering out of the room, down the corridor and into the kitchen. The living room was beginning to resemble an abattoir.

Peter Thomas came to with someone blowing into his ear and whispering, 'Cooee, cooee, wakey wakey, Peter.' He grinned and giggled, opened his eyes, and through a fish-eye lens saw a ginger-haired man smiling at him. As he had entered the room, Ally had seen Thomas slumped in a chair at the far end and had barged past Piggy, Bovril and Pizza to get him, shouting. 'Thank you, God, thank you.' Thomas frowned as he looked at Ally and tried to remember where he knew him from.

'Hello, Peter,' said Ally sweetly, 'remember me?'

'No,' he replied sourly. 'Who the fuck are you?'

His vision was clearing and he could now identify the copper's uniform the man was wearing. It wasn't that stumpy Jock, was it? 'You're not that fucking Jock, are you?' he said.

'Fucking right I am,' screamed Ally. 'Have some of this, you little cunt,' and venting all his pent-up hatred of niggers, wops, spies, ab dabs, Catholics, Australian barmaids and anyone taller than himself, he brought his truncheon down across the top of Thomas's head with a sickening crack. The man's scalp split and he slumped back in the chair with a torrent of blood obscuring his face. Ally stood back and briefly admired his handiwork before he became aware of Piggy watching him closely.

'What?' he barked aggressively.

'You OK? Feel better for that, Ally?' Piggy asked.

'Much,' he snapped.

'What the fuck was all that about?'

'Personal business. One all,' Ally replied simply. Piggy shrugged. There was no point pursuing it with Ally in this sort of mood.

Pizza had never seen anything like it. He had seen the Brothers take out Baker and Driscoll, and watched with an ever-widening mouth as his colleagues had appeared to go mad. There was blood everywhere and the six bodies on the floor looked as though they'd been attacked with a chainsaw. He really didn't know how to react and from time to time glanced at Bovril who appeared quite unconcerned, glancing at his watch, impatient to be elsewhere. The four detectives had watched the attack with an air of resignation, but as they stepped gingerly further into the room to look at their prisoners, a horrible realisation dawned on them. They looked at each other simultaneously.

'Where the fuck are their clothes?' asked Benson for all of them. For the first time the uniforms took stock of the bodies on the floor and noticed that none was wearing trousers, shirts or shoes. They looked at one another and then at the detectives. Clarke had his eyes closed, head down, rubbing his temples as he spoke.

'They've dumped their clothing, everything. We've got no fucking forensic. We're bolloxed.' He turned away in disgust and walked to the kitchen. As he walked in he found Psycho at the fridge, busy completing another of his rituals with his cock in a milk bottle. Every time he was involved in a house search he would find time to get to the fridge and have a piss in a half-full bottle of milk. He would later laugh himself to tears imagining the house occupants discussing whether the milk was off as they looked at a suspect cup of tea or bowl of cornflakes. It was the tomcat in him, making sure that people knew this was his territory. Clarke shook his head as he saw him carefully shake the last drops into the bottle and shut the fridge door.

'Jesus Christ, Psycho, we've got real problems without that. They've dumped all their clothes somewhere. Tear this shit pit apart, see what you can find, will you?'

Psycho couldn't give a toss about the lack of evidence in the flat. He'd had his fun with Anderson, but now he could do a bit of damage whilst he searched. As Clarke walked out of the kitchen, Psycho pulled the doors off a cupboard with a loud splintering noise.

As Clarke returned to the living room where Lloyd, Benson and Thomas were ensuring that the prisoners were being cuffed and given an arresting officer with requisite evidence of arrest, Pizza came bounding up to him like an eager puppy. He almost put his hand up to speak.

'Their clothes, their clothes . . .' he spluttered.

'What about them?' said Clarke impatiently. He was quickly getting pissed off with this spotty woodentop.

'I think I've found them,' Pizza said loudly. The piano player stopped as the saloon doors swung open and all eyes in the room turned to Pizza.

'Found them? Where?' said Clarke slowly, taking hold of Pizza by the shoulders and looking him in the face.

'I was in the garages earlier, and I found a bag full of bloodstained clothing . . .' he started before Clarke interrupted him.

'What garages, when? Start from the beginning – don't miss anything out.'

Pizza took a deep breath, keenly aware that for the first time he had the full attention, and, he hoped, the respect, of his colleagues.

'I went to the underground garages here about six thirty this morning to see if any motors had been dumped. There weren't any, but as I was leaving I found a bin liner in one of the garages. Someone had tried to set fire to it but it's so wet down there it hadn't caught.'

'Yes, yes, go on,' said Clarke excitedly.

'I got it outside and had a look. It was full of bloodstained clothes.'

'What sort of clothes?'

'Trousers, shirts, couple of pairs of boots. The blood looked quite fresh.'

'Where's the bag now?' said Clarke nervously.

'Back at the nick. I logged it all in.'

'You fucking beauty,' whooped Clarke, grabbing Pizza by the cheeks and pulling the flesh until it hurt. 'They've fucked up big time. That clothing's theirs and we'll match it to them no problem. What a result! Fucking good job . . . what's your name?'

'Alan Petty.'

'But we call him Pizza,' said Bovril, walking alongside and placing a friendly hand on his shoulder. Pizza looked at him, saw Bovril smile at him and give a barely noticeable nod. He knew what it meant. He looked at the others and thought that they too were looking at him differently. The Brothers were staring at him. They said nothing but their glares were definitely softer. He had arrived; they had accepted him as one of them. He swelled with pride, felt the hurt and rejection slide off his shoulders like a heavy blanket and was worried he was near to tears.

'Good job, Pizza,' continued Bovril, patting him on the back. 'Your little find sounds like it's going to make all the difference. You must be feeling quite pleased with yourself.'

Pizza couldn't speak because of the lump in his throat, but nodded.

'Should do too,' agreed Clarke, 'but we're still one light. Where's Baldwin?' No one spoke. 'Anyone done the bedroom yet?' Clarke continued. Again, silence.

'We'll do it,' said Bovril. 'Come on, Pizza,' and guided him out of the living room.

The bedroom door was shut and Bovril opened it gingerly, located the light switch and stepped into the room ahead of Pizza. They stood together and looked at Myra, still lying under the duvet in the foetal position. She lay looking at them with her eyes sparkling and her lips drawn back over her teeth in a dry smile. Bovril knew her of old, Pizza only by reputation.

'Up you get, Myra,' said Bovril gently. 'You're all nicked for GBH. You know the score.'

She didn't move or change her expression, but her breathing had quickened. Bovril frowned as his sixth sense told him that something was wrong.

'Come on, Myra,' he repeated, slightly less confidently as he felt the hairs on the back of his neck stand up and his stomach begin to churn. Pizza had felt his new friend's confidence and bonhomie vanish and was looking from him to Myra and back with a puzzled expression on his face.

'What's up, Bovril?' he whispered anxiously.

'Something's wrong,' Bovril replied quietly without taking his eyes off Myra. 'Go and get some help in here. Don't startle her, just go quietly.' He was struggling to keep his composure. His instincts told him to turn and run away as fast as he could. Get away from this strange, evil, grinning bitch. Run away now – something is wrong. You're in danger. But how could he run away in front of Pizza, a brand-new probationer who was looking to him to do the right thing, show him how to do the job properly? But the right thing to do was to run away, live to fight another day. What would Pizza think of him, running away like a scared child from a woman lying under a duvet? But something's not right, her eyes are telling you things are very seriously not right. Get the fuck out of here – now.

'Get some help in here, Pizza,' he said again as his brain raced madly. As Pizza began to edge past him to the door, Myra sat upright on the bed, the duvet falling from her shoulders, still covering the hand holding the gun. She was still smiling and staring at Bovril, unaware of Pizza's presence. She knew why he was in the room; it was what every man was after but she was determined that it would never happen again. If he took a step towards her, she would kill him. Bovril moved nearer to the bed with his arms outstretched.

'Listen, Myra, I'm not here to give you any grief. Just get yourself dressed and we'll be on our way.'

He froze and the colour drained from his face as she quickly pulled her arm from under the duvet and levelled the gun at his chest.

'Jesus,' he whispered, as his heart leapt into his throat and his breathing became frantic, 'Jesus, no.'

Pizza heard him and half turned to see what she had done now, and watched what followed transfixed. He couldn't speak, or shout out or move. His body and all his senses except his sight stopped working. He saw Bovril's lips move again as he spoke to her, saw his face etched with fear, his eyes fixed on her, saw him stretch both his arms out in front of him, hands up, take a step back and mouth the single word 'No'.

Myra pulled the trigger without altering her expression or taking her eyes off Bovril. Pizza saw the flash and recoil, saw Bovril tilt forward slightly, grab at his stomach and then collapse like a deck of cards on to the floor. It looked as though all the bones in his legs had suddenly been removed and the muscle and flesh had collapsed under his weight.

The 158-grain jacketed soft-point round, travelling at 1300 feet a second, had passed through his tunic like a hot knife through butter. It struck the bottom rib on his left side, shattering the bone, and fragmented into four pieces, the largest of which began to tumble up into his body, pulverising his liver and tearing through the aorta before lodging in his spine. He was haemorrhaging massively before he hit the floor, still conscious and feeling as though he'd been heavily punched in the solar plexus. He felt no other pain but knew what had happened and began to pant as he panicked and struggled for air. He could feel liquid escaping inside him.

Myra looked at him, still with the strange smile on her face, and then put the barrel of the gun into her mouth and pulled the trigger. Nothing happened. She frowned, looked down at the gun and pulled the trigger again. With his sound still off, Pizza watched as the back of her head exploded. Pieces of skull like coconut shell, blood and brain tissue sprayed against the wall behind her and she slumped forward, her face distorted, eyes bulging as the bullet's gases escaped from every orifice in her head. She lay in a kneeling position with the hole in the back of her head pumping blood over her shoulders onto the bed. The pair of pants was still stuffed between the cheeks of her backside, and, bizarrely, it crossed Pizza's mind that she looked like a rooster from hell. Only five seconds had passed since Myra had first pulled the trigger, and now she lay dead on the bed that was changing colour as she drained into it, and Bovril was dying on the floor.

The two shots in quick succession momentarily stunned the other officers out in the living room. Benson reacted first, looking at Clarke, asking, 'What the fuck . . .' and running into the corridor. Psycho came out of the kitchen holding a cupboard door, looking stunned. He looked at Benson.

'What the fuck?'

Without answering him, Benson burst into the bedroom. It was a gruesome scene. Pizza had recovered from his paralysis and was kneeling on the floor alongside Bovril, who lay on his back with his hands pressed to his chest. He looked deathly pale and his eyes were wide and staring at the ceiling. Pizza was talking desperately to him, telling him to hold on, tears running down his face.

'What the fuck happened?' said Benson, looking towards Myra on the bed and the gore on the wall behind her.

'She shot him,' answered Pizza tearfully. 'Get a fucking ambulance, for Christ's sake, he's been shot.'

Benson turned and shouted to the group who were now gathered behind him at the door. 'Someone get an ambulance on the hurry up and tell Control this has gone to fucking rat shit.' Piggy hurried out into the living room to make the call on his personal radio.

Benson knelt down next to Bovril and looked closely at him. He could see very little blood around the hole in his tunic. Bovril's eyes were opening and closing and his lips were moving.

'Stay with him, keep him awake,' he instructed Pizza, who had his ear close to Bovril's mouth as his lips moved. Benson stood up, went over to the bed and looked dispassionately at Myra's corpse.

'Fucking bitch,' he snarled and spat into the still-bleeding hole in the back of her head. Then he saw the pistol lying by her right knee and called Clarke over to him. He and the ashen-faced detective quickly discussed what to do next.

'We haven't got long, Bob. We're going to have to make the best out of this that we can. This gun'll come in handy.'

'How?' asked Clarke, glancing over at Bovril. He was consumed with guilt, incapable of thinking straight. He repeated his question.

'What's happened in here is tidy. This bitch is dead, but we can still score some points. Some more fingerprints on the gun would come in handy, wouldn't they?'

Clarke still didn't understand.

'We can tie someone else in to the gun, Bob,' said Benson urgently, picking it up with a Biro stuck up the barrel. 'Driscoll's prints on the shell cases would go down a treat.'

At last Clarke nodded his understanding as Benson took a handkerchief from his pocket and spread it on the bed next to Myra. Then, using the handkerchief, he opened the chamber and ejected one live round and the two spent cartridges. He glanced over his shoulder and saw that one or two of the group were watching him.

'Get them out of here, Bob. Fewer people who know the better,' he whispered. 'Find something for them to do while I get this sorted.'

Benson wrapped the bullets in his handkerchief and walked back into the living room. Driscoll and Baker still lay unconscious side by side and obscured from the other groaning Mafia by the sofa. Kneeling alongside them, he quickly forced Driscoll's right thumb and forefinger on to both of the spent cartridges, and for good measure did the same to Baker with the live round. Smiling grimly, he walked back into the bedroom, where he found Clarke kneeling alongside Bovril and Pizza. The others had disappeared. Clarke looked up as he entered.

'OK?' he asked.

'Done and dusted,' replied Benson, going over to the bed and carefully replacing the live round and the spent cartridges in their original places in the chamber. Snapping the pistol closed, he threw it alongside Myra's body. 'That should fuck them,' he said quietly, turning back to the group on the floor. 'How's he doing?'

Bovril could feel the liquid running even faster inside him, almost gurgling like a stream in flood. He felt cold and dizzy and was still struggling to breathe. He couldn't focus his eyes but was aware of people around him. One of them was Pizza. Pizza was talking to him but he couldn't hear him, the buzzing in his head was too loud. Lisa. Lisa. He had to get a message to her. He had to tell her he loved her. Perhaps Pizza would pass it on. He'd tell her himself when he got out of hospital. There was only one bullet inside him, he was sure he was going to survive. But what was that gurgling sound? Why was he so cold? Why couldn't he hear or see properly? Pizza, Pizza, listen to me, you have to tell Lisa something for me. Nobody knows about her yet, but I love her and I need her to know that. You have to tell Lisa that for me. Pizza, Pizza, can you hear me? You have to tell Lisa. Lisa. And Bovril slipped into unconsciousness, bleeding to death on the floor of a dingy bedroom in a squalid flat in the arsehole of the world, a whispered name on his lips.

He opened his eyes in a very dark place. He didn't know where; it was so dark he couldn't see his hand in front of his face. He turned slowly round in the dark, but dare not move any further. A few minutes passed. Then he noticed that he was beginning to cast a shadow in front of him and he turned to see a bright light some distance away. Despite its intensity, the light didn't hurt his eyes and he began to walk uncertainly towards it. The light warmed him and as he got closer he saw a figure silhouetted deep inside it. He strained his eyes and then smiled with relief as he recognised the figure. Bovril ran into the welcoming, warm light, all fear and pain gone. The light closed around him and he was gone.

# Chapter Fourteen

It was still raining when they buried Bovril two weeks later; no one could swear that it had ever stopped. Low, scudding, leaden clouds, whipped along by a biting northerly wind, added to the melancholy air in the small churchyard a few miles west of Horse's Arse. The surrounding trees, stripped of their leaves, thrust their branches into the sky like blackened, arthritic fingers and bent against the chilling blast. Circling rooks added their menacing tones to proceedings, completing the depression that hung over the churchyard.

Situated on the side of a hill, the place offered little defence against the elements, and the crowd gathered around the grave huddled closer for protection. The thousand-year-old oak at the far corner of the graveyard, however, had provided cover for mourners and revellers alike for as long as the church had stood. In the summer, its heavy, low branches, which touched the ground in places, provided solace from the beating sun, and now it protected the slim young girl from the wind and rain as she watched the proceedings below her.

The gravel path to the church door was lined with uniformed officers wearing white gloves. They had stood silently to attention as Bovril's coffin, draped with the Force flag with his helmet balanced on top, had been borne along the path and into the church by a party made up of the Brothers, Piggy, Pizza, Andy Collins and Psycho. Ally was still sulking, as he'd been thrown off the original party on account of his height, which caused the coffin to tilt alarmingly. During a dress rehearsal, they'd dropped it. The church had been packed to the rafters with officers from all over the county and Bovril's relatives. Some of those, Psycho had noticed happily, were well worth a shag and he'd resolved to get after them once the funeral was over. Most of the officers there had no idea who Bovril was and had certainly never met him, but his funeral was a great opportunity to get away from tedious divisional duties elsewhere. But the 'B' Division officers who knew of him and the Horse's Arse officers in particular, who knew him well, were there for all the right reasons. The Chief had given his eulogy prompting one or two raised eyebrows, but generally decorum was preserved. Even Inspector Greaves at the back of the congregation was on his best behaviour, though he very publicly needed his wife with him as an emotional crutch.

The service over, the coffin party had crunched along the

path to the prepared grave where they gathered round for the service of interment. Pizza had deliberately absented himself from the throng and stood on his own with his back to the driving rain. He wanted to be alone with his thoughts. He'd felt like that since the shooting, preferring his own company and so far refusing to discuss the matter with the rest of the group. The CID officers who'd investigated Bovril's murder had found Pizza bloody hard work when they'd questioned him. It wasn't that he was stupid or being awkward; he really couldn't talk about the death of his friend. His find in the garages had proved crucial in tying Driscoll and his cohorts in the flat to the attack on the pub landlord. All fourteen were now languishing on remand in Strangeways charged with the assault; Driscoll and Baker also faced additional charges relating to the gun used by Myra to murder Bovril and the assault on her revealed by the post-mortem. They were all looking at substantial prison sentences with luck, but Pizza drew no comfort from his part in their downfall. As he snapped out of yet another flashback to that fateful day, he gave a deep sigh and looked beyond the huddle at the grave to the oak tree at the far corner. He could see a young girl sheltering under its branches and covered his eyes from the rain to see if he recognised her. He didn't, and out of idle curiosity walked slowly over to the tree and joined her in its shelter.

'Hello. My name's Alan Petty,' he said quietly. 'Were you a friend?'

'Yes, sort of I suppose,' she said hesitantly.

'He was my best mate,' continued Pizza, growing quickly in confidence with this apparently vulnerable and very attractive girl. 'I was with him when he was killed, in the same room.'

'With him?' she said, suddenly very interested and looking intently at him. 'What happened, can you tell me? Are you allowed to?'

Pizza sighed, looking at his shoes and then towards the grave as his throat tightened and his eyes filled. 'It's difficult for me. I'm sorry, but sometimes I can't talk about it,' he said hoarsely. 'He was my best friend and I was standing next to him when she shot him.'

'It must have been very frightening,' she said softly, slipping an arm through his. 'Did he suffer at all?'

'No, I don't think so. He was alive for a few minutes after, but I don't think he really knew what was going on. He was sort of delirious, I think, in and out of consciousness, and then he was gone.' His throat began to ease.

'How long had you been friends?' she asked.

'Not very long really, but we were really tight, know what I mean?'

The girl had moved round to face Pizza and began to gently probe his memory and remove the layers that tried to cover the nightmare.

'What happened in the flat?' she asked softly.

Pizza swallowed hard as he remembered. He wanted to

tell her everything. Strangely, he felt better as he talked to her.

'We were there to nick this mob for GBH, but he and I kept out of all the aggro. We went to search the bedroom and she was in there. He tried to talk to her. He was really pleasant about things and then she shot him. Just like that, and then she blew the back of her own head off.'

'Why didn't you get involved at the start?' she asked, sensing somehow that it was significant. He shivered as the wind gusted hard and thrust his hands deep into his coat pockets.

'Don't know really. He didn't seem interested, didn't want to be there. He had something on his mind, I think.'

'What makes you say that?'

'Well, before we went in he was miles away and I asked him what was up. He just said that he'd forgotten to tell someone something important. No, not forgotten, "bottled out", that's what he said, and it was a woman. He was going to tell her whatever it was later, but Christ only knows what it was all about.'

The girl smiled sadly. 'Did he say anything else?'

'No, I don't think so, not until after he'd been shot and he was delirious. His voice was really quiet, almost a whisper. I had his head in my lap when he died. He was trying to talk, looking at me like he was desperate to tell me something. His lips were moving but I couldn't hear what he was saying.'

'Nothing at all?'

'No, he was too quiet. It sounded like he was saying a name or something like that, but I couldn't make it out.'

'A girl's name, do you think?'

'Could have been, but I couldn't hear him properly. It sounded like "Leaf" or "Leach" or something like that but it didn't make any sense.'

He noticed that the girl's eyes had filled with tears and she was quiet, looking back at the ceremony at the grave. 'Are you OK?' he asked gently.

'I'm fine. Thanks for being so kind and telling me about things. I'm glad you were with him when he died. I know he'd have got a lot of comfort from you.'

'Do you think so? God, I hope he did,' sighed Pizza. 'He was my best friend. How did you know him, by the way?'

She laughed, and smiling said, 'I only knew him a short time, but he had quite an effect on me. We were good friends.' She paused before continuing, 'It looks as though they're finishing up down there. You'd better join them, hadn't you?'

'Suppose so,' said Pizza. 'It's been nice talking to you. See you again, I hope.' He pushed his way from under the tree and walked back to the grave. As he walked away, head bent against the rain, Lisa smiled and stroked the life growing inside her. Bovril had certainly had an effect on her, but had never known how much.

\*

After the service, long after everyone else had departed, 'D' Relief had hung around the gates to the churchyard, oblivious of the drizzle, not sure what to do with themselves, not wanting to go home, not yet. They had all been due to join Bovril's family at their house for afternoon tea, but Psycho's stalking of one of the spinster aunts had changed that. During the service, the unfortunate woman had made the fatal mistake of catching Psycho's eye. He'd seen her and interpreted her look of horror as one of unadulterated lust. As they'd stood around the grave later, Psycho had sidled up behind her, eased his trousered diamond cutter of an erection against her bottom and breathed beerily into her ear, 'It's your lucky day. Guess who, sweet thing?' Only Andy Collins's intervention had prevented her from screaming the place down and he'd ushered the sullen, scowling Psycho away, explaining to onlookers that this was how he dealt with his grief.

'What the fuck is the matter with you?' he said furiously once he'd got him out of view.

'She was begging for it, absolutely gagging,' protested Psycho. 'What else could I do?'

'Jesus fucking Christ,' exploded Collins, 'by the fucking grave? Are you completely fucking mad?' Then he realised that he was and stormed away to placate the family. The invitation to afternoon tea was icily withdrawn.

Psycho broke the silence when he spoke to no one in particular.

'That's that, then. See you Monday night then?'

'Fucking hell, nights again Monday,' said Jim. 'Comes round quick, don't it? That'll do me as well. You in Monday, H?'

'I'll be there, Jim,' replied his partner as they walked slowly to their cars parked nearby and returned to their other lives for a while. The others took their cue from the Brothers and also began to drift away. Only Psycho remained, soaked to the skin, nowhere to go, no one to go to. Even the Blister walked away.

'Anyone fancy a drink?' he called plaintively. 'No? Well bollocks to the lot of you.'

# Chapter Fifteen

Acting Chief Inspector Kevin Curtis drew himself to his full, less than impressive height and surveyed the assembled Night Turn officers in what he imagined was the fashion expected of a man on the way to the top.

'Fuck me, the circus is in town,' said a loud voice from the back of the group. Sitting at the desk alongside him, Andy Collins realised what was coming and lowered his head in case someone threw something. 'D' Relief glared at Curtis with an intensity that could fry a rump steak. He decided not to make an issue of the insult, smiled benevolently and walked into the heaviest shitstorm he would ever experience.

'Before Sergeant Collins starts, ladies and gentlemen, I'd just like to say a few words,' he began confidently, completely misinterpreting the venomous looks he was getting. Never one to miss an opening, Chief Daniells had instantly recognised that Gillard's demise was the opportunity he needed to get rid of his ludicrous staff officer. Within hours of Bovril's death, Curtis had found himself in charge, albeit temporarily, at Horse's Arse. Across the county, other relieved Chief Inspectors went on the piss to celebrate their lucky escapes. Curtis's wife's reaction to the news had been extremely odd. Rather than jubilation at his promotion in the field, she'd caustically remarked that his chances of success were on a par with those of a chocolate fireguard, before slamming down the phone. He'd subsequently made a point of attending Early Turn and Late Turn musters, but had really fucked up by arriving for 'D' Relief's first night duty since Bovril's funeral. Nobody had seen fit to warn him about 'D' Relief. Strange, that.

The other groups of officers had received him in sullen, disinterested silence, which he had interpreted as respectful deference to his new rank. Whilst he was vaguely aware of what Horse's Arse was all about, he really had absolutely no idea just how bad things were.

'Some of you might be wondering who I am,' he continued in the same light-hearted manner.

'No,' shouted Psycho belligerently from the front, his arms folded across his chest, 'no, we weren't at all . . . sir,' he finished with a sneer, managing to make 'sir' sound like 'cunt'. The others sniggered and forgave him for his faux pas at the cemetery. Collins dropped his head into his hands and despaired at the insanity of it all.

'You weren't?' said Curtis hesitantly, wringing his hands

together and glancing down at Collins, who was now shaking his head. He'd have to speak to Collins later, he decided; clear lack of support for a senior officer. That wouldn't do at all. He still didn't recognise the danger signs that were obvious to everyone else in the room. All that was missing was an air raid warning siren.

'Who are you anyway, and why are you here?' continued Psycho, who was delighted with the response he was getting from the others. He knew he'd gone too far at Bovril's funeral and now he had the chance to rectify things at this twat's expense.

'I'm Chief Inspector Curtis . . .' he started in a fluster before Psycho interrupted him.

'No you're not. You're only an inspector. You've only got two pips up.'

'*Acting* Chief Inspector . . .' Curtis corrected himself, wondering what the hell was going on. This shouldn't be happening. He was in charge.

'Sarge, sarge,' shouted Psycho, 'are we sure this bloke is really in the Job? He doesn't seem to know what rank he is or anything.'

Collins decided that enough was enough as a chorus of dissent rose from the chairs in front of him and Curtis stared at the rabble like a rabbit frozen in a car's headlights.

'Shut the fuck up, Psycho, and listen up everyone,' he said, getting to his feet and towering over Curtis. The noise ceased. 'This is Acting Chief Inspector Curtis. He's taken over from Mr Gillard for the time being as Mrs Bott is still incapacitated.' At this, he noticed the Brothers lean forward and pat the beaming Psycho on the shoulders. It confirmed his suspicions about what had happened to Bott, but he had no intention of acting on them. The stupid cow was well overdue and Psycho had probably done them all a favour. 'Mr Curtis will be with us until further notice,' he continued, 'so be gentle with him,' he finished with a laugh.

'What's that supposed to mean, Sergeant?' interrupted Curtis haughtily; furious that Collins had intervened, completely missing the fact that he had stepped in to save him from a real kebabing.

Collins fixed him with a withering stare, leant down closer to his face and growled, 'Just wind your fucking neck in, guv, and you might get through this.'

Curtis was speechless as Collins turned back to the Relief and began to assign them to their beats and vehicles for the night. How dare the grey-haired old dinosaur speak to him like that?

I'm not having this, he said to himself, resolving to step in at the next opportunity with some news that would really sort this shower out. Oh yes, just watch. He laughed quietly.

The group were listening attentively to Collins, taking a few notes about items of interest, getting their pocket notebooks up to date for what would, without doubt, be a busy night. Bovril's murder was still an open sore with them, and none of them had mentioned him as they had changed before starting duty. The only thought they could console themselves with was that Driscoll and his hardcore Mafia were banged up on remand. Bovril's death wouldn't be a complete waste if that pond life went away for a very long time. It was the only positive thing any of them could draw from his death.

'That's all I've got for you,' concluded Collins; 'unless Mr Curtis has anything to add,' he said out of professional courtesy, flaring his eyes at him to say, *Don't say a fucking word, arsehole.*

'Thank you, Sergeant,' said Curtis imperiously, getting to his feet and motioning for Collins to sit.

'Oh shit,' said Collins quietly, settling back into his chair and hanging his head in his hands again, 'oh shit.'

Curtis surveyed the once again simmering mob, paying particular attention to the large, unshaven, ugly brute at the front who'd been so rude to him.

'I don't mean to add to your problems,' he lied, 'but I'm afraid I have some news that is going to upset you.' The Relief fell silent and waited. Curtis cleared his throat before continuing, beginning to sweat until his podgy, pink, boyish face resembled a freshly glazed bun.

'I had a communication from Division this afternoon concerning Mr Driscoll,' he said, eyeing them cautiously to try to gauge how they would react. They now sat in rapt attention and he pressed on, beginning to feel that he had them eating out of his hand. 'It seems that he's found a judge somewhere who was prepared to grant him bail. He arrived back in Handstead this afternoon with a condition of residence and reporting twice a day to us starting today.' He paused to let this news sink in and surveyed the group, who appeared thunderstruck. No one spoke. Curtis continued in an almost distracted tone, as he desperately wondered why they were behaving like this.

'Yes, well, that's it really. He's back, got to live with his parents, be home between nine p.m. and nine a.m. and sign on here every day, morning and evening.' He waited for someone to say something but the silence was almost overpowering. His heavy, sodden shirt clung to his back like an amorous ape, and he was beginning to wish he hadn't tucked it so far into his underpants. The group stared at him as though he'd just announced he was a closet arse puncher – a mixture of disgust and fascination. He looked down at Collins for some moral support and saw that he had raised his head and was looking at the group like a man approaching the biggest firework ever made that had fizzled out.

'Oh shit,' said Collins quietly again.

'You're fucking joking,' bellowed Ally, getting to his feet in the middle row and advancing through the front chairs to stand about six feet from Curtis. The inspector stepped back behind Collins for protection and stood clutching the back of the chair with both hands, looking wide-eyed at the shitstorm he had whipped up. The rest of the group had also got to their feet and were shouting and swearing loudly, pointing aggressively at Curtis, blaming him for allowing Driscoll to get bail.

'You useless bastard,' screamed Ally. 'He helped murder one of us and now he's got bail; you must be fucking joking.' There was murderous intent in his eyes, his face was dangerously flushed and he stepped closer to Curtis, fists clenched. His voice had risen an octave and a red mist had descended on him. Collins got quickly to his feet, completely obscuring the trembling Curtis.

'That'll do. Sit down all of you,' he thundered, glaring at them, daring them to take him on. Ally halted his advance and stood breathing heavily, looking through slitted eyes at Collins, weighing up his chances, which he quickly assessed as less than none. He sighed, shrugged his shoulders and returned slowly to his seat as the others, equally reluctantly, retook their places and silence returned. Collins allowed a minute to pass before he spoke again.

'You might as well go, sir,' he said over his shoulder. 'I'll finish things up here.' There was no reply.

'I said you might as well go, sir,' he repeated loudly. When he again received no reply, he turned to see what the hell Curtis was doing. He was still holding the back of the chair, looking desperately at his hands and making little choking noises. He looked up at Collins and then back to his hands. 'What the fuck's wrong?'

'I can't move my hands,' whispered Curtis.

'What d'you mean?'

'I can't move my hands, they won't work,' Curtis hissed. In his fright as the group had verbally attacked him, he had gripped the back of the chair so hard that the muscles in his hands had gone into spasm and locked. No matter how hard he tried, he couldn't free himself.

Collins reached down with his huge, spade-like hands, and with one tug pulled Curtis free. Curtis yelped and stood looking at his fingers, which were still in spasm, locked in shape. He looked desperately at Collins, who snorted loudly, and then at the others, who had begun to laugh. Pushing past Collins, he ran for the door, which he opened with difficulty, and fled along the corridor holding his crippled, claw-like hands in front of him, the sound of their mocking laughter following.

I can't do this, he thought to himself as he climbed the stairs to his temporary office. The place is a madhouse.

Back in the muster room, Collins had whipped the lions back on to their display boxes where they roared and pawed the air. He was desperate to find something to placate them and get them out on the ground in a better frame of mind. Turning the pages of the large, leather-bound General Occurrence Book, he quickly scoured the entries for something of interest. As its name suggested, the GOB was used to record pretty much any item of interest that took place during a 24-hour period, and included arrests, sudden deaths, domestic disputes, unsatisfactory business transactions and the like. All the daily detritus of life in

Handstead went into the GOB. Collins glanced briefly at the few entries recorded for the day so far, but initially saw nothing of great interest. 'The pikeys are back on the Bolton Road industrial estate,' he announced conversationally. 'Late Turn were up there giving them a hard time, so make sure you do likewise.' He glanced up at them with raised eyebrows to ensure that his message had been received and understood. Psycho's broad smile answered in the affirmative and most of the others had also cottoned on. Gypsies got short shrift when they moved on to the Division and it was remarkable that they kept coming back; but, as H had been heard to comment, like a bad dose of the pox, they did.

'Late Turn took an interesting call to a flat in Upminster Close,' said Collins, quickly reading ahead. 'Couple of homos shoving their pet hamster up each other's ring-pieces through a toilet roll holder when the hamster disappeared from view inside one of them.' The room exploded with laughter.

'It gets better,' continued Collins, delighted with the change in their mood. 'The one with the hamster up his arse lies down so Dorothy's friend can have a look. Of course it's a bit dark so the friend lights a match, holds it closer and suddenly his arse explodes.' Pandemonium ensued and it was some time before Collins could go on.

'Apparently there was a pocket of gas in his arse which ignited,' he said, wiping a tear from his eye, 'which shot the hamster out like a bullet into the face of the bloke with the match. He's in hospital with a broken nose and the other one's got severe internal burns.' He had to sit down as hysteria ensued.

'How's the hamster?' asked the Blister in all seriousness, which prompted another bout of heads-back laughter.

As they calmed down and swapped insults and quips amongst themselves, Collins continued to quickly read through the GOB. The last prisoner nicked by Late Turn had been a drunk found unconscious at the railway station. He was about to pass the entry by until he glanced at the surname – Middleton. That name alone prompted him to look at the entry more closely and a broad grin spread across his face.

'You're going to fucking love this one,' he announced, before he began to read aloud.

Chief Superintendent Geoffrey Middleton commanded neighbouring 'C' Division. With his circular, wire-rimmed NHS spectacles, mad, staring blue eyes, nervous facial tic and clipped, almost East European accent, he could be, and was regularly, mistaken for the infamous Nazi, Dr Joseph Mengele. The nickname 'Mengele' had followed him throughout his service and perfectly suited his cold, aloof, sinister personality. He appeared to float and hover when he walked, which added to his menacing, spectral qualities. His preferred greeting, 'you're doing a great job', would usually be followed by the unmistakable feel of a knife being furtively inserted into the back. 'You're doing a great job' was tantamount to the vote of confidence a chairman of a struggling football club would give his beleaguered, doomed manager.

Loathed by most of the officers he had come into contact with over the years, only his senior position within the Freemasons had ensured regular promotion within the police, where the funny handshake club looked after its own whatever their shortcomings as human beings. His strange accent was the result of his ridiculous attempts to lose his native Birmingham patois, which he thought common and likely to hold him back in his remorseless climb to the top, both in the Lodge and in the Job. The outcome was his hilarious, clipped delivery, and there were those in the Force prepared to swear that they had heard him interview a prisoner in the past with the words, 'Ve haf vays ov makink you talk, English pik.' To say he was not well liked was to describe Attila the Hun as 'a bit rough'.

It was not altogether surprising that his eldest son, Jason, had inherited one or two of his more unpleasant personality traits. Coupled with the legacy of his mother's alcoholism, they had ensured that Jason had developed into an eighteen-carat shit with a serious drink problem. To his father's immense embarrassment, he had been arrested twice, once in Manchester, once in Handstead, for being drunk and incapable. Drunk and unconscious would have been a more accurate description of his condition on the occasion of his previous arrest at Handstead. As he'd sobered up, he'd become more obnoxious and aggressive, and only frantic string-pulling by Middleton Snr had avoided a court appearance the following morning. Middleton had collected Jason from Handstead in the small hours and dragged him out to his car under the withering glares of the officers who'd nicked him and wanted to take things further. The account of his arrest and his father's machinations had quickly passed around the nick and Jason Middleton had gone on to the unwritten list – 'If you ever see the bastard, nick him for something'.

Now the stupid little shit had done it again and lay deeply unconscious in the drunk cell, snoring loudly, covered in his own vomit and urine. He was back in play. The Late Turn custody sergeant hadn't bothered to let Mengele know that his devil's spawn was locked up, and Sergeant Mick Jones was in no hurry to do so when he took over at 10 p.m. He decided to ring him about 3 a.m. when he was most likely to be in a deep sleep.

Fuck him, thought Jones, who feared he was in for an absolute bastard of a night.

# Chapter Sixteen

Bovril's murder and the arrests of the fifteen Mafia members including Driscoll and Baker had stunned the Park Royal estate. As the headline news spread around the estate, groups of would-be future members had gathered in all the usual places that bored, idle, arrogant youth gathers, and discussed their downfall in shocked whispers. The murder of the copper barely rated a mention. There was general agreement that a snout had to be behind the arrests, and in the following days, as the news filtered through that Morgan was being held in voluntary isolation in Strangeways, his name began to appear amongst the graffiti on the walls around the estate. The latest scrawls also included taunting references to Bovril's death for the Old Bill's benefit.

Morgan's family began to pay for his forced confession. First the words 'snout' and 'grass' had been daubed on the front door and walls of the family home, and a day later his

12-year-old sister had been attacked on her way home from school. Her attackers were all female and tore clumps of hair from her head as she was kicked and punched to the ground and left bleeding and crying. Despite the fact that the Morgan family were very much part of the cheap fabric of the Park Royal, they were quickly ostracised. Despite their own impressive collection of convictions, Mr and Mrs Morgan soon became social outcasts and the message being sent to them in the form of their terrified daughter was clear: 'We can't get to him but you can. Tell him to keep his mouth shut or this gets worse. Much worse.' The Morgans got the message immediately; they understood these things, and began to try to arrange a visit to Danny. But that had been anticipated by the police, and when the ever-helpful prison service informed the officer in charge of the case that a visit had been arranged, he simply arranged for Morgan to be brought to Handstead 'for further questioning' on the day in question. Morgan's parents endured a fruitless visit to Strangeways and finished up standing outside in the cold cursing the system they themselves regularly tried to buck.

But their excuses for their lack of success with Danny cut no ice with what remained of the Mafia. After a petrol bomb was thrown at the house, the Morgans decided that enough was enough and crept away in the dead of night to a sister-in-law in Leicester, abandoning Danny to his fate. Thus he found himself in the strange position of almost welcoming the offers of help he began to get from the police. His brief was proving as much use as men's tits, continually encouraging him to cooperate and accept the offers. After all, he had signed a confession, naming names.

'They fucking forced me to sign it. How many fucking times have I got to say it? They forced me,' he screamed during one of his solicitor's visits.

'But that is your signature? They haven't forged it?'

'No, I told you, they forced me.'

'And what's in the interview record is substantially correct?'

'Yes, but so fucking what? I didn't want to sign it; they were whipping me with those fucking rubber bands. It was fucking agony – I'd have signed anything. Jesus Christ, how many fucking times?'

'Are we able to prove they assaulted you? Are you injured in any way?'

'I've still got loads of bruising around me arse,' he replied, standing up and pulling down his trousers to show the brief. The brief shook his head sorrowfully and motioned for Morgan to pull them up.

'Not enough there for us to do much with. You should have seen a doctor immediately. Didn't you ask to see one at the police station?'

'Fucking right I did,' said Morgan, tucking his shirt back into his trousers. 'I asked for loads of things and got fuck all. Two right big fuckers decked me in the cells and I suppose fuck all's going to happen about that?'

'Did you make a complaint?'

'I tried to but they told me to fuck off. You don't get fuck all when you're banged up at Handstead.'

'I can't see that we can do much more than throw ourselves on their mercy. You were arrested trying to escape from the scene of the crime, covered in what turned out to be the landlord's blood and glass fragments from the bottle used to stab him. I'd be very interested to hear what possible defence you think I could run on your behalf.'

'Fucking hell, you're the brief, you must be able to come up with something.'

'And you admitted it all during a contemporaneous interview which you signed.'

'They forced me,' he replied sullenly, but without the same conviction as before.

'And you implicated and named everyone else involved in the attack in your interview, which you signed of your own free will as a true and accurate record,' continued the brief, rubbing salt into the wound.

'They fucking forced me,' shouted Morgan, before burying his head in his arms on the tabletop.

'But your confession is, for the most part, true?'

'Yeah, suppose so,' said Morgan sulkily.

'So we have to make the best of a very bad job, don't we?'

'What d'you mean?'

'The police have indicated to me that in return for your evidence against the others, they might be prepared to reduce the seriousness of the charge against you, down to a straightforward grievous bodily harm, as opposed to a "with intent". That could substantially reduce any sentence you subsequently receive. But you'll have to give evidence against the others.'

Morgan was silent for a moment, as the gravity of his situation became clear. As he'd languished in the cells at Handstead he had admitted to himself that he was well fucked. What he hadn't appreciated was how well.

'The others know I'm here and what I've done, don't they?' he said quietly after a long pause for thought. His thin, pale face was showing the strain of solitary confinement and what little colour it had had been quickly bleached under the all-enveloping fluorescent lights of the prison.

'Do they?'

'Yeah. The cons who bring me my food have been threatening me, passing on messages, you know.'

'What sort of messages?'

'Guess, why don't you? Fuck me, they're threatening to top me, what the fuck do you think? They're saying my mum and dad and sister are on offer; we're all going to get some unless I keep quiet.'

His brief had not yet told him of events back at Handstead and decided that now was not the time to enlighten him. 'Threats like that are commonplace in prison; happens all the time. But you shouldn't lose sight of the situation you're in and the way out that may present itself.'

'Give evidence against Bobby and the others, you mean?'

'That's right. We may even be able to make a good case for getting you out on bail if we agree to help them. I can't see you getting out otherwise and the trial is at least three months away.'

Morgan gave a deep sigh, sat back in his chair and gazed over his solicitor's head into the far distance. 'I don't want to stay in solitary here,' he said flatly.

'Well, you can rule out ever joining the rest of the prison population, so your choice is quite clear, Mr Morgan. Cooperate with the police, which might get you bail and a lesser charge, or stay in solitary here until your trial when in all likelihood you'll get a substantial gaol sentence and have to serve that sentence in solitary confinement. My job is to best serve your interests in the prevailing circumstances. My advice would be to cooperate, and get the best deal you can while it's still on offer.'

'What do you mean, still on offer?'

'It's not imperative to their case that you give evidence but it'd certainly help. They've got other witnesses and forensic evidence, but turning Queen's evidence would be the icing on the cake. They won't be feeling in such a generous mood for ever.'

Morgan sighed deeply again. 'Fucking hell. I mean, giving evidence against Bobby. Do you know what that means? Fuck me, I'm dead. I couldn't stay in Handstead; I'd have to fuck off miles away.'

'I could speak to them about getting you relocated permanently after the trial, looking after you before and during the trial, if you like.'

'And I put Bobby and the others away?'

'That's about it, Mr Morgan, otherwise you take your chances, and I have to tell you, they don't look particularly good. What do you want me to tell them? It's your choice.'

Morgan was silent for a moment as he weighed up his options. Dense as he was, even he could see that his prospects were bleak. He was going to prison, he knew that, but the thought of a long stretch, all of it in solitary, did nothing to improve his black mood. His brief rummaged in his pockets for a packet of cigarettes and lit one for each of them. 'You need to come to a decision sooner rather than later,' he said, blowing the smoke towards the high ceiling as he spoke. 'Time is of the essence.' Morgan hardly heard him as he drifted off in his private hell. The brief realised he'd been talking to himself and shook his head. 'You need to make a decision soon,' he said loudly, startling Morgan back to the here and now.

'Yeah, yeah, I know,' he replied wearily. 'When will you see them next?'

'I can contact them as soon as you come to a decision. Today, if necessary.'

'Christ, this really chokes me up, know what I mean? Grassing the others to make myself a deal, fucking hell.'

'Do you have a choice?'

'No, I suppose not, fuck it.'

'Well?'

'Well what?' snapped Morgan.

'Your decision,' replied the exasperated brief. There was a long pause before Morgan spoke again.

'Tell them I'll give evidence but I want some bail and a deal on the charge otherwise they can poke it.'

'I'll pass that on, but don't forget you're in no position to make demands. I'll get what I can for you, but don't hold your breath. They aren't relying on you.'

'Whatever, but I'm not giving evidence for fuck all. They've got to give me something.'

'I'll do what I can,' said the brief, getting to his feet and walking to the door. He knocked twice and walked back to the table. 'As soon as I've spoken to them I'll contact you. In the meantime say nothing to anyone and keep your head down.'

The door was opened by a warder who stepped into the interview room and looked at the brief. 'We're all finished here, thank you. Mr Morgan can return to his cell,' said the brief. Morgan got slowly to his feet and shook the brief's hand.

'Take care of things, OK?' he said earnestly. 'I'm relying on you.' The brief smiled grimly but said nothing as he watched his client leave the room ahead of the warder, who shut the door behind them. He listened to the rattling of keys, a gate opening and closing and echoing footsteps disappearing into the bowels of the prison before he threw his cigarette to the floor and ground it out with his shoe. He placed a few pieces of paper into his briefcase, which he snapped shut, and glanced at his watch. They should still be waiting for him if he hurried.

He left the room and a few minutes later was walking down Southall Street. He turned into Great Ducie Street and stopped, carefully surveying the parked vehicles. He saw the red Mark Two Ford Granada with two men sitting in it about fifty yards ahead of him, the exhaust pipe billowing a large cloud of smoke in the cold afternoon air. He walked briskly up to the passenger window. The window was down and the heavy, middle-aged man in the passenger seat looked up at the brief and smiled thinly.

'Well, how'd it go, Simon?' asked Detective Chief Inspector Harrison. The brief leant forward so his head was inside the car and rested his left arm on the roof.

'Yeah, OK, he'll give evidence against the others but he wants a deal.'

'What sort of deal?' said the DCI, his smile disappearing.

'Bail, Section 20 GBH and help with relocation after the trial.'

The DCI chuckled, looked at his driver, who was smiling and shaking his head, and said softly, 'You're having a fucking laugh, aren't you, Simon? I hope you've not made him any promises you can't keep, because he can bang that list up his arse. Help with relocation after the trial? Who the fuck does he think he is, Judas Iscariot?'

'I know, I know,' said the brief hurriedly, glad he'd been careful to play down the prospects. 'I told him exactly where he stood, but he's already been threatened on the basis of that dodgy interview you got him to sign. He's terrified about going back to Handstead —' The DCI interrupted him.

'Dodgy interview? What the fuck are you going on about? Is there anything in there that's untrue? Tell me that.'

'No, but as you very well know, that's not what I mean. He was assaulted to get him to sign it.'

'Any evidence to support that, Simon? Independent witnesses, medical evidence, anything like that?'

'Of course not, you were very thorough as usual, but you know as well as I do that force was used to get him to sign it. If he gets up in the box and gives evidence to that effect it could cast an adverse light on any other evidence.'

Harrison paused as he considered what the brief had said. 'Bollocks,' he snorted after a moment. 'He can say what the fuck he likes in the box and I'll still chop his fucking legs off with identification and forensic evidence. Fuck it, I don't need him, Simon. Would've been nice, but I don't need him, catch my drift?'

Simon did catch his drift; all too clearly, things were not going as he had hoped.

'Perfectly, thank you. I'm only passing on what he said to

me. I've told him not to set his sights too high and to take what he's offered, but you know what these people are like. Hugely inflated opinions of themselves. He'll give evidence against the others, don't worry about that, but a bit of bail would really help make his mind up.'

Harrison looked up at the flabby, perspiring brief and smiled. 'You tell him what's good for him, Simon. Make an application for bail and we won't oppose it. But you make fucking sure he understands that if he doesn't do the business I'm going to shit down his neck. He'll be begging Driscoll and the others to hide him. That clear?'

'Quite. Leave it with me. I'll get an application in the day after tomorrow.'

'There's something to be going on with, Simon,' said Harrison. He took an envelope from his jacket pocket and passed it to the brief, who quickly opened it and frowned as he saw the banknotes. He slipped it into his own jacket pocket.

'It's not all there,' he protested.

'You'll get the full monkey when he's given evidence,' said Harrison flatly, looking straight ahead.

'That's not what we agreed. How much is in there?'

'You've got a ton in there. You'll get the rest when your scumbag client gives evidence against the others, understood?'

'How very Christian of you, Mr Harrison,' said the brief sarcastically as he stood up and stepped back from the car. 'I should have known better than to trust you, shouldn't I?'

'Don't get all fucking righteous with me, Simon,' snapped Harrison. 'You're earning nicely for doing not very much, so don't fucking start. You'll get the rest of your dough when Morgan stands up in the box and flaps his gums. In the meantime, you've got a ton to be going on with.' He turned to face his driver and motioned with his head that it was time to go. The big car roared away leaving Simon Edwardes looking bitterly after it, shaking his head. Picking up his briefcase, he wandered down Great Ducie Street towards Trinity Way, pondering his next move.

He and Harrison had done business on numerous occasions in the past and it had not been a surprise when he'd been contacted shortly after he'd taken on Morgan's case. A complete moron could see that Morgan was fucked, but there was clearly scope for a little earner if he could be persuaded to support his statement and turn Queen's evidence. Edwardes expected Harrison to make the approach and he hadn't been disappointed. He was, however, seriously pissed off about being £400 light as he stood hailing a cab in Trinity Way. There'd been no mention of withholding most of the money until Morgan had given evidence, but grudgingly he accepted that Harrison had to cater for every eventuality and this would certainly ensure that he put body and soul into making sure that Morgan did the right thing. It wasn't as if they were looking to fit up anyone decent, after all. Morgan was scum and so were the people he would help convict. They deserved each other. Fuck them.

Amidst the heavy late afternoon traffic, he spotted a cab with its yellow light piercing the fading winter gloom, and whistled loudly. As he settled into the back seat and they crawled in heavy traffic towards Manchester Piccadilly station, he decided to play along with Harrison. There was no risk involved and £500 was a decent drink in anyone's money. The only issue of any concern to him was whether acting for Morgan would have an adverse effect on his business with the scum of Handstead in the future. Whilst not quite on a retainer with them, he had something of a reputation as a 'defender of the slag', after several spirited defences of some of Handstead's more unsavoury residents. That had ceased once he'd met DCI Harrison, who had encouraged him to keep taking them as clients, and keep Harrison up to date on their defences. All at a price, of course, and he'd needed very little persuading.

As he stood on the packed train back to Handstead, he mused on the strange ménage à trois he was now part of. A villain defending one villain against another, whilst at the same time taking a bung to ensure that the villain from the CID convicted his villain and his villainous accomplices. He preferred not to dwell too long on it; it was the sort of arrangement that could really do your head in. He shut his eyes and decided to strap hang all the way, swaying like a drunk and occasionally brushing against the pretty young girl behind him. She looked with obvious disgust at the obnoxious, sweaty, middle-aged man with thinning black hair plastered to his head. His thick pinstripe three-piece suit was shabby and shiny around the elbows and seat, and the cheap plastic East European shoes he was wearing had badly worn heels and large holes in the soles. She was sure he was the sort of man who'd had very waxy ears at school. His gaunt face and parchment skin reminded her of Chalky from the Giles cartoons, and after a few minutes of his unwelcome interference, she got off at the next stop and got into the next carriage. There was an aura about Simon Edwardes that caused most people, not just women, to react like that. Something that made the skin crawl when he was near. That probably explained why he still lived at home with his elderly, senile parents who believed their indulged only son was a respected High Court judge. Even DCI Harrison could barely bring himself to spend more than a few minutes in his unctuous company, and found their occasional meetings in anonymous pubs onerous. There was something of the sewer about him.

# Chapter Seventeen

Upstairs in the CID office, Bob Clarke and John Benson sat at their adjacent desks, sorting through the piles of paper that threatened to engulf them. There were supposed to be in and out trays somewhere on the desks, but they had finally been swamped weeks ago by the ever-increasing piles of blue prisoner files and manila files for crimes still undetected. Larger piles of typed paper balanced precariously alongside their desks. These were the jobs committed for trial at the Crown Court, which took painstaking weeks to put together. First everything would be typed on to 'skins' (the only clerical assistance given) and then each page roneoed and paginated by hand. Each file could run to hundreds of pages, and then copies had to be made. One for the judge, two for the prosecution, two for the defence and six for the jury, until the total number of pages ran into the many thousands. South American Indians hacking down their rainforests seven days a week could barely keep up with the demand for paper. It was not uncommon to see officers attending Crown Court with a porter's trolley to ferry the reams of paper their job had generated.

Clarke and Benson would generally assist one another with committal files, but it was an absolute ball-breaker of a task. Without doubt, it was the side of the job that all detectives hated. The nicking and interviewing was great, but the paperwork – fucking hell, the paperwork.

Their desks were as they'd left them at 6 a.m. that morning after another horrendous night. They'd got out shortly after 10 p.m. to nick a local for a series of supermarket burglaries, but after booking him in with Custody had spent the rest of the shift dealing with a serious assault that at one stage looked as though it might become a murder inquiry.

The robbery victim had fortunately been found in time by what passed for a Good Samaritan in Handstead, who'd phoned anonymously for an ambulance before relieving the unfortunate man of his watch. The animals who'd fractured his skull with a tyre wrench had made do with just his wallet and the takeaway curry he'd been carrying. He now lay in a coma at the local hospital and Clarke and Benson had spent a long night getting the scene of the attack preserved and examined and forlornly looking for witnesses. Needless to say, none had been forthcoming. In the small hours of the morning the victim's wife had confirmed that her husband's decent Omega watch was amongst the property missing and

Clarke and Benson at last had a line of inquiry to pursue. By that time, though, the watch had changed hands twice in a club, and even if they ever managed to trace the original supplier, they would only ever lay their hands on the Fairly Good Samaritan. Unaware they were pissing into the wind, they had left instructions for the Early Turn CID to start getting into known local fences.

Amongst the paper debris, Clarke found the note he'd been looking for. He read it quickly and said in disgust, 'Early Turn got fucking nowhere with the watch. He's still in a coma and surprise, surprise, still no witnesses.' He tossed the note back on to his desk. Benson gave a grim, hollow laugh without looking up from his pile of paper.

'No change there then. You got any of the paperwork for Gough?'

'Gough?' replied Clarke absently.

'We nicked him first thing, remember?' said Benson, tapping the side of his head. 'The supermarket burglaries?'

'Oh, fuck me, yeah. No, not a thing. Didn't you hand him over to Early Turn to deal?'

'Don't think so. Can't remember speaking to anyone about him, can you?'

'No, I don't. We booked him in, brought him up here, stuck him in the cupboard and then we got the shout to the robbery. We didn't get a chance to speak to him.'

'So where the fuck is he then?'

They said simultaneously, 'The cupboard,' got to their

feet and went to a large, double-doored, built-in cupboard at the far end of the office. A key hung from a hook on the wall beside it and Clarke used this to unlock the door. He peered inside. It took a second for his eyes to adjust to the almost complete darkness within, before he could make out the shapes of two people sitting inside on the floor. The whites of two sets of eyes looked hopefully up at him.

'Mr Gough?' he called.

'That's me. About fucking time too,' said a voice from the darkness.

'You ready to be interviewed?' continued Clarke, looking back at Benson and mouthing 'Fuck' at him.

'I can't fucking move, I've seized up,' said the voice. 'No fucking wonder, I've been in here so long. What time is it?' What day is it would have been a more appropriate question, but Clarke ignored it anyway.

'Never mind the fucking time, we've got a few questions to put to you and we're expecting some answers. Otherwise it's back in the cupboard with you. You ready for interview?'

'Yes, yes, I've had enough of this bollocks. I'm coming out, for fuck's sake, just give me a moment.' There then followed the sound of groaning and moaning and the cracking and snapping of stiff joints, before Lance Gough, burglar of the parish of Handstead, emerged on all fours, blinking in the harsh light and shading his eyes as he tried to see his arresting officers. 'Where the fuck have you two been?' he said. 'I've been ready for hours but none of the others would talk to me. I'm busting for a piss. Can I go before we start?'

'Come on, I'll take you,' offered Benson, moving alongside him, expecting him to get to his feet. Instead, Gough began to shuffle across the floor on his hands and knees towards the door.

'Through there, is it?' he called as he increased his speed before his bladder, now the size of a beach ball, burst.

'On your feet,' bellowed Benson.

'I can't. My fucking back's seized solid. Does this sometimes, but I'll be OK in a couple of days. I'll need a hand in the khazi, though.'

'You can fuck right off if you think I'm holding your knob,' grumbled Benson. 'You can piss up the wall like a dog if you have to.' The human turtle hurried out into the corridor as Benson opened the door.

'Can I come out now as well?' said another voice from the pitch-black cupboard. Clarke screwed his eyes up and peered in.

'Who are you?'

'David John Hegg,' the voice replied formally in the manner of someone used to being locked up regularly.

'Who's dealing with you?'

'DC Adams and DC Smith.'

Clarke recognised the names of two of the Early Turn officers he'd seen at 6 a.m. that morning, not due in until 6 a.m. tomorrow.

'What you nicked for?'

The voice mumbled something in reply.

'I can't hear you. You'll have to speak up,' Clarke shouted.

'Flashing,' shouted the voice.

'You dirty cunt. You can fucking stay put for a while. Teach you to wave your old man about,' bellowed Clarke, slamming the door shut and locking it.

'Let me out. I'm sorry. Let me out,' cried the voice in the dark plaintively.

'Shut up, you dirty bastard,' shouted Clarke, giving the door a kick, 'shut the fuck up or you're out the window.' The voice trailed off into silence; its owner knew about the windows at Handstead police station. From the first floor up, every window at the station was barred, not as might be expected to stop the locals breaking in, but to stop prisoners being dangled out by their ankles to encourage meaningful dialogue. Whilst no one had ever been dropped, too many complaints had been made for the matter to be ignored. Rather than issue a memo to the effect that prisoners should not in future be dangled out of windows, the Divisional Commander had arranged for the gradual installation of bars on the upper-floor windows at Handstead. It was a tacit admission that the practice went on, but he stopped short of a witch-hunt that would have resembled the British Raj's attempts to outlaw suttee. But the fact was that Handstead was the only nick in the Force with windows barred for the benefit of its reluctant visitors.

Hegg had been out of a window at Handstead before, and had no wish to repeat the experience. Captured three years earlier showing his blue veiner to a jeering junior school playground, he'd been encouraged to admit to a few other offences, some real, some imagined, by two detectives who'd hung him out of a fourth-floor window at the back of the nick. Contemplating the long drop on to the roof of a police car below, he'd happily have put his hands up to drilling holes in the hull of the *Titanic*. It had been a sobering experience and Hegg still shuddered as he debated which had been worse – dangling, stark bollock naked, out of a window over a sixty-foot drop, or having his meat and two veg crushed as the detectives dragged him back into the room over the window sill. He hadn't managed a blue veiner for months afterwards.

As the CID officers began their interview with the recidivist human turtle, the uniformed officers of 'D' Relief were collecting their car keys and radios from the front office. Blister was handing the radios out on receipt of a signature, and having dealt with the Brothers was now impatiently waiting for Ally to sign for the radio he was cramming into his coat pocket.

'Come on, Ally, I haven't got all night,' she snapped, eager to get back to her Barbara Cartland bodice-ripper.

He looked at her and smiled, but said nothing, signed the register and turned to walk away. Then he stopped, turned back, put one hand on his hip, threw his head back and began to pout his lips, swaying his hips from side to side, lisping loudly, 'Come on, baby, love that camera for me, love it, baby, love it, lick your lips for me, baby, hmm, love it.'

The rest of the group began to bray like donkeys, with the notable exception of Psycho who stood horrified, looking from Ally to the Blister with the expression of a man having a catheter fitted by a blind, arthritic cobbler. For a moment Blister was nonplussed by Ally's performance, but gradually the lights came on and she fixed Psycho with a stare guaranteed to thicken blood.

'You fucking dirty, slimy, sick bastard,' she hissed venomously, her face turning crimson with rage as she puffed her fat little body up like a Louisiana bullfrog. Psycho didn't bother to play dumb or deny what he had done – he turned and fled along the corridor as the rest of the group cried with laughter and the Blister steamed, swearing dreadful revenge on him at the top of her voice.

Ally finished his display, which rather disturbingly he was quite good at. He'd noticed the dark looks he was getting from the Brothers as he minced and swayed around the front office, and decided to call it a day. The Blister spoke for the Brothers when she said, 'You look like some horrible old drag queen, Ally. Not a poof, are you?' It was an innocuous, inconsequential question that could and should have been swatted away contemptuously, but instead produced absolutely the wrong response.

'Course I'm fucking not. I got crabs from that Aussie barmaid I shagged, didn't I?' he announced proudly. Not everyone on the group had known about Ally's dash with the infested barmaid, but they did now, and erupted in another bout of belly laughs.

'Crabs?' shouted the Blister, shrewdly seeing the opportunity to change the focus of attention from her unfortunate photo session. 'Fucking crabs?' she repeated. 'You dirty bastard.'

'Don't get holier than thou with me, you old cow,' shouted Ally desperately above the laughter. 'At least Psycho didn't shag me and then take pictures.'

'Sure about that, are you, Ally? You were mincing about there like a real shit-stabber. Wouldn't surprise me at all if he'd given you one by mistake when he was pissed.'

Pizza, who was standing nearby, cringed as he recalled the horror he'd felt when he'd woken in Psycho's bed and believed for a while that the hose monster had rethreaded his kitchen towel holder. He wandered away from the uproar and into the relative calm of the custody area where Mick Jones sat grinding his finger into his ears, looking through the custody records he'd inherited from Late Turn.

'Hello, sarge. Got many in?'

Jones glanced up briefly, examined the finger, and then looked back at the papers. 'Just the two at the moment.'

'One of them's Mr Middleton's son, I hear.'

'That's right. So what?'

'Nothing, sarge. Just wanted to know if he was still here,' Pizza replied, the beginning of a plan suddenly forming in his mind.

'Be here a while yet. Still pissed as a fart,' said Jones distractedly as he read Middleton's custody record. 'I'll be phoning his dad a bit later. Got to make arrangements to get him home eventually.'

'But not straight away?'

'No, not for a few hours, that's for sure.'

'Thanks, sarge. See you later probably, hopefully with a prisoner.'

'Great,' said Jones sourly, and Pizza departed in search of Psycho. He'd had an idea that he knew Psycho could help him with.


The Brothers also drifted away from the maelstrom engulfing Ally and the Blister. They had something much more important to discuss.

'He should be at home now,' said H, looking at his watch.

'Yeah. I can't believe he'll break his bail conditions first night out without some help. We've got to find a way to get him out of the house and then we can sort him out.'

'First up, let's make sure he's fucking there. There's a phone book in the report-writing room. I'll give him a bell first.'

They made their way to find the phone book, the first step in their quest to capture Bobby Driscoll and get him back where they felt he belonged.

'If he's in, how the fuck are we going to get him outside?' mused H as he flicked through the phone book until he found the number he was after. Picking up the phone, he got an outside line, dialled, and then waited as the phone rang and rang. He was about to put it down when a very sleepy woman's voice answered it with an irritated 'Hello?'

'Bobby there?' said H curtly.

'Who wants to know?' replied Driscoll's mother suspiciously.

'Jimmy Anderson,' he said, giving the name of the brother of one of the Mafia on remand in Strangeways. She knew Des Anderson well and knew he had a brother, but not his name.

'Yeah, he's here, Jimmy,' she said, her doubts about the caller allayed.

'Can I have a word? It's important.'

'Hold on a moment.' H then heard Driscoll's mother call, 'Bobby, phone.' After a few moments he heard Driscoll ask 'Who is it?', his mother reply 'Jimmy', and Driscoll repeat the name in surprise as he picked up the phone.

'Hello?' he barked.

'You piece of fucking shit, I'm going to rip your throat out before the end of the night. Die, you cunt,' said H pleasantly.

'Who's that?' shouted Driscoll.

'Your worst fucking nightmare, you scumbag. I'm going to set fire to you, then cut your mummy's throat from ear to ear and skull fuck her while she bleeds to death,' said H, warming to his task and oblivious of the concerned looks Jim was shooting him.

'You fucking bastard,' screamed Driscoll, covering his phone with spittle. 'When I find you you're fucking dead,' he added rather impotently.

'Don't go to sleep, Driscoll. I'll be over later to gut you like a fish,' said H calmly, before he put the phone down and sat back with a contented sigh.

'You've done that before, haven't you, you fucking headbanger?' said Jim, looking closely at his colleague.

'Certainly not,' replied H indignantly, but not altogether convincingly. 'Inspiration came to me, that's all. Got him going, though, didn't it? Fuck me, he was foaming, but we've still got to get him out of the house somehow.'

'A fire might do the trick.'

'Yeah, right, Jim, we'll set fire to the house,' replied H, shaking his head mournfully.

'No? Well, give the impression that it's on fire, then. Get something smoking nicely, evacuate everyone and have him away outside somewhere.'

'We can't be seen anywhere near the house. We've got to be able to say we nicked him miles away.'

'Or have him away then, keep him somewhere safe and produce him hours later having just found him.'

'Yeah, I like that, Jim. Keep him somewhere until much later. Yeah, I really like that. Where could we keep him, though?' said H thoughtfully.

'Boot of the car?'

'We'd never get away with it. How the fuck can we get him out of the house?'

'Don't fancy the fire, then?'

'Nah. Even if it got him outside, there'd be too many people about who'd see him and there's no way he'd wander off too far. He'd hang around the garden or on the pavement. We've got to get him some distance away from the house on his own. Come on, Jim, think. What would get him away from the house at this time of night in breach of his bail conditions?'

Outside, as the temperature hovered around the freezing mark, it had begun to snow. Not the big, fluffy, cotton-wool snow beloved of Hollywood film producers, but thin, wet snow driven by an icy wind that stung the face and eyes, forming a treacly black film on everything it touched after dark. Only a villain or a copper would venture out in weather like this. The rest of mankind took one look at it, muttered 'Fuck that', and shut the front door. Those coppers unfortunate enough to be working in shit weather regarded it with mixed emotions. It was no fun being out and about in it, especially on foot, but it was a truism: only they and the villains would be out in it. The chances of pulling a completely innocent Joe Public were substantially reduced. Lazy old lamp-swingers often solemnly intoned that 'bad weather was the best copper of them all', because it kept most people at home out of trouble. Elsewhere perhaps, but not in Horse's Arse, where the villains mistakenly believed that the Old Bill would be tucked away in the warm and dry, and repeatedly got locked up on what they regarded as 'dead cert' jobs. The Old Bill had worked it out, but the villains had still to see the light on the road to Damascus.

Pizza found Psycho lurking in the locker room with a hunted look on his face.

'Christ, thank fuck it's only you,' he'd sighed gratefully as Pizza had entered suddenly. 'I thought it was the Blister.'

'Teach you to keep it in your trousers, won't it?' said Pizza.

'I've only done her a couple of times,' complained Psycho, 'and now look at the shit I'm in.'

'Putting her meat shots on public display was probably not one of your best moves, Psycho, but listen up. I need your help with something. I've had a blinding idea.'

Psycho remained seated with his head in his hands. He didn't look up, or say anything.

'Psycho, will you give me a hand?' repeated Pizza, slightly louder.

Psycho raised his head and stared intently at him. 'What sort of idea?' he asked slowly.

'Not here. I'm town centre foot patrol. Pick me up in ten minutes outside the cemetery, OK?'

Psycho was still dubious and unwilling to commit himself far. 'Hold on, hold on. What sort of idea?' he insisted.

Pizza sighed loudly and looked conspiratorially around him. 'Jason Middleton,' he said quietly, beaming like the Cheshire Cat.

'What about him?'

'For fuck's sake, Psycho, not here. Pick me up in ten minutes if you're interested. If you're not there I'll assume you've lost your bottle and I'll do it on my own,' and with that he turned and hurried out of the locker room, the bait laid.

'You spotty little cunt, I've pulled more fucking stunts than you've had shags,' Psycho called after him. Fucking nerve of the little sprog, calling him out like that. Him, King of the Stunts, the man responsible for Hilary Bott's demise. He resolved to pick Pizza up and show him what a proper stunt was all about. Saucy little twat. He turned back to his locker, rummaged through the junk inside and finally found what he was looking for. Sitting down, he unzipped the black plastic rifle case and carefully pulled out his .22 air rifle with telescopic sight. Reaching inside the case, he located a tin of pellets and grinned. He patted the stock affectionately, checked the sight, and then carefully replaced the weapon in the case. If he had a few minutes to kill, he planned to shoot up the gypsy site on the industrial estate, keep the fuckers on their toes and encourage them to move out of town. With virtually no legislation to deal with them, the officers at Horse's Arse had developed their own way of dealing with gypsies and Psycho had taken things a step further as usual. Other officers contented themselves with round-the-clock harassment; he preferred the more direct approach, and the last time gypsies had arrived in town he'd shot out the windows of six caravans. His campaign against them culminated when he set fire to one of their Transit vans parked across the entrance to their unofficial site. Realising they were dealing with someone more dangerous than themselves, that particular group had moved on the next day.

He grabbed some items from his locker and made his way cautiously out into the corridor, listening intently for Blister's shrill voice or the sound of her little pig's trotters on the polished lino floor. There was no sign of her and he hurried out into the back yard and located his vehicle for the night, Bravo Two Delta One. Delta One took the Park Royal estate and Psycho decided he'd take Pizza up there later to show him the ropes.

Three cars up, Ally sat seething in the passenger seat of Delta Two. He'd been crewed with Piggy again and had made no attempt to disguise his anger and disappointment when the crews for the night had been read out.

'Fucking hell, not again,' he'd shouted. 'How come I always get the fat bastard? Why's it always me? What have I done?' Collins had ignored his protests, again.

Despite his outburst, Piggy had merely smiled cheerfully and wiped the remains of the huge curry he'd eaten before he left home from around his mouth. He looked as if he'd let a child apply orange lipstick to his face, and now, even worse for Ally, his guts were starting to bubble up nicely.

'I'm a bit windy tonight, I'm afraid, Ally,' he belched, before lifting a leg and letting rip with a fart that bleached the curtains in the muster room.

'You do that in the car, you fat cunt, and you're dead,' Ally hissed venomously as he joined the desperate dash to find fresh air.

Now, as he sat waiting, he saw his obese partner rolling towards the car through the sleet. As he watched, Piggy paused, lifted his leg again and farted loudly enough to be heard through the closed windows. Ally closed his eyes and wondered how long it would be before he punched Malone very hard.

'Better out than in,' announced Piggy brightly as he opened the driver's door and began to ease his bulky frame inside. The remnants of his gastrointestinal disturbance followed him into the vehicle and Ally furiously wound down his window and hung his head out in the freezing night air.

'I'm going to fucking kill you, fat boy,' he gasped. 'As soon as I can breathe properly, I'm going to fucking kill you.'

As Psycho manoeuvred his vehicle towards the back gates, his headlights picked out Ally hanging out of Delta Two. He wound down his window as he got close and called out, 'You up for a bit of sport with the pikeys later? I'll give you a shout.'

'I think I touched cloth with that last one,' said Piggy cheerfully as he settled himself into the driver's seat and began to wriggle around. 'Yeah, I think I followed through.'

Ally closed his eyes and allowed his forehead to drop on to the door sill. Tomorrow morning seemed a long way away.

Driscoll had hurled the telephone back on to its cradle after H had rung off and stood cursing in the hallway, occasionally rubbing his still-throbbing, extremely painful kneecaps. Nervously, his mother opened the kitchen door and asked, 'Who was that then?'

'Fuck knows,' bellowed Driscoll, 'probably the Old Bill, bastards.' He limped towards the kitchen still swearing revenge at he knew not whom and demanded his mother get the kettle on and make a brew whilst he calmed himself and contemplated his unexpected period of freedom. As the kettle boiled he ran over in his mind what needed to be done to ensure his freedom became permanent. First thing tomorrow he'd show himself around the Park Royal to let people know he was still in charge. It was very likely attempts would be made to fill his place in his absence and it was important that he showed he was still the main man. And then there was the trial to sort out. He was cursing the fact that he'd trusted the moron Baker to get rid of the gang's bloodstained clothing, which he'd spectacularly failed to do, and now the Old Bill had some strong forensic evidence against all of them. The eyewitnesses could be dealt with easily enough – only Morgan was a real problem, though Driscoll was confident he could be persuaded to change sides again. He'd got Danny completely wrong. Thought he'd be OK when the wheels came off, but the Old Bill had really done a number on him and got him to roll over. They'd also given him and Baker a tidy fitting up with the gun Myra had used to kill the copper. Driscoll had not known of its existence but the Old Bill had got his prints on to it and the ammo. That was down to Baker as well – the idiot had not told Driscoll about it and now they were both in deep shit. Driscoll sat at the breakfast bar fuming. He and Baker were also in the frame for the attack on Myra in the bedroom. He regretted that now, but her death had had little impact on him. If anything, it had been quite convenient, because she had the potential to be a nuisance. She was so unstable there was no way anyone could be sure what she'd say or do from one moment to the next. Morgan really bothered him, though. The little bastard had given the Old Bill chapter and verse about the attack on the pub manager. He'd even embellished the story a little to further implicate Driscoll and Baker, albeit at the interviewing officer's behest. It would be very useful if Morgan suddenly found himself dead as well. Driscoll decided to get word to Baker and the others on remand in Strangeways to take care of it. His evidence could be very damaging and Driscoll couldn't allow that. He'd get his instructions into Strangeways via a visit Baker was due from his mother in two days.

As he sipped at a mug of milky, heavily sugared tea, he nodded to himself, satisfied that he was getting his train back on the tracks.

The phone in the hallway rang again and he put his mug of tea down in surprise. Who'd be calling so late unless it was another threatening call? His mother made no move to leave the kitchen and answer it, so he eased himself off the chair and limped out into the hallway.

'Fuck off, you cunt,' he screamed into the mouthpiece, assuming it would be the same sort of call as before. It wasn't. This time the caller adopted a very different tack.

'Bobby, is that you?' the voice whispered urgently.

'Who the fuck are you?'

'Bobby?'

'Yes. Who the fuck are you?' shouted Driscoll again.

'Alan Morgan, Danny's dad,' came the reply.

There was a stunned and lengthy silence. Driscoll knew virtually nothing about Morgan's family, other than that they had been driven out of Handstead in the aftermath of the Mafia's downfall.

'What the fuck do you want?' Driscoll finally asked sullenly.

'Listen, we need to talk,' continued the whispering voice. 'I know what Danny's done and I can't live with it. We're paying for what he's done and it's not right.'

'So fucking do something about it then,' interrupted Driscoll loudly.

'That's why I'm ringing, Bobby. I can do something about it but we need to meet. I don't want to talk on the phone. I'm back in our old house in Deacons Drive. Can you come over so we can talk?'

'Bollocks,' shouted Driscoll. 'I'm not going fucking anywhere. You deal with the little shit before I do.'

'Bobby, we need to talk,' continued the voice in the same urgent whisper. 'I'll be at the house until just after midnight, then we're gone for good. If you don't come I'll assume you're not interested. That'll be a shame, because I can sort things out. Take care, Bobby,' and the phone was put down quickly.

'Fuck off,' screamed Driscoll, before pulling the phone line out of the wall socket and hurling the whole phone at the wall.

Back at Handstead police station, H and Jim hurried out into the back yard, where it was still sleeting heavily, and got into Yankee One. Jim had the keys for the evening, and he settled himself and waited whilst H got comfortable. H had been restored to full driving duties following Bott's demise, but tonight was Jim's turn to drive, H to do the paperwork.

'Ready?' he asked.

'Let's go, Jim,' responded H, picking up the main handset to book on. 'Delta Hotel from Bravo Two Yankee One, show us on watch please,' he said quietly.

'Thank you, Yankee One,' responded the operator. 'Good hunting, boys,' she added.

The Brothers looked at each other and grinned as Jim took the car out into Horse's Arse to find Driscoll. Hunting was definitely the appropriate term.

The temptation to confront Morgan's father had been too good to resist and Driscoll had quickly dressed to go out.

'Where are you going so late?' asked his mother as he buttoned up his coat by the front door.

'Out,' he snapped without looking at her.

'Where? Who was that on the phone?'

He tapped the side of his nose by way of reply and opened the front door, slamming it shut behind him. The sleet and chill wind took him by surprise and he gasped involuntarily as the cold hit him, and hunched his shoulders to keep warm. He hurried down the path, crossed the deserted street and made towards the industrial estate on a short cut to Deacons Drive. The bitter chill made his damaged knees ache more than usual, but he soon found that the exercise eased them and he lengthened his stride. He was looking forward to the confrontation with Morgan senior and began to formulate what he intended to do and say. Depending on how big Morgan senior was, he might even give him a slap. It depended very much on his size, though, because at heart Driscoll was an abject coward and generally depended on Baker to do his muscle work. He walked quickly along a rubbish-strewn alleyway and out on to the industrial estate, glanced left and right and began to cross Wheatcroft Drive to walk to the alleyway opposite which would cut out having to walk right through the estate. As he crossed the road he was startled by two figures that suddenly emerged from the darkness of a building to his right. He stopped in his tracks as they closed on him.

'Hello, Bobby,' one of them said. The pair walked under the weak street lamp and into the pale yellow light.

Driscoll recognised the Brothers immediately. His blood ran cold as it dawned on him that they had phoned him on both occasions and he was now completely at the mercy of these two mad, dangerous bastards. H had been absolutely right. The one thing Driscoll really needed to know was whether Morgan would give evidence against him and he had walked straight into the trap. Driscoll's mouth was dry and he swallowed hard as they stopped under the light and grinned at him.

'You should be at home, shouldn't you, Bobby?' said H. 'I was sure your bail conditions said you had to be at home in the evening. That's right, isn't it, Jim?'

''S right, H,' answered his colleague, 'and there's a power of arrest for breaching the condition. It's back to Strangeways for you, Driscoll, for a very long time. Where are you off to at this time of night anyway? It's a bit late to be going visiting, isn't it, H?' The Brothers laughed and stared at Driscoll, relishing the moment for a while longer.

Driscoll knew he'd been had and that his ill-gotten liberty was about to be whisked away from him before he'd had a chance to enjoy it or sort things out. Dodgy knees or not, he decided to have a go. He took off like a greyhound for the opposite alleyway, catching the Brothers completely off guard.

'Fuck it,' shouted H, starting after him. 'Get round the other side quickly, Jim, cut him off.'

As H raced after Driscoll down the unlit alleyway, Jim ran back to Yankee One parked at the rear of the building and raced away to try to intercept the foot chase on the other side of the industrial estate. Deliberately, he did not use the radio to summon assistance; there was no way he and H were going to give up their prize to anyone else.

Back in the alleyway, H was closing on Driscoll, but still about thirty yards behind him. Driscoll's knees were not up to anything as energetic as a foot chase, but he could see the lit road up ahead at the end of the alleyway and kept going. He could hear the copper panting behind him and knew he couldn't afford to get captured. Too much depended on his remaining at large.

# Chapter Eighteen

Jimmy Martin and Dave Chance had escaped from the car park at the Hoop and Grapes and, because they had not gone back to Baker's flat, had avoided the police round-up. Now they sat in a clapped-out Ford Capri listening as Martin revved the engine until it screamed.

'It's absolutely fucked,' he shouted above the din to his partner in crime, who nodded his agreement. 'Be all right for a bit of a burn-up, though,' he added.

They had stolen the unregistered and untaxed rust bucket from outside the owner's house about an hour ago and brought it down to the industrial estate to do some handbrake turns and then set fire to it. It was what they always did with every car they nicked. They were nothing if not predictable and consequently had previous convictions as juveniles as long as the proverbial arm. Both wannabe Mafia, they came from the Park Royal estate and had been involved in car theft and other petty crime most of their young lives. Aged only fourteen now, they were very well known to the local police and had only one aspiration: to move into the ranks of the Park Royal Mafia as full-time members; to become Bobby's boys. With their backgrounds, they were condemned to that fate anyway, regardless of any other aspirations they might subsequently harbour.

Martin put the Capri into first gear, revved the engine again until it sounded as though it must explode, and then let the clutch in fast, causing all four wrecked tyres to smoke before the vehicle careered forward. The boys were whooping and cheering as the car roared along the empty road, both anticipating the handbrake turn in the cul-de-sac at the other end.

Neither H nor Driscoll heard the screaming engine from within their alleyway above their own laboured breathing and thumping hearts. Driscoll had his head back, eyes fixed on the enlarging square of light ahead of him that meant possible escape. He emerged out of the darkness into the light without slowing, was across the pavement in a single stride and into the road and the path of the speeding Capri. Still in the pitch-black alleyway, H saw the collision perfectly framed for a split second in the square of light as the stolen Capri hit Driscoll side on at 60 m.p.h with a sickening thud, who then disappeared from view as though flicked by a giant finger. H came quickly to a halt, still in the darkness, panting deeply and unable to fully appreciate what he had just seen. He heard the car engine slow slightly and then the screech of tyres as the vehicle turned in the cul-de-sac and then flashed back through the square of light. From where he was, H was unable to even establish the colour of the vehicle, let alone its make, or the identity of its occupants.

As the sound of the engine died away, H walked to the edge of the darkness and peered out into the road. All the buildings in his view were in total darkness and the road was deserted. There was a vast amount of broken glass spread around, but of Driscoll there was no sign at all. For one moment H wondered if he had been picked up by the occupants of the car but he quickly dismissed the thought. He was expecting to see body parts all over the place, but there was nothing to see other than the broken glass. He had begun to walk towards the cul-de-sac when he heard the sound of a speeding engine coming towards him and he turned to see a pair of headlights approaching him. Momentarily fearful it might be the bad guys returning, he was relieved to see it was Jim in Yankee One.

'What's happened? Where the fuck's Driscoll?' Jim asked urgently, looking at the glass on the road. H knelt down by the car window, and paused to catch his breath and compose himself.

'Fuck knows. He got taken out by a motor and he's vanished. He's got to be dead, the speed the car was going, but Christ only knows where his body is.'

Jim got out of the car and continued to survey the glass-littered road surface. 'Jesus, it's everywhere,' he said, squatting down and examining one of the thousands of square pieces of windscreen glass. Holding it up to the street light, he peered at it closely before announcing, 'It's covered in blood. Got to be a chance he's inside the motor that hit him.'

'Christ, I hope not,' replied H. 'Be much better if we found him here. Besides, I'm sure I saw him thrown clear.'

They walked slowly together towards the cul-de-sac until Jim stopped and looked over a low wall outside a cable manufacturing company.

'Over here, H,' he called quietly. H joined him and there behind the low wall, lying motionless on his back and wide-eyed, was a very dead Bobby Driscoll. He lay on a small patch of grass with both legs at odd angles and his left arm tucked under the small of his back. An ever-increasing pool of blood was forming under his head, fed by a heavy flow from both his ears and his nose.

'Dead as a fucking doornail,' remarked Jim. 'Best we fuck off before anyone sees us.'

'Did you pass anything when you came in?'

'Not a thing. They must have pissed off up Balmoral Road. Did you see what it was?'

'No. Come on, let's make ourselves scarce. There's nothing to tie us in with this so let's keep it that way.'

Nothing else needed to be said. The Brothers returned to

Yankee One and left the industrial estate quietly, confirming for themselves that they were unobserved and the only living souls there.

Driscoll had died almost instantly, his last conscious thought being one of puzzlement as he was flipped across the Capri's bonnet before his skull was crushed against the windscreen cross beam. He continued upwards in a spin, his right leg, hip and arm and all the ribs on his right side fractured. Both his lungs were punctured, his liver ruptured and his gall bladder collapsed mid-air before he landed behind the wall, breaking his left leg. He was dead before he hit the ground; both lungs quickly filled with blood and his liquidised brain began to ooze through the top of his head and ears on to the grass. He remained undisturbed for another six hours until a cleaner arriving for work at the cable manufacturing company noticed him when she stood in a puddle of blood and brain tissue at the front door.

Martin and Chance, the wannabe Mafia, had not hung around to find out whom they had run over. They too were puzzled by the lack of a body when they had turned round in the cul-de-sac and were making their escape. Driscoll's body had slammed across the bonnet and smashed the windscreen before disappearing over the top, but they were not minded to make further inquiries as to its whereabouts. They got away from the industrial estate as quickly as possible, discussing hysterically what they should do. They agreed they had to dump the Capri quickly and get it burnt to destroy all trace of their presence in it. As petty criminals tended to do, they headed for home ground to dump and burn the car before they vanished into the labyrinth of tight alleyways on the Park Royal estate.

Two minutes later they passed Delta Two parked up in a bus stop with Ally and Piggy arguing furiously. Ally was waving a clenched fist at Piggy, screaming, 'Next one you're going to fucking die, you fat cunt,' before plunging his head out of the car window into the fresh air. Martin and Chance took in the extraordinary sight of a ginger-haired policeman hanging out of a police car gulping in air, before Martin floored the accelerator and made a run for it.

'Come on, you fat cunt,' shouted Ally, coiling himself back into the car. 'Come on, get after them quickly.'

'What?'

'The fucking car with two little scrotes in it, no lights and a smashed windscreen,' screamed Ally. 'GET A FUCKING MOVE ON.'

Reluctantly, Piggy got their panda car rolling, Ally withering his ears with constant exhortations to go faster. As they got behind the Capri, Ally put the blue light on, grabbed the radio handset and began to broadcast.

'Delta Hotel from Delta Two, we're chasing a red Ford Capri along Tavistock Place towards the Park Royal estate. Vehicle has what looks like accident damage, no lights, two up, failing to stop for police.' He read out the vehicle registration number.

There was a pause before the operator informed them that the vehicle had no current keeper and had not been reported stolen. Other police vehicle crews began offering help and moving towards the chase.

'FUCKING KEEP UP,' screamed Ally at Piggy, forgetting he was still transmitting on the radio. 'We're not going to lose these little fuckers. Thanks, Delta Hotel, still towards the Park Royal, still failing to stop, speed is 55 m.p.h.'

The main set operator took the opportunity to tell Ally he had an open radio microphone before she opened the channel completely to talk through as the chase developed.

In the clapped-out Capri, Martin knew the wreck had little chance of outrunning the police car behind him and decided to dump it before they got to the Park Royal. He recognised where he was and realised he was travelling alongside the Valley Forge Golf and Country Club, which lay on the right side of the railway tracks. He lurched the Capri left on to a service road that ran up to a greenkeeper's storage shed alongside the twelfth fairway, closely followed by Delta Two. Ally knew where they were as well.

'Delta Hotel, he's off the main drag on to a dirt road up to the Valley Forge Golf Club. Decamp is imminent. Is there a dog unit available?'

'Negative, Delta Two. The only dog unit this side of the

county is assigned at Foxtrot Sierra, continue commentary please, now towards the Valley Forge Golf Club.'

'Fuck it,' shouted Ally, again forgetting he was transmitting, 'get up his fucking arse, you useless cunt. Delta Hotel, we're still on the dirt track which is a dead end, vehicle slowing, doors open, decamp, decamp.'

Martin and Chance bailed out of the Capri as it was still moving, allowing it to run into the side of the concrete greenkeeper's shed, and sprinted out on to the twelfth fairway, disappearing into the inky sleet.

'Come on, you fat bastard,' roared Ally, throwing the microphone on to the floor and flinging open his door to follow them.

'They'll be well away by now. There's no point,' whined Piggy, who didn't fancy a run at the best of times, but certainly not on a freezing cold, pitch-black night.

'Get out of there and help, you bastard,' hissed Ally, leaning back into the car and going nose to nose with him, eyes blazing. Reluctantly, Piggy eased his corpulent frame out into the cold and lumbered off into the night after Ally. It was no good. After only fifty yards he had lost sight of him, and, worse, his stomach was starting to rebel against this unwelcome exercise. Fearful however of further abuse, and possibly physical attack by Ally, he broke into a fat person's run/jog and carried on into the dark. Disaster struck shortly afterwards as his sphincter, unable to cope with the huge quantity of curry in his gut and the totally alien exercise, lost the good fight and Piggy shat his pants 250 yards up the twelfth fairway from the competition fee, a good wood shot distance, and adjacent to a deep fairway bunker.

'Bollocks,' he bellowed, standing bandy-legged and soaked in the dark. 'Thanks a fucking lot, Ally.' He was unsure what to do next. Soaked to the skin anyway, he couldn't go on in this state. Eventually, he took his shoes off, dropped his trousers and gingerly eased his soiled bundies off, kicking them away in disgust before having to retrieve them to clean himself up as best he could with the unsoiled areas. Once he had redressed, he looked round to see where best to dispose of his filthy underwear. His eyes lighted on the fairway bunker. He kicked his pants into it, climbed in himself, scooped a deep hole and then buried his pants, scraping the sand back over them with his shoes. Stamping the sand flat and satisfied the evidence had been disposed of, he wandered disconsolately back to the vehicles by the greenkeeper's shed,

Ally returned about twenty minutes later in a foul mood and without a prisoner. 'What the fuck happened to you?' he said darkly to Piggy.

'I had a good look round. We must have got separated in the dark. You had no luck, then?'

'What's it fucking look like? If you'd been up their arses we could have had them. Bollocks. Have you had a look in the motor yet?'

'Erm, no, not yet. I was just about to though,' Piggy lied.

Ally didn't say anything, but walked over to the abandoned Capri and peered in. Both doors had remained open and the interior was now soaked.

'There's no current keeper for it, is there?' he said. 'No one's going to claim ownership of this pile of shit, are they?' Frustrated, he took out his truncheon and began to smash the windows.

'What the fuck are you doing?' asked a startled Piggy, who never ceased to be amazed by Ally's sudden outbursts of extremely violent temper.

'Well, fuck it,' said Ally, 'look at it – no keeper, no tax, no insurance, fuck all. Who's going to want it back? Who's going to come complaining that it's been nicked and trashed?'

'Well, no one I suppose,' agreed Piggy uncertainly, 'but all the same, I mean . . .' He trailed off as Yankee One rolled to a halt behind the panda car and the Brothers got out and walked over to view Ally's handiwork. They had listened to the brief chase, put two and two together and prayed that Piggy and Ally didn't nick either of the occupants.

'Didn't get them then?' said H casually.

'No, fuck it,' snarled Ally, glaring at Piggy, who looked away, ignoring him.

'Get a good look at them?'

'Couple of young scrotes, that's about it. Got to be from the Park Royal.'

'What about if you saw them again?'

'Not a hope. Never got close enough, did we, Piggy?' added Ally pointedly.

Again, Piggy ignored him and wriggled uncomfortably.

'No keeper or anything, is there?' continued H.

'Fuck all.'

'Give it the treatment then, shall we?'

Without another word, H and Jim went to either open car door, unzipped their trousers and pissed all over the seats and dashboard, then drew their truncheons and trashed the inside of the Capri. If anyone ever queried it, they would simply claim that was how the thieves had left the vehicle. More importantly, what they had done was dispose of any evidence linking Martin and Chance to the vehicle. Barring unlikely fits of conscience, they would never be brought to account for Driscoll's death. The Capri was left where it was, open to the elements, and it would be another three days before officers investigating Driscoll's death connected with it. By that time the trail was cold. Driscoll's ironic demise would remain unsolved. The only people who could ever throw any light on it were not inclined to discuss it.

As agreed, Psycho had picked Pizza up outside the cemetery on the edge of the town centre, and, still bridling at Pizza's insolence, had driven in silence out to the Bolton Road industrial estate where the gypsies had taken up residence. The silence didn't bother Pizza one bit. He had quickly learnt that being out of the wet and cold was worth any price.

'What've you got planned, then?' asked Pizza, breaking the silence as Psycho turned off the car headlights and pulled up in an unlit lay-by about a hundred yards from the half-dozen caravans. A row of tall conifer trees completely concealed the police car from anyone who might have been watching from the site.

'Just watch and learn, boy,' Psycho replied very smugly, getting out of the car and going round to the boot. Pizza joined him and watched with increasing anticipation as Psycho pulled out an air rifle with the largest telescopic sight he had ever seen. The illegal .22 German-made rifle had been brought back from Hamburg by Psycho after a trip to the city's fleshpots a few years earlier. Producing a muzzle velocity of 17 foot-pounds and firing steel-cored Prometheus hunting pellets, it was an absolutely lethal weapon. It had a massive kick when being fired and it took a strong person to use it effectively.

'Jesus, Psycho, what are you hunting, elephants?' Pizza asked. 'What sort of range have you got with that thing?'

'Fuck knows,' replied Psycho, 'but what I do know is that I can't miss with it. Look at this.' He flicked a small switch on the side of the huge sight and a low humming noise started. Pizza saw a green light start to glow from within the sight.

'What's that then?' he asked, genuinely impressed.

'Night vision sight,' Psycho replied proudly. 'Look at that, bright as day and clear as a bell.' He held the sight to Pizza's eyes to prove the point. The gypsy camp appeared in the sight as clearly as Psycho had claimed and Pizza whistled his approval.

'Lovely looking bit of kit, Psycho, but can you use it?' he challenged.

'Can I fucking use it, can I fucking use it?' repeated Psycho. 'Watch and learn, boy.'

He broke the barrel, pushed a pellet into the breech, locked the barrel shut with a satisfying clunk, and wrapped the strap around his left arm. He then walked to the other side of the vehicle before he rested his left arm across the roof and tucked the butt into his right shoulder. Settling himself, he closed his left eye and moved his right eye into the cushioned sight, quietly cursing the incessant drizzle.

'Right then, you pikey bastards,' he murmured to himself, 'who wants some?'

He swept the sight across the unofficial gypsy site, but the occupants were either all having an early night or, more likely, out thieving. Not a thing moved nor a light shone in any of the caravan windows.

'Fucking hell, where are they all?' he complained as Pizza leant, bored senseless, against the bonnet, an ear cocked for the radio which had burst into life some minutes earlier.

'Piggy and Ally are still chasing that Capri,' he said hopefully.

'Going the other way. No chance for us,' said Psycho, who had no intention of going anywhere until he'd shot someone. Pizza sighed and pulled his head deeper into his coat, debating whether he should get back into the car but knowing that Psycho would get the hump.

'Hurry up and shoot something, will you?' he complained. 'I'm bloody soaked. The whole idea of getting a ride with you was to keep dry.'

'Can't hurry these things,' answered Psycho, who was himself beginning to doubt he'd ever get the opportunity.

'They've decamped at the golf course,' interjected Pizza, going back to the radio. 'A couple of toe-rags across the golf course,' he reiterated, looking over at Psycho, hoping he might get the reaction he was looking for.

'Won't come this way,' said Psycho, still not lifting his eye from the sight.

Pizza puffed out his cheeks in defeat. The golf course was only a little over a mile away, but in this mood he knew Psycho wasn't going to be moved. He resigned himself to getting very cold and wet until Psycho had purged his blood lust.

Fifteen minutes later he suddenly heard Psycho hiss 'Yes' triumphantly and saw him stiffen into his firing stance, slowly moving the barrel of the rifle left and right as he fixed on a target.

'You little beauties, let me see you,' he whispered, as if the prey might somehow hear him and run away. In his sight he now had two bedraggled, unkempt youths, carefully picking their way through fairly dense undergrowth over to the east of the gypsy camp.

'Been out poaching or robbing,' he whispered to Pizza, who had moved behind him, hoping to witness the cull. 'Stand by, stand by, stand by,' he muttered slowly to himself. Pizza looked oddly at him; he really was the maddest person he'd ever encountered.

Jimmy Martin and Dave Chance were lost, but not overly worried because they were now quite sure the Old Bill weren't behind them. They'd stuck together across the fairway of the golf course but had become disorientated in the dark and were now headed away from their intended destination, the Park Royal estate. Still, they'd lost the Old Bill and now intended to stay off the main roads as much as possible until they hit home ground. They were pushing their way through thigh-high shrubs and undergrowth and stumbling over rubble on some waste ground when Martin, who was slightly in front, stopped as he saw something up ahead.

'Fucking gypos,' he whispered back to Chance. 'We must be on the Bolton Road estate. This lot moved on a couple of days ago.'

'Bolton Road?' hissed back Chance. 'We're going the wrong fucking way then.'

'Yeah, I know. Still, at least we know where we are now.

Give these bastards a bit of room, though,' he cautioned. 'They catch us, I heard they'll do you up the arse and keep you as a sex slave in one of their caravans.'

Chance looked saucer-eyed at his friend and hurriedly followed as he moved over to the left, giving the camp a wide berth, and casting anxious looks towards it.

Then something ripped off the tip of Martin's nose, causing him to throw both hands to his face and drop to his knees. Such was his shock that he didn't scream or yell. He took his hands away from his face and even in the dark could see they were covered in what was obviously his blood. Chance saw him drop and called out quietly, 'What's up?' He received no reply, so moved towards him. His friend was staring at his own outstretched hands and reaching up to touch his nose.

'What's wrong?' hissed Chance anxiously. 'Stop fucking about.'

Martin turned to look at him, and Chance saw the ruined nose and fearful, heavily bloodstained face. Martin's eyes were wide with fear and he was struggling to breathe properly.

'I've been shot,' he stammered.

'Shot?' queried Chance, a split second before a second pellet embedded itself into the hard bone above his temple. As he fell poleaxed to the ground, blood flowing from the wound, Martin began to scream like a hunted hare. Chance had not lost consciousness when he was hit, and as he rolled around in the undergrowth, clutching at his head, he too began to scream.

Psycho stepped back from his rifle sight and grinned over at Pizza, who was looking admiringly at him and glancing over in the direction of the hysterical screaming.

'Got both of them,' he boasted happily as he packed his rifle away in the boot of the panda car. He glanced over towards the gypsy caravans as he noticed lights coming on in one or two. 'Time we made ourselves scarce, Pizza.'

He slammed the boot shut and hurried round to the driver's side. Pizza followed suit; Psycho started the engine up and drove quickly out of the lay-by, not putting the headlights on until they had put some distance between them and the camp. He was beaming contentedly and hit the steering wheel several times in celebration.

'Fucking brilliant, fucking brilliant,' he repeated before quietening down, turning to Pizza and saying, 'So tell me, Pizza, what's your little stunt all about then?'

Back on the waste ground, Chance and Martin were not screaming quite as loudly, and ceased altogether as they heard voices approaching them. Getting to their feet they saw lights on in the caravans and figures moving towards them in the dark, some of them clearly rather large dogs.

'Gypsies,' screamed Martin, 'and fucking dogs.'

'NOOOOOOO,' shrieked Chance, who viewed the

prospect of ending up as a gypsy's 'special friend' with an arsehole like the top end of an old Wellington boot with absolute terror.

'NOOOOOOO,' shrieked Martin as well, as both youths momentarily forgot their injuries and grew wings as they fled from the approaching gypsies.

The dogs pursued the pair for some distance, eventually catching them in the lay-by recently vacated by Psycho and Pizza where they administered a dreadful savaging. Eventually losing interest in their blubbering prey, the dogs returned to the camp, leaving Martin and Chance to reflect painfully on a night they would never, ever discuss with anyone else.

Psycho brought the car to a skidding halt and looked over at the beaming Pizza.

'Pizza, that's fucking brilliant,' he shouted delightedly, 'absolutely fucking brilliant. How are you going to get down to him, though?'

'That's where you come in,' Pizza replied. 'I need you to get Jones out of Custody for about five minutes, that's all. That'll give me plenty of time to get Middleton done.'

'OK. Any ideas how I get him away?'

'I hadn't really given it a lot of thought. I was hoping you'd come up with something, Psycho.'

Psycho recognised the challenge immediately. Pizza was really pushing his luck, though he had to admit that the boy knew which buttons to press. A bit like himself, really. Psycho began to feel a little glow of professional respect for him.

'Not a problem,' he announced brightly, inspiration coming quickly. 'You tell me when you want Jones out of the way and it'll be done.'

'Lovely,' replied Pizza, reaching forward to turn up the hopeless heater to try to dry out a bit. As the car moved off again, he settled back into his seat and allowed himself a broad grin at the thought of what was about to happen.

In his desolate office on the third floor at Handstead police station, Acting Chief Inspector Curtis stared at the phone he had just put down, before he put his head in his hands and slumped forward. Taking advantage of Curtis's temporary promotion, the appalling Chief Superintendent 'Mengele' Middleton had just phoned to berate him about his son's continued detention in the drunk cell. Sergeant Jones had relented and phoned Mengele just after 1 a.m. Mengele had been on to Curtis immediately afterwards.

'I take it there won't be any question of his being charged, Acting Chief Inspector,' he hissed at him. Curtis had not even been aware that Middleton Jnr was in his cells. He tried to stall.

'Oh, well, I don't know what's planned for him,' he tried as an opening bid. 'I'll need to speak to the arresting officer.'

'Don't know what's going on?' shouted Mengele. 'You're

supposed to be in charge there, Acting Chief Inspector. This is a very inauspicious start to your career in a position of some value and importance. All I need from you is your agreement that my son won't be charged and I'll be over to pick him up later when it's quiet and get him out of your hair. No need for anyone else to get involved. Any problem with that at all?'

Curtis's complete lack of operational experience or backbone betrayed him and he answered limply 'No, sir' before Mengele abruptly slammed the phone down to avoid further discussion. Curtis kept his head in his hands for some time as he considered alternative careers. He finally picked up the phone and spoke to Sergeant Jones in the custody block, telling him that Middleton Jnr was to be released into the custody of his father without charge. He expected a row, but was surprised when Jones merely responded, 'You're the boss. I'll mark up the custody record with your instructions,' and hung up.

Curtis contemplated the implications of what Jones had said for a while and weighed it against what Mengele had implied. He eventually decided that he could probably cope marginally better with the unbridled contempt of the officers at Handstead than the malicious politicking of Mengele and the effects that could have on his fledgling career as a high flyer. He was, after all, part of the palsied future for the Job.

*

Half an hour later, Sergeant Jones looked up from his
newspaper as he heard the door to the custody block open
and saw Psycho smiling at him. He was relieved to see that
the unshaven brute had not got a prisoner with him.

'Yes?' he asked.

'Spare me a minute, sarge?' said Psycho politely. 'I'd really
appreciate a couple of moments for a chat about something
personal.'

Fucking hell, just what I don't need. I've got enough of
my own problems, thought Sergeant Jones, but he replied,
'Sure, come on in. It's pretty quiet at the moment.'

'Not here, sarge. I don't want us to be interrupted. Can't
we use the sergeant's office? I've checked and it's empty.'

'OK,' sighed Jones, getting wearily to his feet and
reluctantly going out into the corridor through the door
Psycho was holding open for him. As the far corridor door
shut behind them, Pizza hurried unseen from the back yard
into the custody block carrying a plastic carrier bag.
He quickly checked the two custody records hanging on
clips on the wall behind the desk to confirm that
Middleton Jnr was alone in the drunk cell. He noticed
that even though Jones was working without a gaoler,
he had kept up to date with his visits to the prisoners,
visiting them only half an hour ago. Apart from his phone
call from Curtis, he'd had nothing to do since he took over
at 10 p.m. Despite his initial fears of a hectic evening, the
night duty officers had yet to bring a body in; both

prisoners were left over from Late Turn. Quietly opening the desk drawer, Pizza was relieved to see that Jones had not taken the cell keys with him. Holding the large bunch tightly to stop them rattling, he made his way stealthily down the corridor to the cells. The passage was lit only by the eerie red night lights in the ceiling, and as Pizza paused by the gate to the cells themselves he could hear only loud, rhythmic snoring. He inserted and turned a key in the gate, which opened without a sound. He crept quietly to the drunk cell and peered in. The cell was devoid of any furniture and its cold shiny stone floor was only blemished by the shallow open drainage channels that led to a shallow hole in the middle of the floor covered with a cast-iron grille, which was bolted into the recessed gap. The design of the cell was intentional and entirely in keeping with its function – in the morning a quantity of industrial-strength disinfectant would be thrown over the walls and floor and a fire hose used to wash all the vomit and shit away. It was a task all the Early Turn gaolers loathed with a passion, though it could be fun if an overnight drunk was still in residence.

Lying helpfully on his side in the middle of the floor, with his head almost in the drainage channel, was Jason Middleton, snoring like a pig and covered in his own vomit, which he had rolled around in as he had made himself comfortable. Pizza gagged at the stench as he opened the gate and walked over to him. He waited briefly to ensure he hadn't disturbed him before he reached into his carrier bag, knelt down beside him and got to work.

In the sergeant's office, Jones motioned disinterestedly to Psycho to sit down in the chair on the opposite side of the only desk.

'What's on your mind?' he asked, suspecting that as usual there would be very little. Psycho wriggled uncomfortably, looking down at the floor and then at Jones before he replied.

'I don't know if you're aware,' he started, 'but I'm gay and I need to run something past you.'

'Gay?' shouted Jones, alarmed and sitting back firmly in his chair. 'Gay?' he repeated.

'Yes, gay,' continued Psycho, pulling his chair closer to the desk as Jones tried to push his through the wall, 'and I really like the way you move and hold yourself. I wondered if you'd like to come over to my place for dinner one night, perhaps make a night of it with a few other friends?'

'No,' bellowed Jones, looking towards the door, planning to make a dash for it if Psycho got any closer. 'I'm no fucking shirt-lifter.' He noticed Psycho frown menacingly at this remark and held up both hands apologetically. 'What I meant was I'm not a homosexualist,' he blustered. 'Sorry, I didn't mean anything by that last remark.'

Psycho ignored the apology. 'Not a homosexual,' he corrected. 'You're not gay. I thought you were single now?'

'Well, yes, my wife's left me, that's true,' admitted Jones.

'We heard she caught you getting banged up the arse at your last nick,' Psycho lied.

'Christ, no,' squealed Jones desperately. 'I had an affair with the wife of one of my PCs; nothing wrong with me. No, I didn't mean that there's anything wrong with you . . .' He trailed off in despair.

Psycho stood up and Jones tried to melt into the varnish on the back of the chair. 'You're definitely not gay?' he asked. Jones shook his head in reply. 'You sure you're not gay?'

'No, no. I'm definitely not gay – I shag women, for Christ's sake,' yelled Jones. How was he ever going to get away from this horror?

'OK,' said Psycho with a shrug of his shoulders, going over to the door. 'It'll be our little secret, but if you ever change your mind, promise me you'll give me a ring?'

Jones nodded.

'Promise me,' said Psycho, raising his voice.

'I promise,' whispered Jones, and Psycho strode out of the room. Jones momentarily relaxed before Psycho put his head back round the door and looked at him.

'Love you,' he lisped quietly at his horrified sergeant.

Jones remained in the office shaking for quite a while, not returning to the custody block for some time. By the time he did, the drunk cell had been locked, the keys returned and Pizza was recounting his stunt to Psycho out in the car, both laughing until tears ran down their faces.

Absolutely jubilant, Psycho decided to take a run down to the railway sidings to see if any of the local toms was having a quiet night and fancied doing him a favour. 'Tanks need emptying,' he announced, to the horror of Pizza, who had heard graphic accounts of Psycho's blow jobs and was appalled at the prospect of having to witness the monster having his plums sucked dry.

Jones tried to settle back into his newspaper but couldn't concentrate at all, constantly jumping as he heard distant doors slamming, expecting at any moment to see Psycho leering at him. The mere thought of it made him shudder.

Mengele appeared in the custody block shortly after 3 a.m., or rather he appeared to float through the wall and hover in front of the desk. Jones was having a horrific dream where a rampant Psycho dressed as Little Bo Peep and carrying a lamb under a hairy arm was chasing him round a bedroom, and quite welcomed the sudden visitor. He didn't recognise him and looked the stranger up and down with barely concealed disdain. He was wearing a beige sports jacket with leather patches sewn on to the elbows, green moleskin trousers and shiny brown leather brogues. Under an open-necked cream shirt was a real eyesore of a red and green check cravat. Two sinister blue eyes glared at Jones through round, wire-rimmed glasses. Whilst faintly ridiculous, there was also an unmistakable air of menace about the man. Jones, however, completely failed to spot it.

'Yes?' he demanded rather rudely.

'Yes?' bellowed Mengele. 'On your feet, you little cockroach. D'you know who I am?'

'No,' replied Jones defiantly, but getting up anyway. He recognised something in the man's tone that said 'senior officer'.

'Chief Superintendent Middleton,' said Mengele testily. 'I've come to collect my son. Go and get him and we'll be on our way.' Jones didn't move quickly enough so Mengele snapped, 'Go on, you cretin, go and get him now.'

Jones coloured up at the insult and wished he had the balls to give the old twat a mouthful back. But he hadn't, so he grabbed the cell keys from the desk drawer and slunk away down the darkened cell passage. As soon as Mengele heard the keys rattling in the call gate, he quickly viewed the three custody records on the clips. Finding his son's, he pulled the papers free, folded them in half and slipped them into his jacket pocket. He waited a couple of minutes before Jones reappeared, walking ahead of a shambling, shuffling figure.

'He's a bit of a mess, I'm afraid, sir,' murmured Jones, belatedly trying to show deference and respect. 'If you'll just sign for him you can be on your way,' he continued, looking up at the empty clip where the custody record had been, and then at his desk in case he'd left it there by accident. Where's his custody record? he asked himself quietly, and then looked at Mengele who was staring aghast at the shuffling figure that had come to a halt and was leaning against the door frame. 'I can't seem to find his custody record,' he said, beginning to open and close the drawers in the desk.

'Jesus fucking Christ,' exploded Mengele, his voice rising a couple of octaves, 'look at the fucking state of him.'

'Yeah, he's a mess all right,' replied Jones, peering into the depths of one of the larger drawers.

'Look at his fucking hair, you moron. What the fuck have you done?'

'Done? What you on about?' said Jones, getting to his feet and walking closer to the stinking figure.

'Look at his fucking hair,' shouted Mengele again, striding towards his son, gesticulating wildly. He grabbed Jason's shoulders and pulled him upright and suddenly Jones saw what he was talking about. The boy's lank, dirty, vomit-covered hair hung limply down to the left side of his head and face, but the right side was as bald as an egg.

'His fucking head's been shaved, you cunt,' screamed Mengele. 'You've shaved his fucking head.' His eyes were bulging madly and the veins in his forehead straining.

'Fuck all to do with me,' sniffed Jones huffily. 'Must have been like that when he was nicked. If I could find his custody record I could tell you. Haven't seen it, have you?' he asked, looking Mengele straight in the eye for the first time.

# Chapter Nineteen

The officers of 'D' Relief were long home in bed and asleep by the time Marjorie Wallace and Rachel Weinberg arrived at the ladies' twelfth tee at the Valley Forge Golf and Country Club. As the Ladies' Captain, Marjorie had to maintain a certain standard, and she was, as expected, dressed to kill. Her motorised trolley contained a set of handmade Max Faulkner clubs in a hand-stitched leather bag, and the cost of her golfing attire – Jack Nicklaus checked slacks, Pringle roll-neck jumper and cardigan, black leather shoes and brand new white leather glove – ran well into three figures. Wearing a Dunlop sun visor she looked the part of the lady captain, but any resemblance to a golfer ended there as her lack of any natural sporting prowess or hand–eye co-ordination rather negated the effect. Her elevation to Ladies' Captain owed everything to her status as the wife of an ICI director who didn't mind putting his hand in his pocket when required. As a member of a private golf club where status and money were everything, it had only been a matter of time before Marjorie rose to the top of the tree, with her own designated parking space at the front of the sumptuous clubhouse.

She had been the Ladies' Captain for the last four years, returned unopposed at every annual general meeting. The rest of the lady members took the very sensible view that while they had a cash cow in post it would be most unwise to offend it. That was, however, until Rachel Weinberg gained membership. Married to a hugely wealthy jeweller with premises in Deansgate, Altrincham and Chester, she had let it be known that she was in a similarly happy position to dole out her husband's cash to the golf club. The ladies' section had split into two camps and the next AGM promised to be a bloody affair after Rachel announced that she had 'graciously acceded to requests from lady members to stand for election to the post of Ladies' Captain'. Marjorie had maintained an icy, furious silence when the two candidates' names had appeared on the advance notices for the AGM around the clubhouse, and the atmosphere around the club became more and more electric as the AGM got closer. It went into meltdown when Marjorie and Rachel were drawn against each other in the first round of the Ladies' Challenge Cup, due to be played a week before the AGM. The incumbent against the heir apparent. Everyone agreed that the result of the match would probably sway the ballot for Ladies' Captain.

The prospect of a real battle ensuing drew a crowd of around fifty as the two silent, glowering combatants drove off into the late-morning mist. Marjorie played off a handicap of 20, Rachel, a slightly better player but prone to spectacular 'blow-ups', off 15. On paper she should beat Marjorie, but Marjorie was nothing if not a tenacious competitor when it came to her social standing. She played out of her skin, matching Rachel shot for shot, hole for hole – going one up, back to all square, one behind, all square again, with never more than a hole between them. It was a riveting match that enthralled the following crowd, evenly split into two very partisan camps.

As they stood on the twelfth tee, Rachel had the honour to drive first, having gone one up at the eleventh, and briefly surveyed the challenge ahead. A 375-yard par four, dog leg right, the only obvious hazard being a fairway bunker about two hundred yards ahead. However, it was a tight, narrow fairway with gruesome rough and out of bounds on both sides to worry about. She was playing sensible, percentage golf and decided to lay up short of the bunker and leave herself a decent iron shot to the flag. She pulled her favourite driving iron out of her bag after a brief discussion with her caddie, teed up her ball and again surveyed the shot ahead. Her choice of club caught Marjorie's attention and she realised that Rachel intended to lay up short of the fairway bunker. It was an opportunity for her, albeit a risky one, but if she could pass the bunker she'd have an easier shot on to the green. She whispered to her caddie and watched intently, plump arms firmly crossed, as Rachel smoothly despatched her ball straight as an arrow down the centre of the fairway. She'd caught it perfectly and watched, frozen in position, as it flew high and true before beginning its fall to earth. For a brief moment she feared she'd caught it too well and it was headed for the bunker, but to her relief she saw it bounce twice and roll to a halt on the damp turf alongside the bunker's edge. Smiling contentedly and graciously acknowledging the polite ripple of applause, she slotted her club back into her bag with a flourish and fixed Marjorie with a withering stare. Marjorie waited for effect before striding out on to the tee carrying her number one wood. Her choice of club drew comment from within the crowd. It was a bold but risky choice. If she caught it right and carried the bunker, she'd have little more than a short iron shot to the flag. Get it wrong and she'd need a machete and beaters to find her ball. Still, she who dares wins, and all that. Marjorie teed up her ball, got her stance comfortable, wriggled her fat bottom twice, and swung for all she was worth. A gasp went up from the gallery as they realised that the shot had not been perfect and that she had hooked the ball badly. It was beginning to curve left from way out right over the out of bounds, and with the extra power imparted by the wooden club plummeted full tilt into the fairway bunker and plugged, the top of the ball barely visible above the sand.

Marjorie watched open-mouthed in horror as her ball flew into the bunker, whilst Rachel turned away, barely able to conceal her glee. Disgracefully, one or two of her supporters had given audible laughs, which drew dark looks and loud 'tuts' of disapproval from the other camp. Things were getting serious. Thin-lipped, Marjorie thrust the wood firmly back into her bag and marched off the tee towards the fairway bunker, muttering inaudibly to herself. She was livid; couldn't believe she had been so stupid and taken such a silly risk. Worse, she hated bunker shots at the best of times and she knew this one would be difficult. Probably plugged in the wet sand and still 175 yards to go to the flag. She would be lucky to get out of the bunker, let alone make any distance. It was very likely she was going to go two holes down with only six left to play. Why had she been so stupid, she fumed. She glanced over at Rachel who was talking animatedly with her caddie and looking very pleased with life. Bitch.

Arriving at the fairway bunker, Marjorie was surprised to see how deep it was, and when she peered over the edge her heart sank as she saw the top of the ball just peeking out of the sand. Worse, whoever had played out of the bunker last had not raked it, leaving huge great footprints all over the place. What was the club coming to, she thought bitterly.

'That's going to be difficult, Marjorie,' remarked her caddie sympathetically.

'Thank you, Grace,' snapped Marjorie unpleasantly,

deciding to blame her for letting her play that stupid shot. 'Any caddie worth their salt would have advised against taking a wood off the tee,' she continued bitterly as she snatched her sand wedge out of her astonished caddie's hand and climbed, grim-faced, down into the bunker. She again glanced at Rachel, who was standing about twenty yards away with a grin so wide it had to hurt. She'd seen how badly the ball had plugged. Gritting her teeth, wobbling her bottom and clenching her buttocks as hard as she could, Marjorie resolved to get the ball out of the bunker if it was the last thing she did. Careful not to ground her club, she took a full swing, dug into the sand behind the ball, felt some resistance as the club head went in, but, as her numerous coaches had instructed her, played through the resistance, under the ball and up. A huge spray of wet sand erupted in front of her, in amongst which she was vaguely aware of a large grey object wrapped around the club head. As she continued with the shot and the club head rose above head height, the grey thing detached itself from the club and landed on her head. It caused her to shriek and let go of the wedge, which thudded against the side of the bunker whilst her ball, barely disturbed by her exertions, rolled slowly to the back of the bunker into a small puddle. Horrified, but as yet not sure why, Marjorie reached up to her head and pulled the dripping object off and stared at it. The gallery and Rachel were now crowded at the edge of the bunker and watched as Marjorie stared quizzically at Piggy's shitty pants before she began to scream hysterically. Realisation had dawned.

It took four male members from the crowd to remove her thrashing, porky little body from the depths of the bunker and get her back to the clubhouse, where she lay in state in the darkened ladies' locker room until her husband was summoned from a meeting to take her home. In the bar, amidst much hilarity, Rachel called for a ruling on what had occurred to determine the outcome of the game. The decision was made that Marjorie had forfeited the game by her refusal to play on, and Rachel progressed into the next round of the competition and the post of Ladies' Captain.

Still deeply traumatised by her meeting with Psycho, and now her public humiliation at the hands of Piggy's pants, Marjorie decided enough was enough. At her insistence, she and her husband moved out of the area and nearer her aged parents in the West Country. She was a changed, almost pleasant woman, as anyone who knew her would testify. Psycho and Piggy were blissfully unaware of the service they had done to the rest of society.

The summons to meet DCI Harrison in the small, secluded country pub they sometimes patronised had not come as any great surprise to Simon Edwardes. They had met there in the past to exchange information or money, and he assumed this meeting was for either or both purposes.

Harrison arrived earlier than the agreed time, as he usually did, and secured a table in the far corner where he could sit with his back against the wall and watch the bar and particularly the only door to the pub. Additionally welcome was the proximity to the large open fire.

He was growing tired of his clandestine relationship and meetings with Edwardes and had it in mind that now was as good a time as any to pull the plug on the odious bastard. It was a big decision. The information on the local villains that Edwardes regularly passed on was absolute gold dust. The results Harrison gained professionally had made him look very good with the CID hierarchy. Promotion to Detective Superintendent in the near future was a real possibility and like it or not, Edwardes had played a big part in putting him in the limelight. The news he had to pass on to him this evening, though, could potentially sour things between them anyway. Ordering himself a pint, he sat down at his table, lit a small cigar and waited and pondered. Keep him or dump him, keep him or dump him. He was far too useful, Harrison finally, reluctantly, admitted to himself, and the thought of someone else running him and getting all the results swayed the decision. Repulsive as he was, Edwardes wasn't expensive to run, even though Harrison paid him exclusively from his own pocket. The Job knew nothing about Edwardes, only that Harrison had a quality snout feeding him eighteen-carat information about the villains in Handstead. They asked no questions whilst

Harrison kept producing results. He quickly patted his overcoat inside pocket, confirming the envelope of cash was still there, and glanced out of the adjacent window, checking that his own car was OK. He never used a Force motor for these meetings, knowing that villains took a keen interest in the unmarked vehicles used by the CID. If he clocked anyone he knew out here, he'd simply leave his car in the car park and get a taxi home. He crossed his legs, sighed deeply, looked at his watch and waited, watching the handful of customers for signs of recognition.

A car pulling into the almost empty car park distracted his attention and he turned to see Edwardes arriving in an almost new Triumph Stag. Harrison frowned. Must be paying the fat bastard too much, he mused. He couldn't afford a motor like that, but at least it wasn't the convertible model. He was relieved to see Edwardes park some distance from his own shabby Datsun before carefully locking what was obviously his pride and joy and walking towards the pub.

Edwardes opened the creaky, black-beamed door, ducked under the low lintel and walked into the warm, smoky, welcoming bar. He paused and glanced round at the other customers before he spotted Harrison at the far table. Harrison merely nodded in recognition, no smile, whilst Edwardes asked with a hand gesture if Harrison wanted another drink. A small shake of his head and a raised hand indicated he was OK with his pint and a few minutes later Edwardes joined him at the table.

'Cheers, Mr Harrison,' he said amiably, slurping the foam off his pint of gassy lager.

'I see crime pays then, Simon,' answered Harrison, ignoring the greeting and gesturing towards the car park with a nod of his head.

'What d'you mean?'

'Nice motor you got there.'

'Oh, I see. Nothing to hide there, Mr Harrison. Bought and paid for by my parents to celebrate my elevation to the Bar.' He laughed.

Harrison knew of the fictitious life Edwardes had created for the benefit of his elderly parents and laughed grimly. 'You're a dodgy bastard, Simon.'

'You've never complained,' answered Edwardes archly. 'Anyway, what did you want to talk about? The trial, no doubt?'

'In a manner of speaking, yes, but you'd better read this,' Harrison replied, pulling an envelope from his coat pocket and handing it to Edwardes. 'Things have changed, Simon; all deals are off.'

'What do you mean?' Edwardes, looking worried, put down his pint and opened the envelope.

'Read it, Simon,' Harrison urged.

Edwardes quickly read through the two-page advice letter from the Director of Public Prosecutions before he laid it on the table in front of him.

'Attempted murder?' he said finally.

''S right, Simon,' said Harrison, reaching across the table to retrieve the letter and envelope and returning them to his coat pocket. 'He reckons there's enough evidence to charge Morgan with attempted murder as well as the Section 18 GBH as an alternative. The manager nearly died, remember, and we've got stacks of forensic and some decent witnesses.'

'What about his evidence against the others?'

'Don't need it,' replied Harrison dismissively, stubbing his cigar out in the ashtray. 'Driscoll's dead anyway – he was always our number one target – and Baker and the others will go away on forensics. We don't need Morgan any more, especially now he's looking at attempted murder. No, I think his usefulness to us is at an end.' He lit another, celebratory cigar, and blew a large cloud of smoke to the grimy yellow ceiling.

'Fucking hell,' said Edwardes, fumbling in his coat pocket for a packet of cigarettes, eventually putting one to his lips with trembling fingers. 'Where does that leave us, then?'

Harrison leant forward with his lighter and lit Edwardes's cigarette, then settled back in his chair and eyed him carefully. 'Your fee, you mean?'

'Don't fuck me about, Mr Harrison,' said Edwardes crossly. 'We had a deal and I was going to keep my side of it. Now this happens.'

'Don't worry, Simon.' Harrison laughed and reached into his inside coat pocket, pulled out the envelope of cash and tossed it on to the table in front of him. 'I know there's nothing you could have done about it; it's not your fault. I trust you,' he lied, 'and I want to keep you sweet, so there's what I promised you originally, OK?'

'What, all of it?'

'Yeah. Our business arrangement still exists, OK? Any of the other Mafia come to you, or any information comes your way, it comes to me – agreed?'

'Agreed,' replied Edwardes, tucking the envelope into his coat. 'Of course, you know this decision is tantamount to a death sentence for young Morgan.'

'Shame,' replied Harrison, pulling deeply on his cigar and exhaling. 'When you going to let him have the good news?'

'I'm instructing Counsel the day after tomorrow and have a visit arranged after that, so probably then. I take it you'll be informing me formally of the new charge in due course?'

'Letter went off this afternoon, Simon,' Harrison replied, 'but I thought we ought to get things straight between us first.'

'Quite right, Mr Harrison. I appreciate the thought.' Edwardes got to his feet and extended a handshake. 'I'll be in touch.'

As Harrison expected, the handshake was cold and flabby, but he took it anyway and bade Edwardes farewell. He waited at his table until he had seen the Triumph leave the car park in a flurry of pebbles as Edwardes wheelspun away, before he satisfied himself there was no one in the pub he recognised and left unobserved.

As he drove home, he considered the remark about the consequences of the DPP's decision on Morgan. Edwardes was right. Everyone knew Morgan had grassed his mates and now he was destined to spend a long time in prison. Unless he spent that time in solitary confinement, one day someone would get to him and exact revenge. It was the way of things, he reflected ruefully; always had been, always would be. There you go. Nothing he could do about it now even if he wanted to.

# Chapter Twenty

The trial opened at Manchester Crown Court three months later on a bright spring morning. Pizza and the numerous other officers with evidence to give, had travelled into Manchester in a Job Transit which they'd parked outside Bootle Street police station. There, they'd had breakfast and discussed the approaching trial. All had agreed it would be a dirty fight, but one they were determined to win. Pizza contributed little to the conversation and banter, and was lagging behind the others as they walked up Bootle Street towards the court. They turned right into Deansgate and into Hardman Street whilst he became stranded on a traffic island in the centre of the road, waiting for a gap in the heavy traffic. He glanced up towards Crown Square, and on the opposite pavement amongst the dense pack of pedestrians he saw a girl he thought he recognised. He stared hard at her as he racked his brain, and then he remembered – it was the girl he had met at the graveyard,

Bovril's friend, the one who had made him feel so much better. Smiling, he leapt into the traffic, causing a taxi to brake suddenly and the driver to hit his horn in annoyance. The blast on the horn made Lisa look up to see Pizza walking towards her, smiling, with his hand outstretched in greeting.

'Hello, he said hesitantly. 'We met at Bovril's funeral, I don't know if you remember . . .'

'Oh yes, I remember you,' she said, taking his hand and shaking it with feeling, 'yes, I remember you very well.'

Pizza was very flattered, but became tongue-tied and coloured up. Lisa rescued him by continuing, 'I suppose you'll be giving evidence. I wanted to see what happens to them all.'

'Yes, I found their clothing which they'd chucked away. It's quite important,' he said proudly. Lisa slipped her arm through his and they began to walk slowly along Crown Square towards the main door to the court.

'You don't mind if I listen to the trial, do you?' she asked.

'Oh, no,' replied Pizza urgently, 'I'm really pleased you're here. You know that the girl who shot him and one of them that gave her the gun are dead, don't you? There's only one called Baker facing any charges in relation to Bovril's murder.'

'Yes I know,' she said quietly, 'but I wanted to see it finished. I need to draw a line under it and get on with life.'

He understood perfectly and glanced down at her now

obviously swelling stomach but said nothing. She saw the glance and answered the unasked question.

'Yes, I'm pregnant.' She smiled happily.

'Is your husband happy about it?' asked Pizza, probing uncertainly for the answers he wanted to hear.

'I don't have a husband – or a boyfriend,' she added quickly. 'I'm on my own now. The father's gone.'

'I'm sorry,' lied Pizza. 'His loss, if you ask me.' They smiled at each other and continued in silence to the main doors, where the other police officers were waiting for Pizza.

'I've got to go now,' he said quietly to Lisa. 'Will you be around at the end of the day?'

'If you'd like me to be, I will,' she said.

'I'd like that very much,' said Pizza, smiling broadly. He released his arm from hers and joined the others, who by the quizzical looks on their faces had lots to ask him. It was going to be a beautiful day.

# Author's note

During the winter of 1975, on a whim, I walked into my home town police station and spoke to the desk sergeant about joining the police. He gave me a couple of forms to fill in and sent me to the local branch of Woolworths where there was a weighing machine which printed out a record of your weight. Shortly afterwards I returned the completed forms to the sergeant with the record of my weight and after passing an embarrassingly simple written test (because I didn't have a mathematics qualification) I joined the Police Service on Monday 2 February 1976. I was eighteen years old. It was that easy. Today the process takes years, with candidates required to fill in numerous forms and still falling foul of quotas and psychological profiling.

My starting pay was £2400 per annum and I would be working shifts, weekends, Bank Holidays, and Christmas. With several other wet-behind-the-ears eighteen year olds, I was despatched to a Police Training Centre in the north of

England where we spent the next ten weeks alongside recruits from Greater Manchester, Merseyside, North Wales, Cumbria, Kent and Surrey. I had led a relatively sheltered life up to that point, and those ten weeks proved to be a real eye-opener. I tagged along with a mate from Greater Manchester to an assembly hall where the Merseyside and Manchester forces allocated postings to their recruits. The officers going to Toxteth, Moss Side and other difficult areas were either enormous, eye-wateringly ugly, or violent, or sometimes all three.

Ten weeks learning definitions and powers of arrest, engaging in 'real life' scenarios and weekly written exams cooled my early flush of enthusiasm, but I persevered and returned to the Force eager to try out everything I had learnt on an unsuspecting public.

Minutes after walking into my first nick I knew the job I wanted to do. It took me twenty-seven years to get it, but I ultimately spent the last three years of my service as a shift inspector with my own group working a busy division in central London. My last three years were as memorable as the first three and I retired on the ultimate high – doing something I had always wanted to do.

Those first three years, before Margaret Thatcher came to power and recognised that she needed the Police Service on board to deal with the unions, left an indelible mark on my memory. Within weeks I found myself with another young officer from a different station, guarding overnight the remains of Janie Shepherd on the desolate Nomansland Common outside St Albans. She was a young Australian who had been abducted in London and murdered. Standing just feet from her I recall being amazed I had a role in a tragedy that was receiving huge media attention. Very soon after Janie was found, the remains of Mickey Cornwall, a London gangster, were recovered from a shallow grave in woods nearby.

Whilst still in my teens I saw life and death at its most base and callous and, like every other officer I know who stayed the course, relied on rough and ready gallows humour to deal with it. I remember walking into a bedroom in a slum flat during the summer of 1976 where a man had died in bed three months earlier and had literally melted into the mattress as he decomposed. My partner that day took a brief look at him and said, 'He's let himself go a bit hasn't he?' It took the horror out of the situation. There were endless occasions when humour took the edge off something deeply unpleasant or difficult. I recall one young probationer (not me!) who was tasked with searching a house by his tutor because the occupant had not been seen for some time. He went upstairs and on returning was asked by his tutor whom he had heard him talking to. He replied that he had located a black bloke on the toilet up there but he wouldn't respond to any of his questions. Puzzled, the tutor had gone to speak to the man only to find the occupier sitting on the toilet, long dead.

Illicit sexual relations occasionally provided some light relief – as always. Officers from my station took a call to reports of a woman screaming for help from the back of a parked car. When they arrived they found an anxious woman whose sexual extravaganza in the car had gone horribly wrong when her boyfriend had sustained a serious back injury and could not be extracted from the vehicle. Eventually they called the fire brigade who cut off the roof of the car to get him out. The woman became hysterical, not as it turned out because of her boyfriend's injury, but because she had no idea how to explain the damage to her husband's car.

The years of Margaret Thatcher were halcyon days for the Police Service. Police officers and their families no longer had to rely on state benefits to get by and we were paid and continue to be paid a reasonable wage. Suddenly men and women began to join the Job to pursue lucrative careers. Despite this, I regard the period of my career from 1976 to 1979 as the last golden age of true vocational coppering. My book is set in that period. It is a work of fiction and should not by any means be regarded as an historical account.

What I hope comes across in this book is that a career in the Police Service involves long periods of mundane routine punctuated by extremes at both ends of the spectrum. Coppers who choose to remain operational see it all. They cope with a dark, sharp, spontaneous humour, not always to everyone's taste – but it helps.

# Belfast Confidential

## Bateman

They say moving house is one of the most stressful things you can do. Well, as far as Dan Starkey's concerned, 'they' can stick it because right now unpacking is the least of his worries . . .

No sooner has Dan moved house, than his best mate, Mouse, is brutally murdered – leaving him to catch a killer, become Editor of scandal magazine *Belfast Confidential*, and compile its much-coveted Power List edition.

But he's not the only one with a hit list to complete. Someone's systematically killing local celebrities and unless Dan can stop them the magazine's going under and so is he . . . by about six feet.

Yep – from where Dan's standing, lugging furniture about looks pretty damn tempting.

IF YOU HAVEN'T READ A BATEMAN NOVEL BEFORE, THIS IS WHAT YOU'RE MISSING:

'As sharp as a pint of snakebite' *The Sunday Times*

'Witty, fast-paced and throbbing with menace' *Time Out*

'If Roddy Doyle was as good as people say, he would probably write novels like this' *Arena*

978 0 7553 0927 6

## headline

Now you can buy any of these other
bestselling Headline books from your
bookshop
or *direct from the publisher*.

FREE P&P AND UK DELIVERY
(Overseas and Ireland £3.50 per book)

| | | |
|---|---|---|
| Run The Risk | Scott Frost | £6.99 |
| Stripped | Brian Freeman | £6.99 |
| Flint's Code | Paul Eddy | £6.99 |
| Dead and Buried | Quintin Jardine | £6.99 |
| Smoked | Patrick Quinlan | £6.99 |
| Copper Kiss | Tom Neale | £6.99 |
| The Death Ship of Dartmouth | Michael Jecks | £6.99 |
| The Art of Dying | Vena Cork | £6.99 |
| After the Mourning | Barbara Nadel | £6.99 |
| Guardians of the Key | Clio Gray | £6.99 |

TO ORDER SIMPLY CALL THIS NUMBER

**01235 400 414**

or visit our website: www.headline.co.uk

Prices and availability subject to change without

notice.